A BABY FOR THE

Firefighter

By Ann-Katrin Byrde

Cover Art by Ana J. Phoenix

Copyright

Dedication

For Jocelyn Smith, who provided the name of the baby in this book. And for all of my other wonderful readers who continue to encourage and enable me.

Prologue

GRIFFIN

The first time I kissed an alpha, I was in my last year of high school.

He came on to me after class, asked me to go to prom with him. I'd never really talked to the guy before. I only knew that his name was Thomas Dayson and he sat in most of my classes. He was kind of hot though, and no one had ever asked me out before. I was sort of giddy about it, really.

What I didn't know at the time was that Thomas was a dick.

We only spent a few minutes at prom, and he didn't even want to dance.

"Let's go someplace else," he said after we'd barely arrived, and then he dragged me outside and round the back to his car.

"Where are we going?" I asked, because I hadn't put on a tuxedo to hide away from all the fun.

"Thought we could have a little party of our own," he said.

I shot him a questioning look, brow furrowing. "What are you talking about?"

He laughed. "It's a good thing you're pretty, because you're not very smart, are you?"

I bristled, but couldn't get any words out before he shoved me back against the car and kissed me as if it was his right.

I'd always imagined my first kiss to be a bit more romantic than that, honestly.

But that wasn't the worst of it. The worst of it was the way his scent drifted into my nose. Not the layers and layers of cheap cologne he'd sprayed on, but his alpha scent. It went straight to some primal part of my brain, awakening some sort of base instinct inside myself that *very much liked* what was happening.

Even as I was starting to *hate* this guy.

"What the fuck are you doing?" I demanded, shoving him off.

"Oh, don't be like that. You said yes."

"Yes to what?"

"Being my prom date. Everyone knows that means sex."

"What?" I blinked. If I'd known that, I would never have agreed to it.

"C'mon," he said, crowding me. "Don't pretend like you're a virgin. Everyone knows you and Dean had something going on before he moved."

I was sure my face was full of question marks by this point. "Dean was my friend." And I missed him, but we'd never... I'd never...

Thomas snorted. "Please, alphas and omegas are meant to fuck. So let's do what nature demands of us." He smashed his lips to mine again as if I'd already given my okay. It wasn't okay, though. This guy was nuts! Didn't matter that he was hot when he couldn't listen. I tried to get away, but he held on, digging his fingers into my hair. And then something came over me. I could feel that part of my brain that had woken up earlier respond to him. My whole body grew hot as if agreeing with Thomas that we should get it on just because he was an alpha and I was an omega. The urge was almost irresistible, like an itch that demanded to be scratched right the fuck now.

"See," Thomas said, finally releasing my lips only to slide a hand down the front of my pants. "I knew you'd come around."

My head swam, doused in hormones. I felt like I had some sort of fever and I had no idea what was happening. This wasn't me. I didn't want this. But it wasn't easy to think while one half of my brain screamed at me to turn around and let the alpha make me happy.

The other half of my brain had a much better idea, though; I pushed Thomas away and ran all the way home. And then I threw up in the bushes outside the house.

Chapter One

GRIFFIN

"You're not lonely living all by yourself in this house, are you?"

I sighed and looked at my brother over the rim of my coffee mug. He'd 'dropped by for coffee', and I didn't mind his presence, but I did mind the questions. "You keep asking that."

He shrugged helplessly. "I guess I still feel bad that we moved out."

By 'we', he was referring to himself and his nine-year old son Jake. The three of us used to live together in this house back when Eli was a single parent. But he'd gotten married to Jake's father now, had another kid, and they'd moved out.

"It's fine. I don't get lonely," I lied. The house *could* get lonely, but it wasn't so bad that my brother needed to worry about me.

"If you say so." Eli took a sip of coffee, and I didn't get the feeling that I'd convinced him in any way.

"I do have friends, you know."

Eli licked his lips, and I could tell by the impression on his face that he was about to ask something stupid. "Do any of these friends ever stay the night?"

And there it was.

I loved my brother, but seriously, sometimes...

"Dude, I'm a little too old to have sleep-overs, don't you think?" I got up from the table and dug through the cupboard for my cookie box. Because you couldn't really enjoy coffee without cookies. At least I couldn't. Opening the lid, I placed it in the middle of the table.

I knew cookies weren't going to make my brother stop asking silly questions, but they were going to make these silly questions easier for me to put up with.

"Actually," Eli said, "I think you're the perfect age to be having some sleep-overs."

Sighing theatrically, I sank back into my chair. "Why oh why do you care so much about my sex life, brother?"

"I don't really care about your sex life." Eli took a cookie out of the box without eating it. "I'd just... you know, like to know that you're not lonely. I feel responsible."

What? I raised an eyebrow at him. "You feel responsible?" And here I was pretty sure that my prolonged virginity was no one's responsibility but my own.

"Well you know the old stories about how omegas need to stay virgins because they imprint on the first person they have sex with? I know that's bullshit, but when I think about it, it looks like that's what happened to me with Matt, so I was scared you'd kind of gotten it into your head that it's true."

"Yeah..." I said slowly, leaning back. "I promise you I don't believe that's true." Eli was right. Those stories were some grade A bullshit made up to keep us omegas docile. I knew that. Looking at my brother, I wasn't completely convinced that nothing like it could ever happen to me, but still... "Trust me, that's not the reason I'm not bringing men home."

Eli nibbled on his cookie. “Then what is?”

“It's nothing for you to worry about, okay? I'm fine.”

“Well, okay.” My big brother exhaled. “But you know you can talk to me when you have a problem, right?”

“Of course I know that.”

But I didn't have a problem.

Did I?

“Are you still taking Jake along to snap some pictures this Thursday?” Eli asked after a moment, distracting me.

“What? Uh, yeah.”

Eli smiled. “He seems excited.”

“I’m looking forward to it too.” I really was. My nephew was awesome and I loved spending time with him. That didn’t mean I was lonely without him around, though.

After Eli left, I put the cookie box back in the cupboard and glanced around the empty kitchen. This house was way too big for one person. The only reason I could afford to keep living here was the generosity of my brother's rich spouse. He'd bought the house for me as a *thank you* for helping raise Jake all those years. As if I needed thanks. But Eli wouldn’t take no for an answer. Honestly, he could be just as stubborn as his alpha mate. The two of them were a match made in heaven.

Still, I was grateful.

And maybe a *little* sad that Eli and Jake didn't need me as much anymore.

I had to think of what Eli had said about having sleep-overs. I was definitely too old for that kind of thing, but... There was no reason I couldn't have friends over to make the house feel a little less big.

I didn't have a lot of friends in town, but there

was one person who came to mind. One person who'd never been far from my mind since he'd returned to town a few months ago.

Without thinking much more about it, I grabbed a light jacket and headed out the door.

I reached the park about twenty minutes later. It was still early afternoon and a warm summer breeze carried the smell of freshly mown grass into my nose as I scanned the area for a familiar face.

My friend was helping his cousin out with his homecare business while staying here, and around this time of day, I often found him taking a walk with one of the seniors he tended to. On a bright and sunny day like this, my chance of spotting him was high. I could have just called him on the phone, of course, but seeing him in person was so much nicer.

And a silly grin threatened to split my face apart as soon as I did. I had no idea what it was about Dean that caused this reaction in me—okay, I had a tiny inkling—but I couldn't help but feel giddy around him. Just as long as I didn't get close enough to feel other things, anyway.

Today, he was walking Mrs. Rosewood, a sweet old lady whom I'd had the pleasure to meet before. She'd slapped my behind and told me to 'go get him, tiger,' referring to Dean. I'd told her that she was misreading the situation, of course, but she'd only laughed.

Lovely lady, really.

It seemed to be impossibly hard for people to understand that Dean and I were friends. We went way back. I'd first met him in elementary school, where we bonded over our mutual love of soap bubbles. His family had moved out of town just before our last year of high school, though, and, much like the soap bubbles of our childhood, our friendship couldn't make it over a long distance. Not with everything else that had happened in our lives. I'd become busy helping my brother raise his child, and he'd become busy firefighting and saving people. I really couldn't fault him for that.

It was kind of hot, actually.

I chided myself for the thought as I watched my friend push Mrs. Rosewood through the park in her wheelchair, but I couldn't deny that he was nice to look at. He'd been handsome when we were younger, and his physique had only become more defined as he grew into an adult.

And his warm, caramel-brown hair and his brilliant green eyes made him fucking edible.

But I would stick to eating his baked goods, rather than the goods he was hiding in his—

Don't even go there.

What use was there in entertaining dirty fantasies I would never act on? I could look and fantasize all day, but truth was, as soon as things got intimate between me and any alpha, the hormone rush became overwhelming and I ran. It had happened with my fucked up high school prom date, it had happened with the two other guys I tried dating after that, and I had nothing to guarantee me it wouldn't happen again.

Not with Dean, though, because Dean and I were just friends.

I closed my eyes, took a deep breath, and walked up to Dean instead of watching him from the bushes like a creepy stalker dude. "Hey."

"Griff!" Dean's face lit up as he saw me and the

smile he gave me made the day feel a little bit warmer than it already was.

"I thought I'd find you here." I turned to the senior with him. "And hello, Mrs. Rosewood."

"Hello Griffin." The old lady regarded me with a foxy smile. "Do you two need some alone time?"

"Oh, no, that's not—"

But she was already wheeling away. I sighed, watching her go.

"I'm sorry," Dean said. "She likes to make up saucy stories in her mind. You should see the books she keeps on her shelves."

"I guess," I said, looking at him and trying not to blush while I pictured what exactly Mrs. Rosewood expected us to do. But that wasn't what I'd come here for. "Am I interrupting? I didn't want to bother you at work, but..." *I really wanted to see you.* I searched my mind for something more reasonable to say, but I came up short. It was difficult to think standing so close to Dean. He had this typical alpha scent that was both intimidating and arousing in ways that always made me feel like I was playing with fire just by being near.

How close could I get without my hormones going out of whack?

"You're not bothering me at all. It'll be good for her to be outside in the sun for a bit." He nodded to Mrs. Rosewood. "She doesn't get out unless I take her."

I glanced at Mrs. Rosewood soaking up the sun, then back at Dean. It always surprised me how little he minded doing this job. Taking care of the elderly was such an omega thing, and here he was, this big burly alpha, tending to a sweet old lady.

But I shouldn't think in stereotypes like that. He'd always been kind. I liked that about him. It was why I was happy to have him as my friend.

Which reminded me of why I'd come here in the first place: not to stare at him but to invite him to hang out. As friends.

So why was it so difficult to get the words out? We'd had sleepovers as kids, for fuck's sake. I could invite him over to my place for one evening.

"Is something wrong?" Dean asked me after another moment of silence from me, a look of concern on his face.

"No," I hurried to say. "I was just wondering if you... uh..." *Jesus, Griff, get over yourself and get it out.* "I was just wondering if you'd like to... come over to my place this weekend. Like, Saturday? I don't know. We could... uh... watch movies or something. I don't know if you've already seen them, but there's some new horror movies up on Netflix. You remember how we tried to get horror movies from the video store but they wouldn't let us? But we're adults now, so I thought... you know..." Great, now I was rambling. I stopped and bit my bottom lip.

Dean wore a curious expression that I wasn't quite sure how to read. He was probably surprised, but surprised that I invited him or surprised that I'd turned out to be a rambling lunatic? Then his features smoothed over and a warm smile spread on his face. "I'd love to watch movies with you."

"Great!" I inhaled. I didn't know why I was so nervous, but suddenly I couldn't wait to get out of the park and get back home. "I'll see you Saturday then."

"At seven?"

"Sure."

"I'm looking forward to it."

"Yeah, me too." I gulped, and then I turned on my heels and left, wondering why I was such a mess. It wasn't like anything was ever going to happen between

Dean and me. There was no way he liked me like that, and even if he did… I sighed.

Even if he did, I was still a blushing virgin with no experience. There was no way I could land a guy as hot as him, no matter what fantasies I held in my heart. They were just fantasies.

Nothing more.

Chapter Two

GRIFFIN

I had to be quiet now. Real quiet. Carefully, I adjusted my camera's focus as I looked through the viewfinder at the bird I was trying to photograph. A blue jay. The lighting was perfect today. Clear sky. Just enough sunlight without being too much. And not a cloud in sight.

Luck was with me.

Or not.

Because the moment I clicked the shutter, a loud noise startled the bird and it took to the air.

I suppressed a sigh. The loud noise was my nephew of course.

"Uncle Griff!" he called out.

"Yeah?" I glanced at the kid, who was pointing downhill from where we were, a short way into the forest behind the town.

"I think I saw a fox! Can we take a picture of it?"

I'd be happy if we could take any *good pictures today.*

Jake had asked me to teach him about photography, and I'd thought it might be fun to take him into the woods, but so far the only thing that kept the nine-year-old's interest seemed to be catching bugs and stomping through the underbrush.

"You know what's important when you're trying

to take shots of animals?" I asked him.

He tilted his head to one side and looked at me curiously. "What?"

"Not scaring them away by yelling your uncle's name is a good start."

"What else should I yell?"

Smart ass. "You shouldn't yell at all!"

"I'm sorry," Jake said. "But there was a *fox.*" He stressed the last word and waved his arm as if I was being ridiculously dense by not seeing how important this was.

"We're in the forest. We'll see tons of critters. If you don't spook them all." But knowing my nephew, I had come prepared. It was time to enact plan B. Reaching around, I dug a little compact camera out of my bag. I'd taken it as a last resort, so to say. I loved Jake, but he was famous for breaking my stuff. Still, he wasn't going to learn anything if I never gave him a camera. I showed it to him. "Next time you see a cool animal, don't tell me about it. Take a picture."

"Ooooh, cool!" He grabbed the small device out of my hand without hesitation.

"Be careful please."

"I'm always careful!"

Right...

We trudged on further up the hill. As we went, Jake stopped pointing out animals. At one point, he even went up close to a tree with a bird in it, but it flew away. I had the hardest time not feeling a *little* happy about his prey getting away.

"Hey, stop laughing!" Jake complained. "This is hard!"

"Sorry. But yeah it is. Makes it all the more rewarding when you snap the perfect shot, though," I promised. Really, that was my favorite thing about these trips. I wasn't in love with hiking, or with the idea of getting up at the break of dawn, but if that meant I could capture the beauty of a perfect sunrise on a photograph? Totally worth the pain. Critters were tricky, because they moved, but I'd hoped that would make the day less boring to Jake.

But even giving him animals to stalk wasn't enough to keep the energetic boy quiet. Not entirely.

"Uncle Griff?"

"Yeah?"

"Are you sad that we moved out?"

One of my eyebrows went up. Had his daddy told him to ask me that? "Are you sad?" I turned the question back on him.

"I miss watching cartoons with you."

Awww. "But we still do that!" I would never give up watching cartoons with my nephew. I dreaded the day he decided he was too old for it.

"But not on Sunday mornings when Daddy wants to sleep in."

He had a point there. My Sunday mornings were pretty boring these days. "Maybe you should stay over next weekend. How would you like that?" His old room was still empty. Honestly, I had too much space.

"How about this weekend?" Jake asked.

"I uh... kind of have plans this weekend."

Don't blush, Griff. You're not doing anything worth blushing over. My cheeks heated up so quickly it was ridiculous. I only hoped Jake was still too young to draw any conclusions from that.

"What kind of plans?" The boy regarded me curiously. "Can I come?"

"I'm doing something with a friend." *A friend and nothing more than a friend.* "Don't tell your daddy about it, okay?"

Jake's eyes went wide. “Is it a secret?”

Oh no, now I'd really sparked his curiosity. “It's not a secret,” I said quickly. “I just don't think he needs to know.” Really, all I had planned was a movie night with a friend, but if Eli heard of it, he would get it all wrong. Dean wasn't my boyfriend, and we weren't going to be a thing, but try telling my brother that. I only had to shake an alpha's hand and Eli heard wedding bells in his head.

Just because *he'd* gotten married. Didn't mean I was going to. I didn't care what people said, there was no reason an alpha and an omega couldn’t just be friends.

Even if that alpha was hot as hell and shaking his hand gave me all sorts of conflicting feelings I didn’t want to think about. Truth was, I'd brought him garlic bread on our last meeting just to make him stop smelling so damn alpha. That smell always made me want to do things I wasn’t sure I should.

Things I wasn’t *brave* enough to do, anyway.

“So can I come?” Jake asked again, pulling me out of my thoughts.

“We'll be staying up very late.”

“I don't mind staying up late.”

Of course he didn't. “Your daddy will mind.”

Jake grinned. “I'll keep your secret if you keep mine.”

My mouth dropped open just slightly. Was my nine-year-old nephew blackmailing me?

Maybe it wouldn't be so bad to have him around. Really, why shouldn't he come? It wasn't like Dean and I were having a date or anything. “Okay,” I said eventually. “You can come, but only if you promise to go to bed after the second movie.”

“Promise.” Jake's grin grew wider, but I knew he

was going to stick to our agreement. He was a good kid when he wasn't breaking my stuff or blackmailing me.

Now I only had to talk to Eli about our weekend arrangements. Make sure he and Matt didn't already have something planned for Jake.

My brother greeted me with a stern look when I dropped his son off at his house after our little hike in the woods. *Uh-oh.* I knew that look. “What, did I do something wrong?” I held my hands up defensively.

“Where were you? I tried to call you an hour ago! I was waiting with dinner.”

“Dinner's ready?” Jake squeezed past Eli into the house while I rubbed the back of my neck.

“You called? I'm sorry, I didn't hear my phone.”

Eli seemed nonplussed by that response. “I called like five times! You know I worry when you take Jake out into the forest. Do you even have your phone with you?”

“Not like anything is going to happen to us in the woods. You don't have to worry.” I went out all the time, and nothing ever happened. And honestly, after all these years, Eli should know that he could trust me with Jake.

“You never know when something's going to happen,” he insisted. “And you shouldn't wander out there without a phone. It's irresponsible!”

“Of course I have my phone!” Or did I? I searched my pockets and came up with nothing. *Damn.* For some reason, I could never remember to take the stupid thing. “Okay, maybe I don't have it. But nothing happened.”

Eli sighed. “I'm going to have to inject a tracking device into you. Or into Jake.”

“A little drastic, don't you think?”

“Just kidding.” He waved me off. “But if that *was* a possibility...”

"Dude."

Eli gave me a half-hearted shrug. "You'll get it when you have your own kids."

That comment stung a little bit. "You know I love Jake like a son."

"I know, I know. I'm sorry. I just can't be laid-back where he's concerned, that's what I meant. It's some omega instinct gone crazy. You'll see what I mean."

Would I?

My silence seemed to make my brother reconsider his words. "I mean, if you want to have kids." It wasn't a question, but it sure felt like one.

I didn't know how to respond to it, though. Yeah, I wanted to have kids someday, but *someday* seemed to be slipping farther and farther away. At this point, I wasn't sure it was ever going to happen. Didn't matter, though, right? Because I could still spend time with Eli's kids. It wasn't some great tragedy if I never had a baby of my own. Not every omega needed that.

It would sure be nice, though...

When I watched Eli with his husband and children, I couldn't deny that I wanted what he had. I had no idea how to go about getting it, though, and so I only shrugged in response to my brother. "Maybe." And because I really didn't want to continue this line of conversation, I changed the topic. "Is it okay if Jake stays over at my place this weekend? Saturday to Sunday."

"If you don't have anything more fun to do on your weekend..."

I wondered if my brother realized his constant subtle attempts at getting information about my love life weren't so subtle at all. "What could be more fun than watching cartoons with my nephew?"

"Watching cartoons with your nephew and your niece?" Eli tried.

I laughed. “Oh no, that's not working.” My niece was just under a year old, and I adored her, but I spent enough of my time babysitting already. “Boy's night.”

“It was worth a try. Oh well. You can have Jake. Just have him in bed by ten.”

“Sure, I will.”

“And don't feed him so much sugar again.”

I cringed as Eli reminded me of the last time Jake had been over at my place. He'd found one of my emergency snack stashes and ate it. All of it. After that disaster, I'd briefly thought about getting rid of my snack stashes, but really... who was I kidding?

“There might be a few cupcakes,” I said before I could stop myself.

“Cupcakes?” Eli's eyebrows shot up.

Damn.

“Is your friend coming?” Eli asked before I could take back what I'd said.

“We're just friends, okay? We're watching movies, that's all.”

“Right,” Eli said in a tone that told me he didn't believe me even a little bit. “Are you sure you want to have Jake over for that?”

“Can you please just believe me that nothing's going to happen?”

“Okay, okay.” Eli held his hands up. “Nothing's going to happen.”

“Thank you,” I said while quenching the nervous flutters in my stomach. I had no reason to be nervous. I was only meeting up with a friend. Right?

Chapter Three

DEAN

Flames licked at the walls and the floor groaned underneath my feet. Smoke hung in the air, and even though I wore a mask, I still felt like it was creeping into my nose, carrying with it the sharp acrid smell of burned plastic. This house wasn't going to last much longer. I knew how these things went. We'd gotten here too late and the fire was too powerful. Any moment now, I'd get the order to retreat.

But I'd heard a cry for help. Someone was still up here, and I wasn't going to give up on them so easily.

I needed to get them out before the fire could consume them. That was my job.

The billowing smoke made it hard to see, and I couldn't find them. Not even with the thermal camera.

Breathe, Dean. Keep calm.

The moment I lost my nerves, it was game over. Panicking was a rookie mistake.

But so was underestimating a burning building.

I took another step forward, and then the floor gave way.

With a *crack*, I tumbled down into the flames below.

And just before the fire could eat me alive, I woke.

Sitting up, I rubbed my face. It had been over a year now since I'd crashed and nearly burned, but it seemed I hadn't quite recovered yet. At least these dreams had become a lot more infrequent since I'd returned to Oceanport. There was just something about this small town that put my mind at ease, and it wasn't *just* my cute omega friend, although I'll admit he played a huge part.

Stretching, I got out of bed, the dream already fading in the morning light. I had a full day of activities ahead of me, and an evening with my best friend to look forward to.

Nothing could really make me feel bad when I had the chance to spend time with Griff. His smiles were so bright that even one would be enough to chase any nightmare away, and I knew just what to do to get one.

I was going to do a little baking today.

The timer pinged and I grabbed my oven mitts to get the fresh batch of cupcakes I was baking out of the oven. Immediately, the smell of sugar, cinnamon and chocolate filled the kitchen. I drew it deep into my nose as I put the cupcakes on the counter to cool. This was my third favorite part of baking.

My cousin came into the kitchen just as I was putting the icing on the cupcakes. "More cupcakes?" he asked. "I can't believe you still haven't given up on that strategy." But even as he said that, he reached for them. "You can spare one for your cousin, right?"

"Sure, go ahead."

Seeing my grumpy cousin smile after taking a bite was my second favorite part of baking. Just last year Shane's omega spouse had passed away, leaving him to raise their two children and manage the business they'd started together on his own. I'd figured I'd stay with him for a while to help him get back on his feet. I'd wanted to get out of Portland anyway, after that last job, and returning home had seemed like the perfect way to do that. *A while* had now turned into several months, but my cousin seemed to be coming out of his shell a bit more lately, and that was good.

"Did they turn out all right?" I asked.

"Sure," he said, leaning against the counter. "Still won't get you into that omega's pants, though."

I barely kept from rolling my eyes. "I'm not trying to get into anyone's pants."

"Sure, sure. So you're not going out to see him tonight?"

Busted. I *was* going to see Griff tonight, but I hadn't made these cupcakes to get into his pants. No, I'd made them because seeing Griff's face light up when he ate one? That was my *most* favorite thing about baking. He was freaking adorable when he was happy. That was reward enough. "So what if I made some of these cupcakes for Griff?" I put two aside. "Give these to Conner and Mary later." Shane's kids. Conner was eight and Mary was almost two, and the two of them loved cupcakes almost as much as Griff did.

"Thanks," Shane said.

"Where are they, anyway?"

"Mary's down for a nap and Conner... Well, you know Conner."

I nodded, because I did know what he meant. Whenever I looked for Conner, nine times out of ten, I'd find him sitting in a quiet corner of the house, nose stuck in a book.

"I don't know where he gets it from," Shane mumbled, then he shook his head. "But anyway, we were talking about your date."

"It's not a date." Even if Griff had kind of

sounded like he was asking me on a date, I'm sure that couldn't have been his intention. He'd mentioned more than once that he wasn't interested in any romantic relationships at this point in time.

Shane gave me a look that was almost thoughtful. "You know, I've heard things about Griff."

"What kind of things?"

"Things that make me think *no one's* been in his pants."

"Can we please stop talking about Griff's pants?" I was so annoyed at the thought of other people discussing my friend's virginity over a few beers. They only did that because he was an omega, and omegas were universally expected to 'put out.' An omega no one had been to bed with? Scandalous. Surely something must be wrong with him.

I despised that kind of talk. Especially since Griff was almost as sweet as the sugar he loved so much. He shouldn't have shit flung at him.

"You can't tell me you're not interested," Shane said.

"Okay." I exhaled in exasperation and ran a hand through my hair. "So I'm interested. So what? What alpha in their right mind wouldn't be interested? He's fucking gorgeous and he smells like heaven. Does that mean I'm going to bone him when he clearly doesn't want me to? Hell no. I'm not going to put any pressure on him." I had few enough friends as it was, and I wasn't going to lose Griff because I couldn't keep my hormones under control.

"Sheesh, calm down." Shane ate the rest of his cupcake and licked his fingers. "I'm only teasing you. And honestly, you've been doing the cupcake thing for months now, so if you *were* trying to get with him, maybe you need to step up your game or try something else."

"I'm not trying anything. He likes cupcakes. I make him cupcakes. That's all."

Shane sighed. "You're hopeless."

"Hey, friendship is better than nothing."

"Is it?" Shane seemed skeptical.

I ignored him.

"You know you could have any omega in town if you wanted. They're all salivating at the thought of a night with the hot firefighter." Shane laughed just a little.

"I don't want just *any omega.*"

Shane shook his head. "Hopeless," he said again. He turned to leave the kitchen, but then he stopped. "Daniel called earlier, asking for you." I looked up at that. Daniel was the director of the local fire department, and I'd successfully avoided talking to him for the last couple of days. "Yeah?" I asked. "Did he say anything?"

"Not really. Just that you should call him back."

"I see." I looked back at my cupcakes.

"Do you know what he wanted?"

I licked my lips. There was probably no harm in telling my cousin. He already knew that Daniel wanted to talk to me, and seeing as he was the director of a fire department and I was a firefighter, it wasn't too hard to guess what he might want. "They need more people at the department."

Shane was quiet for a moment, and I wondered if he feared I might take the job and stop helping him out with the business. "Are you tempted?"

I shrugged. "Not really."

Shane raised a single eyebrow. "Not even a little bit? I know how much you love your job. Your actual job, I mean. Not taking care of seniors. I appreciate you coming down here to help me, really, but... it's been almost a year, man. I don't want to hold you up forever."

"You're not holding me up." Far from it. "If I wanted to go back to firefighting, I would go back to my old department." But I was glad for the excuse to stay.

"Does that mean you don't want to go back to firefighting?"

Shit, did I say too much?

"Of course I want to go back to firefighting." I laughed and hoped it convinced him. "Just not right now and not here. I've got your back, Shane."

Shane looked like he didn't believe me a hundred percent, but he nodded anyway. "Okay, then."

I suppressed a sigh of relief that we were done with this topic. Sooner or later, I would have to face my demons. But not for as long as I could avoid it.

An unfamiliar face greeted me when I knocked on Griff's door, cupcakes in hand.

"Uncle Griff!" the little boy called out. "Your friend is here!"

So this must be Jake. I recognized him, of course. Griff had shown me pictures. Tons of pictures. I hadn't known the kid would be with us tonight, though.

"Come in!" Jake took me by the arm and dragged me inside before I could even utter a greeting. "I'm Jake, by the way."

If I hadn't heard tales of the boy's energy levels before, I would have wondered if Griff fed him a ton of sugar before I arrived.

"Oh hey!" Griff got up from the couch when Jake led me into the living room. "You're early!"

I was only five minutes early, but to someone like

Griff who was perpetually at least twenty minutes late to meetings, that must have felt like an hour. I gave him a smile–it was so easy to smile at Griff. "I guess I just couldn't wait to get here." I still couldn't believe he'd invited me for the evening.

Of course, I hadn't thought that *Jake* was invited as well.

What, did you think this was going to be a date? Get over yourself.

I bit back a sigh.

"I guess we're not watching horror movies after all?"

Griff gave me a pained smile and rubbed the back of his neck. "I'm sorry. I forgot that we talked about horror movies. But there's some really good anime on Netflix that we could watch. I mean, if you want to?" His voice took on a cautiously hopeful tone at the end that was nothing short of endearing. God, he was cute. I remembered the first time I noticed that about him when I hit puberty and my alpha genes started to express themselves. I'd spent a few days out of town on a family trip, and when I came back, he'd startled me by throwing himself at me in a hug. I could never forget the way he'd smelled that day. Like all of my favorite treats combined. I'd wanted to pull him closer and *lick* him. And when he broke away he left me feeling confused as hell. I hadn't known how to handle my sudden attraction to my omega friend back then–and I still didn't.

"I don't mind watching anime," I said when I realized that I'd been quiet for too long. Truth was, as long as I got to spend the night with Griff, I didn't care *what* we were doing. Shane was right. I was pining for this omega to an unhealthy degree. *Especially* considering he was my friend.

But there was nothing I could do about it. Nothing I really *wanted* to do about it.

"I brought you something," I said, holding the box I was carrying out to Griff.

Immediately, his face lit up. "Oh, is it cupcakes?"

"Cupcakes?" Jake perked up.

Thank God I'd made more than enough for all of us. "I tried something new, going for a cinnamon taste. Tell me how you like it."

Griff took the box and looked into it. "That sounds awesome! I'm sure your bakery is going to be awesome when you open it."

I had no idea why I'd told him that I thought about opening a bakery someday when I had no intentions of doing so. I just needed a reason to keep feeding him treats without him growing suspicious.

And I really sucked at lying when I had to make something up on the spot.

Griff handed a cupcake to Jake and then bit into one himself. And the expression on his face when he did so...

He looked like he was about to have an orgasm.

How could I stop baking when it made him look like *that*?

"These are *amazing*," he exclaimed. "You definitely need to make more of them!"

Oh, I would.

Jake seemed happy too, finishing his cupcake off in record time and digging into the box for more.

"Hey," Griff addressed his nephew. "Don't eat all of those."

I had to laugh. It was good to know my sweets were worth fighting over. I'd grown up as one of seven siblings. When I was a child, Griff was the first person I met who truly managed to make me feel like I was special—and he continued to do so to this day. One of the many reasons I loved him—maybe more than I should.

"I'll surrender my share," I said, not *really* wanting the two of them to fight.

My generous gesture pleased both Griff and his nephew and they split the cupcakes evenly between them. Then we could start our movie night. Or, anime night, as it had turned out.

I wasn't really into anime, but I was totally into the way Griff responded to the show. He *lived* the experience. He laughed when the characters did and he bit his lips when any of them were in danger, completely absorbed in what was happening. Even more so than his nephew.

In fact, Jake passed out on the couch between us just around 10pm.

"Should we turn off the TV?" I asked Griff, nodding to the sleeping boy.

He waved me off. "It's fine. Once he's asleep, he's out. That's my favorite thing about him," he joked, although it was obvious how much he loved his nephew. He'd told me so many stories and showed me so many pictures. He was a great uncle, and someday, I was sure, he was going to be a fantastic dad.

And whoever the lucky bastard was who'd eventually put a claim on him, I was already jealous.

"I'm sorry I sprung Jake on you," Griff said quietly. "I was going to tell you, but..."

"You forgot?"

He gave me a sheepish smile. "Got caught up in this new project I'm working on. It's kind of awesome. They want a lot of nature shots."

"It's fine," I said, even though I had been a *bit* disappointed that we weren't going to be alone. That was only due to my fantasies of starting something with him. In the end, it had been good to finally meet the kid I heard so much about. He was obviously a major part of my friend's life. “He seems like a sweet kid.”

“He is.” Griff smiled. “Lots of energy.”

“That's good.” I leaned back into the couch and inhaled. “I wish my cousin's child could be a little more like that.”

“Conner?”

“Yeah. He's only a year younger than Jake, but he spends all of his time hiding away with a book. Not that there's anything wrong with a child who loves books, but... it's all he ever does anymore since Ron passed away.”

“It's difficult to lose a parent,” Griff said with so much sympathy in his eyes I almost wished I hadn't brought the topic up. The evening had been so lighthearted up to now. But Griff made it easy to talk about difficult topics. There wasn't a judgmental bone in his body. He'd always just wanted everyone to do what made them happy.

Even in school, he'd offered his friendship to every outcast and bullied kid he could find. It was no surprise he'd done everything he could to support his brother when Eli became pregnant.

I wanted to be there for my family too. “I just wish I knew how to help. Nothing can replace Ron.”

“No, I guess not...” Griff trailed off, his brow furrowed deep in thought. He always got this faraway look in his eyes when he was thinking, and I wondered where his mind wandered off to.

“I know it's not a long-term solution, but what if we took the kids out to do something fun? “

“The kids?”

“Yeah. Jake and Conner. Jake doesn't have too many

friends, I'm sure he'd love to get together. And maybe some of his natural enthusiasm will rub off on Conner."

Lord, I hoped it could work like that. "That might not be a bad idea."

Griff beamed at me as if he'd just solved the world's most complex problem—and gotten a cookie for it too. "So let's do it!"

"Yeah, let's." I gave him a soft smile. "But do what, exactly?"

"I don't know." Griff waved his hand as if he could grab the answer out of the air. "Something fun. What's fun to do? Oh, I know, it's supposed to be hot next week. We could take them to the lake." His expression turned nostalgic. "Remember how we used to go to the lake as kids? That was fun."

I only nodded, because I did remember. I remembered the whole thing getting kind of awkward as we became teenagers and I developed this stupid attraction to my friend. But I could hardly tell him that now. He was *so* excited about his lake idea.

"Is next weekend good for you?"

"Sure," I said, hoping he didn't plan on skinny dipping or anything. He'd done that one time when we were younger and didn't have swim wear with us. I'd had the hardest time controlling my hormones around my naked friend, and I didn't want a repeat of that.

Or did I?

Maybe I wanted it *a little*, because I wasn't making any counter suggestions. Besides, it might be difficult to see Griff naked, or even half-naked, but I'd still be seeing him naked. I was sure the sight would more than make up for any difficulty I had to face.

God, I really was hopeless, wasn't I?

Chapter Four

GRIFFIN

Why oh why had I ever thought going to the lake would be a good idea? Yeah, it was hot, and yeah, the kids were loving it—at least Jake was, Conner still seemed skeptical of all the wet stuff—but I was having the hardest time not staring at my friend and making a total idiot out of myself.

I'd noticed even when he was clothed that Dean had shaped up nicely since high school, but now that he stood in front of me in just some swim shorts?

Holy shit.

I used to laugh at people who used the words 'sex on legs' to talk about men, but I only had to take one look at Dean now to know he was the whole reason the phrase had been coined. Just to be able to describe him.

And if he went into that lake now and got himself wet I was gonna fucking lose it. I was sure of it.

Look at something else, Griff. Anything else but his abs. Good, good, watch Jake. You're a responsible, non-sex-obsessed uncle.

While I was doing my best not to pay attention to him, Dean spread a blanket out on the grass leading up to the lake and put the basket he'd brought on top of it.

"Griff?"

I nearly jumped when Dean tapped my shoulder from behind. "Yeah?" Jesus, his alpha-scent was strong today, mixing with the day's sweat. I drew in a breath, wondering if all omegas got funny thoughts in their head when they caught a whiff of a hot alpha and why I seemed to be the only one who had a problem with it.

I leaned away a bit, hoping he wouldn't notice. He hadn't said anything when I made Jake sit between us for movie night.

"Do you need sunscreen? I packed some. We should probably get the kids."

"Yeah. Good thinking." I rubbed my face with the heel of my hand.

Snap out of it and focus.

Barely looking at Dean, I took the tube of sun cream out of his hand and walked up to the edge of the lake. "Jake!"

The boy had swum out a little bit, but he turned to me at the sound of his name.

"Come here!"

I turned to Conner while my nephew swam back. The boy was still wearing a shirt over his swim trunks, just dipping his feet in the water. He was super pale too, and probably not just because of his Irish background. The kid really needed to get some sunlight on his skin—and apply three layers of sunscreen.

I bent down in front of the eight-year-old. "Hey, Conner."

"Hey."

"You want to put on some sunscreen so you don't burn your skin?"

"Sure," he said without any enthusiasm, like he knew it was the only acceptable answer. Like he just wanted me to go away again.

He'd hardly said a word and my heart was already breaking for him. Kids his age should be running around and having fun, not saying whatever adults wanted them to say so they could go back to suffering quietly.

But before I could say anymore, something cold and wet hit my side.

I glared at Jake, who looked at me with the biggest grin on his face.

"Got you!" he exclaimed. And then he ran, because he knew that I would want to get revenge. I chased him across the uneven, grassy shore, until he stumbled, laughing, and I wrestled him back into the water where I dunked him for a split second. He came back up panting, but still in good spirits.

"Got you back," I said. "Now let's get out so we can get sunscreen on you."

"Okay." And as we waded to the shore he asked, "Isn't Conner gonna swim?"

"I don't know." Actually, I wasn't even sure if he *could* swim. If he couldn't, that would at least explain why he wasn't getting in the water with any part of his body other than his feet.

I *really* hadn't thought this lake idea through.

When we got to the grass, I dried Jake off with one of the towels we'd brought and rubbed some of the sunscreen on his arms.

"Can Conner swim?" Jake asked. It seemed he'd been having the same thoughts as me.

"I'm not sure. You'd have to ask him. But be nice about it." I tapped a finger with sunscreen on his nose.

"I'm always nice!" he insisted. "And if he can't swim, I could teach him."

Good. I was going to be so busy making sure nobody drowned that I wouldn't have time to ogle Dean. *Speaking of...* I glanced around to see him talking to Conner, though I couldn't quite make out what they were saying.

Conner finally took his shirt off, though.

Good. He could stand to get a bit of a tan.

When I was done with Jake, I applied some sunscreen to myself—just cursory, really, I didn't burn easy—and then I patted Jake on the back and handed the tube to him. "Go and bring that to Dean."

He went off obediently while I busied myself with checking my phone and not looking at Dean.

When I glanced up, I saw that Jake was trying to strike up a conversation with the other boy.

"Do you want to swim?"

"I can't swim."

"But it's really easy! Look! I'll show you." Jake sprinted into the water again.

"Don't swim too far!" I yelled after him. Yeah, I was definitely going to be busy watching Jake.

"Try to catch me!" Jake yelled back.

I groaned, but then Dean stepped up to the task before I could. Muscles rippling, he jumped into the water and caught up to my nephew within moments. He dragged him back onto the grass, hauled him up over his shoulder and carried him to me, Jake's legs kicking. "Express delivery," he said, setting the rascal down in front of me.

"Not fair!" Jake complained.

"What's not fair?" Dean asked, while I watched as a single drop ran down from his chest to his abdomen and past his belly button. My brain nearly short-circuited.

It was definitely not fair for anyone to be that hot.

How was I supposed to keep my cool?

"It's not fair because you're like... super fast," Jake said.

"Well, in my job, I have to be."

"What's your job?"

"He's a firefighter," Conner said, startling me, because I hadn't heard him approach.

"Really? Coooool." Jake's eyes lit up. "Do you like, save people from burning buildings?" He gazed at Dean intently, clearly starstruck.

"It's not always that dramatic." Dean laughed, but something about it sounded forced. Like there was something haunting him that he didn't want to talk about. I wondered what it was.

Dean changed the topic too quickly for me to latch on to anything.

"What do you say we teach Conner how to swim?" he said to Jake. "It's an important skill."

Jake agreed, and Conner simply went along with the two alphas' shenanigans. I got the sense that he was a good kid, just a bit disappointed by the world.

He didn't learn how to swim that day, not really, but I did hear him laugh once or twice, which was good. This was why we'd come here after all, not so I could freak out over Dean's half-naked body.

It was a little better now that he was half-submerged in the water, if only slightly. How could it be that I wanted to touch him and run away from him at the same time?

I bit my lip, hard, and told myself to focus on something else. Dean and the kids made a lovely picture together, splashing in the lake. I dug out my camera to take a few snapshots.

"You have to come visit me, I'll show you my dog." I heard Jake say later when they waded back out.

Conner nodded—a bit hesitantly, but still. I smiled. My nephew was the best.

"Who wants some food?" Dean asked, reaching into his basket again. Apparently, he'd brought sandwiches. He was also the best.

Even so, I ate mine mostly facing away from him. It was the only way I could get myself to eat with him being so naked next to me and smelling like *that*.

I hoped he didn't think I was trying to avoid him, even if I was. And I also hoped he wouldn't ask about it because I had no idea how to explain to him that he was both too gorgeous for me to think straight, and too alpha for me not to lose my shit if he got close. I wanted him. But I also knew that as long as I couldn't get a handle on my issues, we were better off staying friends.

And that hurt more than I wanted to admit.

Chapter Five

DEAN

"I'm telling you, he just wouldn't look at me for longer than five seconds at a time."

Shane stirred his coffee without looking up. "Did you do something to him?"

It was the same question I'd asked myself over and over since parting with Griff the day before. What had I done? Had I creeped him out somehow? I'd tried my best not to stare at him or be weird in any way, and I liked to think that I succeeded too.

"I can't think of anything. I spent most of the time playing with the kids, honestly." The memory put a smile on my lips. It had taken Conner a little bit to warm up, but in the end, it had seemed like he was having fun. Griff and I had accomplished our mission. "You should have seen Conner. He actually laughed."

Shane looked up at that. "He did?" His features softened. He put on a tough façade most of the time, but he did care about his kids. He was just a bit lost on what to do sometimes, but then, so was I. "That's good," he said. "Mary spent a whole day yesterday singing a new nursery rhyme she's learned. She's a lot like Ron, you know. He'd sing all the time."

"I remember." I hadn't met Ron often, but his vibrant personality was hard to forget, and I sincerely hoped Mary would keep his spirit alive.

God knew this family needed all the cheer it could get.

"It would be good if Conner could make a friend," Shane said.

I had to agree. The boy needed to get out more. "Jake invited him to his house," I mentioned. "Maybe you should call his dad and see if you can set something up. Griff told me Jake doesn't have a lot of friends either. I'm sure they'd be happy to have your boy over."

"I'll do that. Thank you." He sipped at his coffee and I did the same. "I've been thinking maybe it really is time for all of us to be moving forward. It's been a year."

"Yeah, I get what you're saying." I had things to get over as well. Though mostly I was just running from them by being here.

"Actually, I kind of have a favor to ask of you."

"A favor?" I raised an eyebrow at my cousin. "You know I'll help with whatever you need."

"Very generous." He grinned. "I guess then you'll have no objections to going on a double date with me."

Excuse me? "A what?"

"C'mon, it'll be fun."

"What are you talking about? Who do you want to date and why can't you go by yourself?"

He sighed. "I would, but you know, I'm rusty, man. I'd probably make a fool of myself."

I shook my head. Where was all this coming from? "Who are you talking about?"

"The Maden brothers from up the street."

I tilted my head, searching my brain for any recollection of those two, but nothing came up aside from maybe passing them on the street once or twice.

"The older one asked me out," Shane continued. "And I know his brother has a thing for you. Then again, that's no surprise. All the omegas in town have a thing for you."

"Not *all* the omegas in town." Specifically, not the one

I wanted and who'd spent all of our outing yesterday avoiding me.

"You need to get over that crush of yours," Shane said, guessing at what I was talking about. "This'll be good for both of us."

I sighed. He might have a point there. I wasn't getting anywhere with Griff. I was only weirding him out and hurting our friendship—and I really didn't want to lose him as a friend, even if I couldn't have him as a lover. He'd faded out of my life once, and now that I had him back, I didn't want to let that happen again. He made my days brighter just by being around. I didn't even have to make out with him to get that effect. Being friends was enough. I just needed to make sure my heart got the message. "Who's going to watch the kids?"

Shane thought for a moment. "I'm sure I can get a babysitter. I could call my mother, if all else fails. She'd be happy to hear I'm dating again."

He was probably right about that. Aunt Stephanie worried a lot about how her son was faring after the loss of his spouse. We all worried, to be honest. He was doing much better now than he had been a few months ago, but I knew the scars on his heart would take longer to heal, and so I had to ask. "Are you sure you're ready, though?"

He didn't answer immediately, and then he gave me a shrug. "Honestly? I don't know. But there's only one way to find out."

I rubbed my temples. There was no way I was going to get out of this without a guilty conscience, was there?

"Fine, I'll go. For you." I wasn't a big fan of blind dates, but if it helped my cousin move on I could suffer one evening.

How bad could it be?

Chapter Six

GRIFFIN

I hadn't talked to Dean in two days and I was getting antsy. Every time the phone rang, I jumped. But it was never Dean.

Impatient for *anything* to happen, I paced around the living room.

Had I pissed Dean off by avoiding him that day by the lake? I must have. Maybe I should call and apologize. But I still didn't know how to explain myself without admitting to my secret crush—which would ruin everything even if it was reciprocated. I couldn't date anyone if my first instinct was to tug my tail between my legs and run like a scared puppy when things turned interesting.

It was absolutely ridiculous. Not every alpha was out to take advantage of me, but the rational side of things didn't seem to matter much to the part of me that was terrified.

Clearly, something was wrong with me.

I wanted to die of embarrassment at just the thought of telling anyone about this. Thank God the one or two people I'd run off on in the past had kept their mouths shut. Nobody liked to talk about how they'd been rejected, I guess.

My cell phone rang and pulled me out of my reverie. Sadly, it wasn't Dean. The caller ID said Eli.

"Hey," I answered the phone. I'd expected my brother to be on the other end of the line, but instead I was greeted by the cheerful voice of my nephew.

"Uncle Griff! Guess what!"

"Your daddy doesn't know you stole his phone?" I joked.

"Nooo. Wrong! Try again!"

"Uh..." I flopped on the couch. "You've decided that you want to become a firefighter?"

"I'm totally going to be a firefighter!" Of course. "But that's not it! I'm going to be in the play this year."

"The school play? That's awesome!" He'd tried to be in it once before when he was seven, but then some misbehavior on his part had gotten him kicked off. It was nice to know he got another chance this year. His behavior in school had improved and he deserved it.

"I have like five lines! I'm a dwarf."

"Awesome," I said again. "I'm sure you'll be the best dwarf ever."

"Yeah! Daddy is helping with the costumes. And you need to help with the props."

I needed to what? "What props?"

"Somebody has to do the uh... wait," he said, and then I heard him yell for his daddy. A minute later, I heard some rustling as the phone was handed over from Jake to my brother.

"Hey, Griff. Everything okay?"

"Yeah, yeah. Everything's fine. What's that I hear about doing props?"

"I'm sorry about that. I offered to help with the costumes, and Jake's got it into his head that you need to be involved too. Matt got off easy. He only has to read lines with Jake, and honestly, there aren't that many lines. He's even tried to rope Olivia into it, but she's having none of it. Just threw all her toys at him. I'm fearing I might have another alpha on my hands."

I had to laugh at that. "Wouldn't that be wonderful?" I asked, remembering all the trouble Eli had gone through with Jake when the boy had first expressed his alpha tendencies.

"Don't mock me." But Eli was laughing too. "Anyway, apparently the guy who usually does the props can't do it this year, so Jake's teacher asked if we knew anyone who could spring in."

"And that would be me?" Lovely.

"C'mon, it could be fun, and it would mean so much to the kids. I remember you used to *love* being in these plays when you were that age."

I cringed, because I remembered too. One year I'd been a mushroom and I'd worn that costume *everywhere*, feeling like some kind of fungal super-hero.

Eli was right. Every kid deserved the opportunity to make memories that would embarrass them as adults.

"Okay, okay, I'll do it."

"Great! There's a meeting at the school that you should come to next Thursday at six. I hope to see you there."

"I'll be there."

"Cool." And that concluded the call. As soon as Eli hung up, I found myself staring at the phone.

Should I call Dean? Shouldn't I?

Oh for fuck's sake, just do it.

Before I could change my mind again, I scrolled through the contact list and hit *call* on Dean's name.

He answered the phone almost immediately—way before I could decide to hang up again.

"Griff?"

"Yeah, hi, it's me."

"What's up?"

"I just uh... kind of wanted to apologize."

"What do you have to apologize for?" Dean asked, and I wasn't sure exactly what to say.

"Just the way I behaved Saturday," I said eventually. "I know I wasn't being super friendly."

"I did wonder about that," Dean admitted. "But thought maybe I'd imagined it."

"No, you didn't. I'm sorry. I wasn't... feeling well." Or, in fact, feeling a little too well when looking at his wet and half-naked body.

"It's okay. I hope you're feeling better."

"Yeah, I am. Thank you." I exhaled, so relieved to be done with this part of the conversation.

"You should know Conner has a play date with Jake this week."

"Really?" That news made me smile. "That's good."

"Yeah. My cousin seems really happy about it too. He's doing better recently. Maybe a little too well." Dean laughed, making me wonder what he was talking about.

"How do you mean?"

"He's decided to put himself out there again."

"That's good." A huge step forward for Shane.

"Yeah, but he wants me to help him, so he's making me go on a double date with him."

That... wasn't so good. Dean was going on a date? With who?

Not that it really mattered, because whoever they were, they weren't *me*. And that was the crux, wasn't it? Even if I didn't want to admit it, I hated the thought of Dean going on a date with someone who wasn't me. Which was, of course, utterly selfish of me, because I wasn't going to date him either.

"Griff?" Dean asked, and I realized that I hadn't

spoken in too long. "Do you have a problem with me going on a date?" His tone turned quite serious, like he would cancel that date if I just said so.

But I couldn't ask that of him, could I?

Shit.

"No," I said, hoping my voice didn't sound as upset as I felt. Damn it, I always knew this was going to happen sooner or later. Dean was too handsome to stay single forever. "Why would I have a problem?" I forced a laugh even though my heart ached. "You should enjoy yourself. When is this date?"

"Saturday."

Saturday... Okay, I needed to put a big bottle of wine on my Saturday shopping list. Or maybe something stronger.

Chapter Seven

DEAN

"How do I look?" my cousin asked, presenting himself in his outfit for the night about half an hour before we were supposed to pick up our dates.

"You look great." My cousin was a handsome man, objectively speaking, and he'd picked out a good outfit. Well-fitting jeans with a blue shirt which accented his light eyes and ginger hair without making him look pale.

"Are you nervous?" I asked because I'd never known Shane to be one to fidget.

"Are you?" he gave back.

I shook my head. I had no reason to be nervous about this date. The only thing that slightly unsettled me was the way Griff had reacted when I'd told him about it. "I'm only doing this for you," I said.

That didn't seem to satisfy him. "It's not like nothing good can come off this date for you."

"I guess." I sighed, rubbing my temples. Griff said he had no problem with me going on a date, even when I'd given him a chance to tell me not to go. That meant he was fine with me dating other people, didn't it? So there was no reason not to make the most of this date, even if I didn't really feel like it. And I *really* didn't feel like it.

"For what it's worth, you look nice too," my

cousin said.

"Thanks." I gave him a smile. I'd put on nice clothes because I hadn't wanted to be disrespectful to my date. I could put in a *little* effort, at least. And I'd been told at least once that my ass looked absolutely edible in these jeans.

I wondered if Griff would agree with that statement. But tonight, I couldn't think about him. Shane was right; it was time to get over this silly crush.

We picked the Maden brothers, Edward and Leonard, up at their house. As Shane had told me, they roomed together to save on expenses. They'd been close ever since their parents died when they were young, leaving them with a rather old-fashioned grandmother. I sympathized. My grandmother still asked me why I hadn't given her a grandchild yet every time I called, and my family wasn't even that big on tradition. I got it from a lot of the seniors at work as well, and if I'd been raised by any of them, I would have clung close to my sibling too.

My date was Edward, the younger of the two. I had to admit, he was kind of cute. The brothers both sported black hair and deep brown eyes, but Edward was a bit shorter and he had a sort of boyish charm to him that I liked. He wasn't Griff, no, but nobody was. It was unfair of me to expect him to live up to the omega who'd made my heart beat faster since my teenage years.

No, I needed to try to forget about Griff for tonight. As much as I didn't want to believe it, the two of us might *never* be more than friends, and if that was the case...

Shane lightly whacked me over the back of my head as we entered the restaurant he'd taken us to. "Stop looking so grumpy," he hissed.

"I'm not grumpy!" I muttered, looking around the restaurant and hoping our dates hadn't heard our exchange.

My cousin had picked the Bella Luna for our date. I say picked, but there hadn't really been much of a choice. Oceanport didn't have a ton of fancy restaurants. There was this, a diner, one or two cafés, and that one really fancy place that belonged to the resort a bit farther out, but only tourists went there, really.

Still, it wasn't a bad choice.

The Bella Luna offered mostly Italian food, even though the owners weren't Italian. The flair was nice, though. Everything *looked* expensive, even when you knew it really wasn't. When I stepped into the restaurant, I knew I was still in Oceanport, but I might as well have been taking a stroll in Milan. Whoever the owner was, they had a good sense for interior design. Griff would have loved this place; he had a great eye for design too, being an artist.

Ugh, I shouldn't think about Griff tonight.

Taking a deep breath, I tried to focus on my date.

Make conversation.

"You and your brother, you live together?" I asked once we sat down at one of the tables by the large window front.

Edward gave me a smile. "Yeah, even though it's a pain."

His brother elbowed him. "Hey! You're the one who's a pain to live with."

"I know that, but don't make me look bad in front of my date!" Edward protested. "Don't you want me to move out some day?"

I had to laugh, loving the light-hearted atmosphere these two were bringing to the table. "Why are you such a pain to live with?" I asked Edward, while picking up one of the menus.

"Because I like to get up early and Mr. Grumpypants over here doesn't appreciate waking up to the sweet sound of my shower concerts."

His brother sighed theatrically. "You have a good voice, but I don't want to hear it at 6am."

I glanced over at my cousin to see if the mention of singing disturbed him. As he told me, Ron had *loved* to sing in the shower. But Shane just stared really hard at his menu.

I looked at mine as well, realizing that neither of us was with the man we truly wanted to be with tonight. We just had to make the best of it. I put the menu aside before I could wonder what Griff would order for dessert and whether he'd like it better than what I made for him.

What was he up to tonight, anyway?

Chapter Eight

GRIFFIN

It was Saturday night, and the bottle of wine was almost gone. I lay on my couch and stared at the ceiling, really wishing I'd bought something stronger. Or just more wine. I glanced at the clock above the living room door and considered going out again. It seemed like a good idea. Go out, have a drink, or maybe one hundred of them. Because I was still thinking about Dean and his damn date, so I clearly hadn't had enough to drink yet.

Maybe I would feel better if I got some fresh air—on the way to the liquor store. Yeah, that sounded like a good idea. Anything that kept me from running circles in my head sounded like a good idea.

I got off the couch with great effort, threw on a light jacket—inside out as I later noticed—grabbed my keys and wallet and went out the door.

It was still early evening and in the sunny weather, lots of people were out and about. Some of them shot me funny looks as I walked by, but that didn't bother me. I was used to people looking at me in strange ways ever since my brother had become the target of the town's gossip back when Jake was born.

The rumors had soared when people learned who Jake's father was last year, but eventually, the public had lost interest in a secret that wasn't a secret anymore.

"You again?" Frankie, the owner of the town's liquor store, asked when I walked in. He was a middle-aged, sometimes grumpy but mostly friendly man. When I'd come here on my 21st birthday, he'd given me a bottle of beer for free. And then he'd refused to sell me any more when I was so drunk that I could hardly tell my hands from my feet since I needed both of them to walk.

Good memories.

"I need another bottle of that stuff you sold me earlier," I told Frankie.

"Are you sure you do?" He eyed me skeptically.

"C'mon, man. I need this right now."

"You look like you're plenty drunk already."

"I'm not," I insisted. Okay, maybe I was a little drunk. But how else was I supposed to cope with the situation I was in? My best friend was back in town, he was hot as hell, and he was dating some other omega because I didn't have the guts to be with him that way.

He probably didn't even know how much I wanted him.

"Tell me honestly, is something troubling you, son?"

"Life *sucks*," I said with emphasis.

"Yeah, life can suck alright." He glanced at the liquor cabinet behind him, then back at me. "Tell you what, you take a nice long walk, and then if you still feel like you need another drink, I'll fix you up. How's that sound to you?"

"Okay." Maybe a walk would help. Or maybe it wouldn't, but then I could still come here. That sounded fair, and I would have liked for something to be fair just then. "See you later," I said to Frankie, and then I walked out the door again.

The sun had sunk a bit in the sky and I figured it

would set soon. It was almost golden hour. I loved this time of the day. It made for beautiful pictures, and I found some solace in the fact that the sun continued to set every day. Even the shitty ones, like this particular Saturday.

I decided to head up to the hill just outside town to watch the sunset from there.

But on the way there, I walked past an Italian restaurant, and, thinking nothing of it, I looked through the window—only to see Dean and his cousin and their goddamn dates.

All thoughts of sunsets fled from my mind. All I wanted to do anymore was to waltz in there and drag Dean out with me. To this day, I'm amazed at the self-control I displayed by not doing that.

Sadly, I can't claim that I had myself so tightly under control for the rest of the night.

As if on autopilot, my feet took me to the foot of the hill, but then I couldn't go on. I didn't want to watch the sunset anymore. I just wanted... I wanted to be with Dean. As stupid as that was. And I can only guess that it was the liquid courage flowing through my veins that made me abandon reason and take out my cell phone. I dialed Dean's number.

It took him a little while to answer the call. He was probably just too engrossed in what his stupid date was saying.

I bit my teeth together. And then I heard a clicking in the line and Dean's deep, masculine voice.

"Hello?"

"Hey, it's me," I said, trying not to slur the words. I wasn't sure how successful I was.

"I know. That's why I answered the phone even though I'm kind of in the middle of something."

"Yeah, uh, about that..." I had to get this out

quickly, because my courage was already fading again and I was starting to feel like the idiot I was. “Remember how I said I had no problem with you going on a date?”

“Yeah.”

“I uh... changed my mind about that.”

“What do you mean you changed your mind?”

Time to be honest. “I saw you in the restaurant and I do have a problem with it. I hate it.”

“You saw?” Dean paused. “Where are you right now?”

“Uh...” I looked around myself. “At the foot of the hill just outside town. Maybe fifteen minutes from the restaurant.” That was how long I’d lasted.

“Stay where you are. I'll be there in a few.” And with that he hung up, leaving me to contemplate what I’d just done, basically confessing my crush to my friend.

With every minute that passed while I waited for Dean, I thought about running away. I wasn't even sure where I would run, just...away. To some place Dean would never find me so I wouldn't have to face him. That was ridiculous of course, and I didn't move, but I did think about it.

In the end, it took Dean about ten minutes to get to me. I knew he'd come quickly, even though I felt like I'd been waiting forever. My heart was threatening to beat out of my chest, and I had the hardest time meeting my friend's gaze as he approached me. Not even the wine could help me now. I was too aware of what I'd done, too sober all of a sudden. Had to be the adrenaline.

“Hey,” I managed to mumble.

“Hey.” Dean gave me a smile so warm my heart couldn't decide whether it wanted to calm down or beat even faster–if that was possible. “What are you doing out here?”

“Just um...” What *was* I doing out here? “I was going to watch the sunset.”

“Really?” Dean glanced up the hill, then back at me. I could see what he was thinking; the hill wasn't very high–we could still get up there and catch the show if we wanted to. Still, I was surprised when he grabbed my hand and started walking. “Let's go then,” he said.

It had been a long time since I'd held hands with anyone, and the sudden contact sent a shiver down my spine. Dean's hand was as warm as his smile as he led me up the hill like he didn't think I was some sort of monumental fool.

We didn't speak until we reached the top a few minutes later.

The sun was really starting to set now, and the sky above us shone in a brilliant gold that I kind of wished I could capture on film. Especially the way it painted the rooftops of the houses when I looked back in the direction of the town. Oceanport seemed so serene in the warm glow of the setting sun, like a place where nothing bad could ever happen to you. I knew the image was deceptive, but I loved it all the same. And I loved standing here with Dean.

“I'm glad you called,” he spoke.

I glanced at him a bit shyly because he still hadn't let go of my hand, and I sort of didn't want him to. “I'm sorry I interrupted your date,” I lied, because I wasn't sorry at all. Embarrassed, yes. Sorry? No.

How could I be sorry when my call had led me here? Watching the sunset with Dean holding my hand.

It was too good to be true.

Dean shook his head. “To be honest, it wasn't

going well anyway." He took his eyes off the red and orange spectacle in the sky to look at me. "I just couldn't get you out of my head."

I stared. My heart skipped a beat. Was he saying what I thought he was saying?

He couldn't *possibly* be saying that.

But he *was* holding my hand. And he'd ditched his date for me, so...

I swallowed past the nervous lump in my throat. "You were thinking about me?" I forced a laugh. "You know I almost ran away after that phone call I was so embarrassed. I wanted to escape somewhere you couldn't find me. Like, hide in the forest or something. Lots of trees to hide behind." I could never stop myself from rambling my way through a tense situation.

Dean took it in stride, though. "Yeah?" he asked, his lips tugging up. Briefly, he scanned the forest that stretched out beyond the hill, then his eyes met mine again. "I would have found you."

That moment, I had absolutely no doubt that he would have. "And then what?" I asked. "Would you have told me off?"

"Oh, absolutely." His eyes gleamed with amusement. "And then I would have dragged you back home and..." He trailed off as heat entered his gaze, ratcheting up my nerves.

"And?" I prompted, because I couldn't deal with the anticipation. He smelled so alpha right then. Like all the things I wanted, and all the things that scared me. I couldn't move, torn between my desire to be with him, and my desire to run from every alpha who got close.

Dean wasn't just any alpha, though. He was my friend. I'd known him since we were children. I wasn't scared of him. I didn't *want* to be scared of him.

So when he leaned in, I didn't stop him. No, I

closed my eyes and focused on the feel of his lips on mine, on the way my heart fluttered at the contact, pumping adrenaline through my veins. Kissing Dean was beyond exhilarating. I felt like I was about to jump off a cliff and like I'd just won the award for best photographer at the same time. I felt like I was standing at the edge of something terrifyingly beautiful—something that would change my life forever.

And then I opened my mouth to him and took the plunge.

The way Dean kissed me wasn't the way alphas usually kissed me. There was nothing aggressive about it, nothing threatening. Just the feel of his lips and his tongue, brushing against mine and making the fine hair on my neck stand up.

This was... *nice*. Better than nice. I was in freefall, and I never wanted to land. I wanted to lose myself. But then I caught another whiff of his scent. I could feel myself respond to it, could feel that need to submit, to be *claimed* rise up in me. Heat rushed though me and my head spun with all the things I wanted this alpha to do to me, and I had to... I had to *breathe*.

I thought I could deal, but it was too much. Too fucking intense. I'd never reacted so strongly to anyone.

"Are you alright?" Dean asked as I broke away from him.

"I'm awesome." *Super awesome.* "Just had too much to drink."

"I see." Dean gave me a sympathetic smile, then he put an arm around my shoulder. "C'mon, I'll take you home. We can talk tomorrow."

Talk, right. I laughed, and hoped the sound wasn't too hysterical.

God, I needed help.

Chapter Nine

GRIFFIN

It was Sunday morning and I was going to die. At least, that's what I felt like waking up and remembering everything I'd done the evening before. In the semi-darkness of my bedroom, I fumbled for my phone and called my brother.

"Eliiii," I whined into the phone as soon as he picked up.

"Griff?" He sounded sleepy. "What's wrong?"

I glanced at the clock on my phone. It was barely past six. No wonder he sounded like he'd just rolled out of bed. For a second I felt sorry, then I went back to being miserable. "I think I'm going to diiiiie." Okay, maybe I was being a little melodramatic, but on top of my love life problems, my head felt like it was going to explode. Goddamn alcohol. I was never going to drink again. Ever.

"What's going on?" My big brother seemed a little more awake now. "You sound like that morning after your 21st birthday."

"It's woooorse." Maybe not the hangover, but everything else. Although to be fair, on the night of my 21st, I'd also made out with a guy. That hadn't ended well either, but at least with that guy, there hadn't been any *feelings* involved.

And dear God did I have feelings now. All the

feelings.

"It's six in the morning, bro, go back to sleep. You're going to be fine."

"No, wait, I need your help."

A moment of silence, then, "What do you need me to do?"

"You told me to tell you if... uh... I had a problem."

"Yeah, but I didn't mean a hangover. What did you even *do* last night?"

"I crashed Dean's date. You know my friend Dean? With the cupcakes."

"You crashed his date?"

I clutched my pillow in my arms. "I told him I don't want him to date anyone else. And now I don't know what to do."

"Oh Griff." My brother's voice was so full of sympathy I almost started to bawl. "Do you want me to come over so we can talk?" he asked.

"Would you?"

"Of course I would. Let me just get dressed and I'll be right over."

"Thank you."

"No need to thank me."

He hung up and I waited. I figured that maybe I should get dressed too, so I heaved myself out of bed. At least the only hangover symptom I was dealing with was a headache, no nausea, so that was good. Still, I brushed my teeth extensively before getting dressed.

How could Dean stand to kiss me the day before? Ugh.

Maybe that was why he hadn't tried again. Because I was gross. I spit into the sink and washed my mouth out.

Better.

Next I put on some clothes and prepared coffee. By the time Eli walked into the house, I felt almost like a person again.

"I'm in the kitchen," I called when I heard him take off his shoes in the entrance.

"Coming!"

I poured a mug of coffee for him and myself and put a more than generous amount of sugar in my own cup. I really needed that this morning.

When my brother came into the kitchen, I handed him his mug and we sat at the counter.

"Tell me what happened?" Eli asked.

"Well..." I closed my hands around my mug. Where to start? "Do you remember Dean?"

"Dean?" Eli furrowed his brow. "Wait, is that the kid you hung out with in school? Who was over at our place sometimes?"

"Yeah."

"That's the Dean you were talking about? He's the one feeding you cupcakes?" Eli's eyes widened, and I tried not to blush.

"Yeah."

"Wow, I thought he'd moved away or something."

"He did. But he came back a couple of months ago." Which Eli would have known if he kept up with the town's gossip at all. Everyone talked about the hot new firefighter in town who wasn't new after all.

"I had no idea. Why did you never say anything?"

"Because I know you. If I'd said anything, you would have assumed I was into him or something."

Eli just looked at me. "And would I have been wrong?"

"No," I admitted grudgingly.

Eli's expression turned sympathetic. "Is having a crush really such a bad thing?"

I didn't know what to say. It wasn't inherently a bad thing; it was only a bad thing for *me.* But how could I tell my brother that without admitting to everything that was wrong with me? I'd called him with the intention of doing just that, but now that he sat beside me, speaking the words turned out to be a lot more difficult than I'd thought.

"Tell me what happened last night?" Eli said when I remained silent.

I took a sip of my coffee to gain a moment to think.

"He went on a date with someone else, so... I got drunk. And then I called him and told him I didn't want him to be on a date with some other omega." It had seemed like a good idea at the time.

"How did he react?"

"He ditched his date and came to meet me."

"But that's great!" My brother's face lit up. "He must like you! From the way you sounded on the phone, I was afraid you'd been rejected."

"No, that's... not what happened." But I couldn't get myself to look as happy as my brother. "He does like me, I think..." I said. "He told me he couldn't get me out of his head... and then he kissed me." And that memory made me blush *furiously.*

"Awwww."

I glared at Eli. He was *loving* this. It was like he'd completely forgotten that he was here to *help* me.

"Did something else happen that makes you look like that?" Eli asked.

"No, it's just..." And this was where I had to explain.

"Your crush kisses you and you look like the apocalypse is waiting right outside the door. What's up with that?"

I took a sip of my coffee. And then another one, but still my mouth was dry. "I'm... I don't know if I can do this."

"Do what?" Eli looked confused. "Have a relationship?"

"It's not just that, it's..." I took a deep breath. There was no easy way to say this, was there? I just had to get it out. "I'm scared."

My big brother leaned in, his face full of concern. "What are you scared of?"

I felt transported back to a time in kindergarten when I'd told Eli about a mean kid who had tried to bully me. He'd been able to help me back then, but I wasn't so sure he could solve this problem. Still, I didn't know who else to talk to.

"I'm scared of... um... You know that feeling you get when you breathe in an alpha's scent and you kind of want to throw yourself down at their feet?"

Eli nodded slowly. "Yeah."

"That scares the shit out of me."

"Really? Is that why you haven't had a boyfriend?"

I hung my head in shame. "When Dean kissed me last night I didn't know whether I wanted to pull him toward me or push him away. I'm so fucked up."

"Oh, no." Eli laid an arm around my shoulders. "You're not fucked up. It *can* be pretty intense and overwhelming. Maybe you just need some time to get used to it. Maybe you and Dean just need to take it slow." He rubbed my back.

"I don't know." I took another deep breath. "How do I even tell Dean? I don't want him to think I find him disgusting or anything."

"I'm sure he won't think that. You two have known each other for a very long time, haven't you?"

"Yeah."

"Did you enjoy the kiss at least a little bit?"

"It was *amazing*. When I wasn't scared."

Eli laughed softly. "You'll be fine. But you and Dean will have to talk about this. Don't make my mistake. Don't let him go because you've convinced yourself you can't be what he needs."

I sighed. "He shouldn't have to deal with my issues."

Eli stroked my hair. "What he wants to deal with is for him to decide. There's more to relationships than just sex, you know."

"Yeah, I know from watching you there's also having babies and getting into fights over who has to take the trash out." I grinned at my brother.

He gave me a playful glare. "Oh, you."

I stuck my tongue out at him.

"Yeah," he said. "You're going to be just fine."

I hoped that he was right about that, but what if he wasn't?

Chapter Ten

DEAN

"Dude, what was that last night?" my cousin grilled me as I walked into the kitchen the morning after our double date. I couldn't really blame him. I'd totally stood him up after getting that call from Griff. I'd excused myself from the table and... never gone back.

Not exactly stellar behavior.

"I'm sorry," I said. "Griff called and I... lost my head."

Shane shook his head, but gave me a small smile. "You're so effing hopeless, man," Shane said, watching his choice of words as he poured a bowl of cereal for Conner.

"I guess I need to call and apologize to Edward."

"Yeah, you should. He was really bummed that you left. But at least that stopped Leonard from trying to come home with me."

"You didn't want him to?"

"With the kids here? Are you kidding?"

"What about us?" Conner asked.

"Nothing, buddy, eat your cereal." Shane placed the bowl in front of his son, and then went on to feed his daughter—who seemed more interested in playing with her food rather than eating it. She threw a fruit loop at me and giggled gleefully when she hit.

"Ow!" I said, just to amuse her. Then I turned to

Shane. “Do you think you're going to see him again?”

“Who are you seeing?” Conner asked.

“I'm not seeing anyone,” Shane said, still trying to get some food into Mary's mouth rather than on the floor. “You don't have to worry. I'm not... ready to date again.”

That seemed to satisfy the boy. I wondered whether he was worried someone could try to replace Ron. As if such a thing was possible.

“Dean might be seeing someone, though,” Shane said, throwing me under the bus.

Conner turned to me. “Are you seeing that man who was at the lake with us?”

The little one was perceptive, I had to give him that. “I might be,” I said. “I don't know yet.” But it was certainly looking good, and so I grinned.

“At some point you're gonna have to tell me what happened last night,” Shane said.

“Not much happened, really. But I think we made a step in the right direction. He was totally jealous of my date.”

“Was he?” Shane laughed. “Told you this date was going to be good for you.”

“I guess you were right. Just not in ways I expected.”

He shrugged. “Still counts.”

“Fine.” I couldn't really be mad. Not while things were going so well. I only hoped that Griff wasn't feeling differently about last night now that he was sober. I had to talk to him soon.

But first, my cousin wanted to talk to me about a surprising idea he’d had.

“You know, Conner had his play date with Jake yesterday,” he started after the children had wandered off into the living room to watch cartoons.

I gave him a smile. "Yeah? How did it go? I mean, did he talk about it?"

Shane glanced in the direction of the living room. "A little bit. He didn't say much, but... I think he had fun. It was good to see him like that. You know... smiling. And I've been wondering."

"About?" I drank the last sip of the coffee that remained in my mug. Now I felt almost ready to face the day. And whatever my cousin was wondering about.

"He seems to really, really like that dog."

I had to laugh. "Fiona?" Griff had told me about his brother's Labrador. She seemed to be a kind, gentle dog, and if she could put up with Jake's energy, she was probably good with all kids.

"Yeah, I think that's what she was called."

"I didn't think Conner would be into dogs."

"Me neither, but I think he should have one."

Both of my eyebrows shot up. Shane had never talked about wanting a pet before. In fact, I could remember him having a pet just once. It was a fish, and he'd managed to kill it pretty quickly. "You want to get a dog?" I asked, just to make sure I was getting this right.

"No need to act so shocked. Do you really think it's such a terrible idea?"

I shook my head. "You act all tough, but you're really just a big old softie, aren't you?" Matter of the fact was, Shane would do anything to make Conner smile more. That was sweet but... "You know nothing about dogs."

He sighed. "Which is why I'm asking you."

"Sorry, man." I shrugged. "I don't really know anything about dogs either." My parents had never allowed us kids to have a pet, and as an adult I'd been too busy to take care of one.

"Yeah, but maybe that omega you're dating

knows something."

"I'm not dating him." Not yet, anyway.

Shane shot me a dirty grin. "But you're hoping to."

Couldn't deny that. "Okay, I'm gonna ask him." Just after we'd talked about all the other things we needed to talk about.

Was I ever looking forward to that.

I made it until lunch time and then I couldn't wait any longer; I called Griff on his cell phone. He answered after a few rings.

"Hey," I said, feeling just the slightest bit awkward. That was new for me. I was used to knowing what I wanted and going for it. Now, I certainly knew what I wanted—Griff, just Griff—but I struggled with the going for it part in a way that was wholly uncharacteristic for me. Something about my friend made me nervous. Maybe because there was more at stake. If I messed things up with Griff, I'd lose him as a friend as well as a lover.

I couldn't stand that thought.

"Hey, Dean." Griff's voice was lacking its usual infusion of cheer. Something was bothering him. I hoped he wasn't regretting last night.

"Do you think we could meet?" Because this was not something to be discussed over the phone. And also because I really, really wanted to see him.

"Yeah, we could meet." Griff hesitated for a moment, then he said, "Could you come over here?"

"Of course. You want me to bring you some

muffins? I made a fresh batch." After all, I'd needed to do *something* to keep the nerves at bay. What a fine alpha I was.

That got a laugh out of him. Such a clear, beautiful sound. I could listen to it all day. "You know the answer to that," he said.

"I'm going to take that as a yes. And I'll be over in a few minutes."

"I'm looking forward to it," Griff said before hanging up, but he still sounded nervous.

Well, at least that made two of us.

Chapter Eleven

GRIFFIN

Oh God, Dean was on his way over. To *talk*. I swallowed, even though my mouth was completely dry. Eli had left a few minutes ago, wishing me good luck, and now I was pacing through the house, trying and failing not to completely freak out.

Normal people didn't feel like this when their crush was coming over, or did they?

I nearly jumped out of my skin when the doorbell rang, heart pounding in my throat.

Breathe, Griff. You're going to be fine. Think of what Eli said. If he really likes you, he won't mind waiting a bit.

But what if he didn't like me enough?

Pulling my lower lip between my teeth, I walked to the front door and opened it.

Dean looked nearly as gorgeous as he had the night before, even though he wasn't wearing those tight pants now. But he *was* wearing a smile and carrying a box with muffins, and if there's one thing you need to know about me, it's that I'd take muffins over tight pants any day. This man really knew the way to my heart was paved with sugar.

"Hey," I greeted him, and somehow, a smile found its way on my lips as well. It was nearly impossible to look at him and not light up—no matter that I had difficult things to explain. "Come in. And let me take those muffins out of your hands."

"Oh yeah, they were really getting too heavy to carry." Dean handed the muffins over gracefully. They smell of freshly baked sweets was heavenly—almost as intoxicating as the scent Dean was giving off. *Almost.*

I led Dean into the living room, where I'd sat with my brother just half an hour ago, watching silly cartoons to relax. I kind of wanted to go back to that, but I didn't think Dean would be open to the suggestion of watching cartoons just then.

Putting the muffins on the coffee table, I sat on the couch and patted the free space next to me. "Sit with me?"

"Sure." He left a few inches between us, unsurprisingly. He'd never been pushy. Even the night before, he hadn't tried to kiss me again after that one time.

What was I so scared of?

"So uh... about last night," Dean started.

"Yeah?" I prompted.

"You should know I've been wanting to do that for a long time."

"Really?" How could that be true? Had we both been secretly pining for each other? "For how long?"

He gave me a pained smile. "Too long, really." Stroking a hand through his hair, he continued. "It kind of started shortly before I moved away. You were the first omega I've ever had a crush on. But then, you know... You were my friend, and you didn't seem like you would be interested in making out. I didn't want to say anything and lose you. And then I left town." He shrugged helplessly. "I thought I was over my crush when I came back here to help Shane, but then I saw you and it all came back. You're even more handsome now than you were when I left here."

Heat spread across my cheeks. I couldn't believe Dean really felt that way about me. I was nothing special. Just a small-town omega who refused to act like an adult. "I had no idea you liked me that way."

Dean only shook his head. "How could I not? You're sweet and funny and... always there when anybody needs help."

I laughed, because I was so embarrassed by all his kind words. "So are you, Mr. Firefighter."

"We make a good couple then," he said, making me pause. Were we a couple now? Was it that easy? "I'm sorry," Dean said when he noticed my confusion. "I'm moving too fast, aren't I?"

"I don't know if you're too fast or I'm too slow," I said honestly.

"I guess we'll have to meet in the middle. I can slow down. It's no big deal," he promised.

I took a deep breath. "How slow can you go? Because uh... I might need you to slow *way* down." I tried not to wince as I said that, and I barely managed to meet his gaze. The only reason I could do it at all was because his eyes were kind and gentle.

"Whatever you need," he said, and there was so much honesty in his voice he almost convinced me. "I know you're serious," he added, "because you haven't even tried the muffins yet."

I had to laugh at that, tense as I was. "You really know me, don't you?"

"I do!" He handed me a muffin. "Eat. You'll feel better."

"Thank you." I took the sugary treat from him and our fingers brushed as I did so. The contact made my skin tingle, and I wondered if he felt that too. Probably yes, judging by the way he looked at me. He wanted more contact just as much as I did, only without the fear I associated with that idea.

I bit into the muffin to distract myself. Dean really needed to know what he was getting into with me—that was only fair. And he'd said I could have whatever I needed, so... I swallowed the piece of muffin, barely noticing the taste, and spoke again. "When I say slow I mean... uh... no... bedroom activities for a while."

I really wished I could have said that without my cheeks glowing, but that wasn't possible. Dear Lord, I wasn't twelve anymore, but I sure acted like it.

"Were you scared I was going to drag you into bed right now?"

"Don't you want to?"

Dean scoffed. "Of course I want to. But I also want to eat a whole batch of muffins and cake for breakfast, and I want to buy a ridiculously expensive car and never work another day in my life. But just because I want to doesn't mean I'm going to do any of those things. I can control myself. I just want to know what's bothering you, so I don't do anything that makes you uncomfortable."

"The thought of sex makes me uncomfortable," I admitted. "That's why I didn't tell you that I like you."

"Really? That's why?" Both of Dean's eyebrows went up. "I was never just going to jump you like a wild animal, you know. We can... work up to it. If you want to, I mean."

I exhaled, and bit into the muffin again. It had a bit more taste now that Dean was being so relaxed about all this. "I do want to. I'm just... I've never been with anyone like that." Embarrassing to admit, at my age. Being a virgin was considered a good trait in an omega—but only to a point.

"That's okay." Slowly, Dean laid an arm around

my shoulders, as if waiting for me to object. I didn't, though. I leaned in to his touch, in fact, glad he was taking all this so well. I'd never thought I'd find an alpha like him, someone not scared off by my issues with intimacy. Maybe I could trust him. *Of course* I could trust him. My fears just needed time to catch up with what my heart already knew.

"How do you feel about kissing?" Dean asked. "Is that out too? Did I step over the line last night? Because I need to know where the line is."

"I'm not sure. I think kissing is okay? Just a little bit?" I could probably handle it if I knew things weren't going to go further than that. Just a little mouth-to-mouth contact. Just a little thrill. I wanted that.

"Can I kiss you? Because I haven't been able to stop thinking about it since last night."

I gave him a smile, and kissed him. Because why should the alpha always be the one to take the initiative? I liked this man, he liked me, so I could kiss him, right?

And actually, being the one to start things off felt really good. There was no pressure, no expectation of submission, or anything. Just the feeling of my lips touching Deans and that small jolt of electricity that went through me at the contact.

Dean seemed to have no problem letting me run the show either. He was *perfect*, opening his mouth when I nudged his lips with my tongue, and then letting me explore without trying to gain dominance over the kiss. So I was free to enjoy the way he tasted, the way he smelled even, all masculine and alpha. But that wasn't scaring me now. For this one blissful moment, all I felt was affection—and a deep, deep longing for time to just freeze us this way, resting our foreheads together. Picture perfect.

But as a photographer, I knew that time always ticked on and the conditions for a perfect shot were fickle, and so even this moment came to an end. Still, when I parted from Dean, I saw the brightest smile on his lips and a look of awe on his face—and that memory would stay with me forever.

"Was that what you were thinking about?" I asked, grinning at him and grabbing another muffin.

He laughed, and there was so much joy in his voice. I really hadn't scared him off with my confessions at all. "Not exactly," he admitted, "but we'll have to do that again."

I smiled at him. "Wouldn't mind that."

He simply smiled back at me. "Actually, I have a favor to ask. Sort of."

"What kind of favor?"

"Don't worry," he said, reaching for a muffin. "It's nothing sexual. It's for my cousin, really."

"Good thing then that it's nothing sexual, because I wasn't going to kiss your cousin." I bit into my muffin. Now that the tension had fallen off me, I noticed a hint of vanilla in the flavor. *So good.* The twelve-year-old part of me wanted to marry this man for his baking skills alone.

"No, nothing like that. I wouldn't want you to kiss him either."

"Oh, are you possessive?"

"Maybe a little bit," he said with a twinkle in his eyes.

"Good to know!" I punched his arm. "Now I know not to let you see me get my muffins from the café."

He put on a shocked face. "You wouldn't dare!"

"I don't know," I teased, feeling brave in the aftermath of our talk. "They're not as good as yours, but you know, a man has needs."

"Are you saying I can't fulfill your needs?"

"I'm saying you'll have to spend a lot more time baking if you want to keep me from trying another man's treats."

Dean only shook his head. "Once you've gotten used to the taste of my treats no other man's will be able to satisfy you anyway."

"Oh yeah? We'll see about that." I tried to look aloof, but couldn't keep up the pretense and ended up laughing instead. It was good to know that Dean and I could still joke around like friends, even if we were also kissing now. "What kind of favor were you going to ask me?"

"Nothing big, really. Shane is thinking about getting a dog."

"A dog?" I raised an eyebrow at him. "Where did he get that idea? And what's it got to do with me?" I wasn't the one studying to become a veterinarian. That was my brother.

"He just thought... because Conner seems to really like Fiona."

"Oh. Did he get to meet her? Everyone loves Fiona." She was a good dog. I missed her a little, to be honest. The house felt awfully empty without her. I'd thought once or twice that maybe I should get a dog too, but hadn't jumped at the opportunity yet.

"Yeah, apparently he was over at your brother's on Saturday."

"That's great." I chewed on my muffin. "Maybe getting a dog is not such a bad idea. Animal company can be soothing."

"You think so? I was thinking you could help because we know nothing about dogs."

I chuckled. "You'll be fine. We can go to the shelter where Eli worked, pick out a good dog that'll get along with Conner and the little one. I can help you get the dog settled. And if you get an older one—"

"I don't think that's a good idea," Dean cut me off.

"What?"

"Getting an older dog. I don't... I don't think the kids should be dealing with death again anytime soon."

"Oh, good point." I rubbed my chin. "Hadn't thought about that. But still, I'm sure we can find a dog that suits your needs. We can go tomorrow if you want."

"That would be great. I'll talk to my cousin." He made to get up from the couch.

"Hey, where are you going?"

"Uh... You don't want me to go yet?"

"Nope." I pulled on his sleeve and made him sit *riiight* next to me. "I know I said we needed to take it slow, but that doesn't mean I don't want to be with you, okay?" Maybe if I could get used to having him close my fears would vanish with time. "You have to stay and eat your muffins, and maybe we can finish watching that show we started last week?"

"You mean you haven't watched any more yet?"

"Yeah, I did, but I want to see it again with you. Pleeease?" I sucked my upper lip in and shot him a pleading look.

"Okay." He laughed. "Anything for you." He leaned in just a bit to kiss my forehead, and I had to laugh too.

Maybe, just maybe, things were going to be fine.

I could only hope so.

Chapter Twelve

DEAN

"You have a nice spring in your step today, son," Mrs. Rosewood commented as I wheeled her through the park Monday morning. "Did something happen with that nice young omega you set your sights on?"

"Nothing happened," I said, following my first instinct. Then I corrected myself, because Mrs. Rosewood was a nice lady and she seemed almost as invested in this romance as I was. "We kissed this weekend," I admitted.

She laughed softly. "You kissed! How exciting. Is that all that happened?"

Okay, now she was digging a little deep. "We're taking it slow," I told her.

That seemed to amuse her even more. "Taking it slow? Boy, if I didn't know better I'd think you were my age! You're too young to be talking like that. Who ever heard of an alpha and an omega in their youth taking it slow?" She laughed again. Well, at least one of us was having a good time.

"We're doing what's right for us," I insisted. As long as Griff wasn't ready, I wasn't going to push him. Waiting was hard when all I wanted to do was sprinkle powdered sugar all over him and lick my way across his body, but I was sure that Griff was going to be worth the wait. I wanted him to enjoy our first time together just as much as I would.

"Pah." Mrs. Rosewood snorted and shook her fist in the air dramatically. "It's time for you to be making babies with that omega."

"Let's not rush anything." Mrs. Rosewood was sweet, but like many of her generation she had some pretty outdated ideas about alphas and omegas and relationships.

"If you don't rush anything, some other alpha is going to claim that omega before you can. Mark my word! He's a pretty thing. It's a miracle no one's put a bun in his oven yet."

I groaned, and not only because Mrs. Rosewood was being crude, but also because the visual she put in my head of a pregnant Griff was pretty damn alluring. Especially if I imaged him being pregnant with *my* child. "No other alpha is going to claim him." And if they tried, they wouldn't leave with all their teeth in their mouth.

Mrs. Rosewood shook his head. "As an alpha, you need to be proactive about these things. The omega is looking to you for cues. I know, my little sister is an omega."

I raised an eyebrow at her. Female omegas were a rarity—and among the most fertile creatures on the planet. Male omegas were amazingly fertile too, but females tended to have multiples with every pregnancy. Twins, at least. I should know, my mother was an omega and I was the only one among my siblings who wasn't part of a set.

"That's nice about your sister. Your family must be very blessed to have her," I said. "But Griff is a different person. He might not feel that way."

She sighed and shook her head as if I was being a stubborn little boy who wouldn't listen. "You young alphas. You have no balls anymore." She said it with so much conviction that for a split second I actually felt insulted before I burst out laughing.

"Maybe you're right, Mrs. Rosewood. Maybe you're right, but times change, and we change with them."

"Pah," she said again. "Even the fact that you're here... Alphas shouldn't be taking care of old people. Aren't you a firefighter? You should be out in the world and saving people."

This time her words made me cringe. "I'm taking a little break." Just until I could think about going back without having nightmares about my last day on the job. But I wasn't going to tell her about that. I wasn't telling anyone. If she thought I was a poor excuse for an alpha now, what would she think if she *knew*?

No, no one could know.

That afternoon, Shane and I met Griff in front of the town's animal shelter. I still wasn't sure where exactly the line was between Griff and me, but since he'd seemed okay with kissing so far, I gave him a short peck on the lips to say hello. From the expression on his face, he didn't mind.

"Hey," he said softly, a smile gracing his features. Then he greeted Shane as well. "So you're the one in the market for a new dog?"

"Yeah. Looking to surprise my son." Shane smiled as well, even if he seemed a little bit unsure. "Something that's going to live for a few years at least." He put that so awkwardly that both Griff and I had to laugh after a moment.

"A dog isn't a thing," Griff said. "And they don't

come with a warranty, but we can look for a young one to increase your chances."

"That sounds good."

"Okay, then. Let's go in."

Oceanport was a small town, and thus, the shelter was comparatively small as well. Still, the few kennels they had were filled with dogs of varying sizes. Some of them yipped excitedly as we walked by, others couldn't be bothered to acknowledge our presence at all.

"You're in luck," the staff member who'd taken us on said. She was a young woman who went by the name of Ava. "Just a little while ago we took in a highly pregnant Golden Retriever lady, and she's had her puppies since. They're almost ready for adoption too."

"That's great." Shane actually sounded enthusiastic now.

"I do have to warn you that puppies are a lot of work, though," the lady advised us. "They need to be house trained and require a lot of attention."

"That's perfect," Shane said, probably hoping the puppy would distract Conner from other things. Maybe he was even hoping that it would distract all of us. I could see that happening.

And when the staff member led us to the kennel with the puppies, it was too late to go back anyway. No one, absolutely no one, could look at those adorable, fluffy little things and not want one.

"We can have any one of these?" Shane asked.

"Take your pick," the shelter lady said. "We're reasonably sure we can get all of these to good homes, but none have been claimed yet." She unlocked the kennel and stepped inside. The puppies who had been crowding around their proud momma a second ago now all came to sniff at her feet. Obviously, she was popular with the dogs.

"Hey cuties," she said, bending down to pick a puppy out of the bunch. All in all, there were four of them, each of them a strong contender for the role of cutest thing ever.

"This one is my personal favorite," Ava said. "He's the fiercest of them all, and fiercely lovable." And just as she said this, the puppy licked her face as if to prove her point. "I'd adopt him myself if I had the space, but he's going to love living in a household with children."

"Good. Can I hold him?" Shane asked while I stood back with Griff.

"Man, I want one," Griff whispered as Ava handed the dog to Shane.

"We're here for Shane and Conner, remember?" I whispered back. "Besides, you have Fiona."

"Fiona doesn't live with me anymore."

"I could stay with you more if you're just feeling lonely." I wanted to grab his ass in a suggestive gesture, but settled on resting my hand on his lower back instead.

Think of the line.

Hell if I knew where it *was*, though. For now, I had to trust that Griff would tell me if I did something that he didn't want me to do.

"You're not a dog," Griff said.

"Good thing, too. If I was a dog, I couldn't bake for you," I reminded him while I watched my cousin pet the puppy he was most likely taking home.

"That would suck. Why can't you shift back and forth between being a dog and being a man?"

"I didn't know you were into furries," I teased.

"Am not!" He whacked me over the head, lips drawn into a pout. God, he was at least as adorable as the puppies.

"Does he have a name?" I heard Shane ask.

"You can name him," Ava said with a smile.

"I'll let my son name him, then," Shane said, the puppy licking each of his fingers in turn.

"Sure. We'll take care of the paperwork and you can pick him up next week. We'll also help you pick out a leash and everything then."

"I guess it's decided," I said to Griff. "Thanks for coming with us today."

"It was no problem. There's no better excuse not to work than looking at puppies."

I laughed. "Guess you're right." I almost wanted one too. I'd always wanted a big house and a dog, and now with Griff standing next to me, I also knew who I wanted to share that house with. But it was too early to be thinking thoughts like that. We'd only just had our first kiss and I wasn't even sure where we stood with each other. But in my heart of hearts, I already knew that there couldn't be anyone else for me. No matter what it took, I wanted this omega.

No other would do.

Chapter Thirteen

GRIFFIN

Entering my nephew's school to do my volunteer work brought back a ton of memories. I'd gone to school here too when I was his age. When I looked out the window of the auditorium, I saw the schoolyard where I'd first met Dean all those years ago.

I'd brought a bottle of soap bubbles to school with me that day. All the other kids had been jealous when I'd taken it out during the break. I'd been open to sharing—I wanted everyone to enjoy the fun with me, really—but not everybody thought sharing was a good idea. Some third grader had stomped up to six-year-old me and ripped the bottle out of my hand.

And that was when I'd first noticed Dean, because he'd gotten it back for me by standing up to the bully.

It was all such a long time ago, but being here really brought the memories back. Dean and I had had a lot of fun the rest of that break, blowing bubbles in each other's faces.

"How's it coming along?" the theater teacher asked me, yanking me out of my reverie.

"Coming along okay," I said. It wasn't hard work. All they wanted me to do was paint an image of a forest and some mountains in the background on a big wooden canvas. Still, as I looked around myself, I realized that I'd stayed longer than all the other parents. Sometimes I just completely lost myself in a task. Especially when there was paint involved.

"Good, good." The teacher nodded approvingly. Him, I knew from when I was still in school too. Eric Zimmerman. He'd been three years above me, and always a bit of an eccentric kid. Liked to stand in the limelight. It was no surprise, really, that he taught theater now. "Say, Griffin," he continued. "It's your nephew in the play, isn't it?"

"Yeah. My nephew Jake."

Eric nodded again. "No children of your own?" he asked, even though he had to know. He regarded me with this half-speculative, half-pitying look that I knew all too well.

"No, no children of my own." I suppressed a sigh. I got this question far too often. People just couldn't fathom that omegas my age would not have children. They weren't wrong to assume that something wasn't quite right with me, of course, but it was still *rude*. What I did with my life was my choice and mine alone, even if I did feel something missing.

"I don't have children either," Eric said. "No partner. Somehow never happened."

"Yeah, but you're not an omega, so it's not expected of you," I said before I could stop myself. To my knowledge, Eric was neither an omega nor an alpha. He was what some people called a beta. There was no weirdly intoxicating scent coming off him to drive me crazy. But nothing about him particularly attracted me, either. Betas just didn't really show up on my radar. A shame, really. Something told me I'd have an easier time dating a beta rather than an alpha, if I was into them at all.

"I guess you're right," Eric said. "Doesn't mean I

don't *want* children, though. I became a teacher because I like children."

"I see." I looked away from him to paint some more green on the canvas.

"Is your nephew looking forward to the play?"

"I guess," I said, keeping my attention fixed on the work I was doing. Didn't Eric have some work of his own to get done? He was starting to get on my nerves for reasons I couldn't even explain.

"Good, good," he said again. "It's good to have him on the team. You know, I've been thinking maybe you and I should get together sometime and discuss our work over a cup of coffee."

What? I turned around. Eric had my full attention again. Was he seriously asking me out? The guy couldn't take a hint, could he? "A cup of coffee?" I asked just to make sure. "You mean like going to a coffee house together and having a cup of coffee?" I must be coming across like an idiot, even though he was the actual idiot here if he seriously thought I'd be going out with him. Then again, he didn't know about Dean, so maybe it was a fair assumption to make?

"Just a cup of coffee, Griffin. Don't make a big deal out of it."

"I'm not making a big deal out of it." Was I? "I'm just asking. I'm not really sure what we would have to discuss. I'm only doing a bit of paint."

"Don't underestimate the importance of your work." He gave me a smile, but it had something sleazy to it, something that creeped me out. What did he want with me?

"Sorry," I said. "I don't think I have time. And actually, I'm done here for tonight." Definitely done. *So* done. "I think I'll have my boyfriend come pick me up."

I saw shock register on Eric's face, but only for a

split second, then he covered it up with the same sleazy smile he'd had before. "You have a boyfriend?" he said it like the idea amused him.

Oh, great, he didn't believe it. I tried not to roll my eyes. "Yeah, in fact, I'm going to call him right now." *Because you're making me really uncomfortable, dude.* I dug through my pockets for my phone and finally fished it out. Eric watched me curiously while I dialed Dean's number.

Fortunately, he answered quickly. "Hey, Dean."

"Griff?"

"Yeah. Listen, could you come pick me up? And maybe hurry? I'm done here now."

"Where are you?" Dean sounded slightly concerned now because we hadn't made any arrangement for him to pick me up from anywhere. But Eric didn't have to know that.

"Yeah, I'm at the elementary school."

"I'll be right there. Are you okay?"

"Yeah. Thank you." I hung up. Thank God Dean wasn't busy right now. Then I would have had to find another way to get rid of the creep.

"Was that the Dean who went to school with us? The firefighter who came back to town?" Eric asked.

"Spot on."

Eric's grin widened. "I remember him. You guys are friends. You're not dating." He sounded almost relieved. Like he'd figured this all out.

Fucker.

"The dating is a recent development," I informed him. "You know we omegas just can't keep it in our pants." *But that's what you were counting on, isn't it?* I suppressed a shudder at the mental image of Eric trying to get it on with me.

Eric looked a bit taken aback at my choice of

words. Served him right for provoking me.

"I'm gonna go wait outside now. He'll be here any minute." It was a good thing Dean didn't live far away. I wasn't sure how much longer I could stand being here.

"Alright. I'll just give you some company until he gets here."

"Oh, that's not necessary." I gave him a tight smile. "Oceanport is a quiet town. Nothing's going to happen to me if I just stand outside the school. Even if I'm a vulnerable omega."

"That's not what I meant to imply," Eric lied. "It would simply be rude to keep you waiting on your own while you're volunteering your time for my play."

"It's really no problem." I grabbed my jacket and started to leave the auditorium. He chose not to believe my words, of course, and followed me anyway.

"What?" he asked, when I shot him a look. "I'm headed home as well." He locked the door to the auditorium behind himself as if he desperately needed to prove his point. I still didn't believe him. Why would I? But I realized it was pointless to argue with him any further.

I hung out by the street lamp in front of the school so Dean would see me when he got here. The sun had just set a few minutes ago, but it was still reasonably warm. A nice summer evening. Or it would have been nice, if I didn't have some pseudo stalker on my trail.

This was not what I'd signed up for when I'd agreed to help make Jake's play better.

I sighed and looked at my phone. A few minutes had passed since I'd called Dean. If he was hurrying, he couldn't be much longer. Meanwhile, Eric was pretending to be busy on his own phone. No doubt he was waiting for Dean to either never show up, or for him to show up as nothing more than a friend.

But he wasn't going to get that satisfaction.

I shoved my phone back in my pocket and glanced down the street, biting my lower lip.

Please get here quickly.

And there he was. I breathed a sigh of relief as I spotted a man walking up the street who could only be Dean. The walk was unmistakable. There was something inherently confident about Dean's step. I might have called it a swagger, but it wasn't *that* pronounced—or douchey.

"Dean!" I waved as he approached, a smile lighting up my face. I was *so* glad he was here. And because I needed to prove a point to Eric—and because I really wanted to—I sprinted up to him, threw my arms around his neck and kissed him. His surprise lasted only a second before he kissed me back, sending a shiver down my spine as his tongue swiped my lips. I wasn't sure about sex yet, but kissing him was awesome—even more so when we were doing it in public where certain people could see.

Dean smiled at me as we parted. "What was that for?"

"Just a greeting." I tapped his nose. "You don't like it?"

He scoffed. "As if. Just didn't expect it."

"Well, get used to it, because I get the feeling we need to be doing it a lot more." I grabbed him by the hand and let him away from the school, up the street in the direction of my house.

"We need to?" Dean asked. "Did something happen tonight? Is that why you called? You had me a bit worried on the phone, you know."

"I'm sorry. I didn't mean to worry you."

"What were you doing here anyway?"

"Oh, didn't I tell you? Jake enlisted me to help with his play. I was working on some of the props tonight."

"Oh, right. I heard about the play. Conner is in it too."

"He is?" That surprised me. I hadn't taken Conner for the sort of boy who would like to be on a stage.

"Yeah, I can tell he's nervous about it too, even though he was in it two years ago as well. But Ron did the props back then."

"Oh." My heart sank as I realized why I'd been given this job this year. The person who used to do it couldn't. Right.

"Anyway," Dean said, as if he wanted to change the topic just as much as I did. "Was there a reason you needed me to get you? Not that I mind..."

"Well." I glanced back at the school. "To be honest, the teacher kind of weirded me out."

"The teacher?" Dean looked confused. No wonder. I would have been too.

"You remember Eric Zimmerman?"

Dean raised an eyebrow at me. "That guy became a teacher? No kidding?"

"Yeah, but you have to admit, he always had a knack for the dramatic."

That made Dean laugh. "No doubt. Still, didn't think he would want to work here."

I shrugged. "Whatever makes him happy. Just wish he hadn't tried to ask me out."

"He tried to ask you out?" Dean furrowed his brow.

I chuckled. "You don't like that idea, do you? Don't worry. I'm sure he has absolutely no baking skills to tempt me with."

Dean shook his head. "Oh, I'm not worried that you could be tempted. I know I've spoiled you."

That made me laugh harder. "What, you're not even a little jealous?"

"No, just hoping the creep knows to keep his dirty hands off you."

"He didn't want to believe that we were a couple at first, but I'm sure that kiss showed him."

Dean looked at me with both eyebrows raised.

"What?" I asked.

"You just called us a couple."

I blushed, because I'd said it without thinking. "I did, didn't I?"

"You definitely did." Dean grinned.

"Guess we're a couple then."

"Guess we are."

Dean leaned over to kiss me, and I opened up to him without hesitation. The fine stubble around his mouth brushed my skin and I felt the tiniest trickle of fear in the back of my mind, but it wasn't enough to stop me. It wasn't enough to combat the joy this moment gave me. Dean was my boyfriend and I was his.

Now we only needed to tackle the rest of this relationship stuff.

Chapter Fourteen

DEAN

The Sunday after our visit to the shelter, and two days after that stupid creep had tried to hit on Griff, Shane and I were going to surprise Conner. The puppy was ready to come home, and my cousin hadn't told his son anything about our plans yet. I was sure the boy was going to be ecstatic, though. I couldn't wait for Shane to get back from the shelter with his furry surprise, but until then, I was on babysitter duty.

"Play!" Mary demanded, banging one of her dolls against my leg while Conner sat in the corner of the living room with a book.

"What do you want to play?" I asked, taking the doll from the little girl.

Wordlessly, she brought me another doll and started banging *that* against my leg.

"Oh, I see. Is that what you want to do? Destroy Uncle Dean's leg? Fun game."

She giggled in response. Evil little thing. At least she wasn't really hurting me, so I let her do it for the time being.

And I was just finishing my coffee when Conner walked into the kitchen. "Where's Dad?" he asked. "I need him to sign something for school."

I glanced at the clock. "He should be back any minute. What do you need signed?"

He shrugged. "We're going on a trip to some museum." It didn't sound like he was looking forward to that. Then again, the boy wasn't looking forward to much these days. I wasn't sure if having a four-legged playmate could change that, but anything was worth a try.

"Sounds like fun," I said. And then I heard a car drive up to the house. Shane, probably. My lips quirked up. Time to see how well this puppy would be received. "Guess your Dad is back. You can show him that thing you need signed."

"I'll go get it." Conner left the room as the front door opened.

I hoisted Mary up on my arm and went to greet my cousin.

"Doggy!" she squealed as soon as she saw the yellow bundle in Shane's hands.

I grinned. "That's right. That's a doggy."

Shane was smiling as well, while the puppy regarded Mary curiously. "You like the doggy?" Shane asked his daughter.

"Doggy!" she said again, happily, reaching one hand out. I stepped a little closer to Shane so she could pet the newest member of the family.

"Where's Conner?" Shane asked.

"Should be here any minute. He just went to his room to get something."

"Alright then. Conner!" Shane yelled. "I got something for you!"

"Coming! I need you to..." Conner stopped short as he stepped into the hallway. "Is that a puppy?" Wide-eyed, he stared at the dog, and the dog stared right back. I got the feeling it was the beginning of a wonderful friendship. Even though it was maybe a bit of a rough start, because the puppy barked and Conner took a step back.

Shane laughed. "He wants to play."

Conner tilted his head, looking at his dad. "Are we keeping him?"

"Unless you want me to take him back?"

"No!" Conner said quickly. "Wait, we're really having a dog now?" Slowly, he stepped up to the puppy in his father's arm, the permission slip he'd wanted signed all but forgotten.

"You can pet him," Shane said. "Your little sister already did."

"Really?" Conner reached a hand out and stroked it carefully over the puppy's golden fur. The puppy seemed to appreciate it too, first sniffing his hand and then licking.

"You have to give him a name," Shane said.

"I have to name him?"

"Yeah, he's your dog, after all."

"He's mine?" The little boy was clearly overwhelmed with all this news, standing almost frozen before his father as if he didn't know how to express excitement anymore.

"Yes, he's yours. If you want him. Do you want him?"

Conner tentatively reached both his hands out to the puppy. "I want him," he whispered almost reverently. "Can I have him?"

"You'll have to walk him," Shane said. "And clean up his messes."

"I will!" It was the most enthusiastic I'd ever heard Conner. "I'll take care of him."

"Good. Just don't call him George, though." Shane smiled and set the dog down on the floor.

Instantly, Mary began to struggle in my arms. "Down, down!"

Laughing, I let her down, where she started crawling across the floor behind the puppy. She knew how to walk, of course, but apparently it was more fun to imitate the doggy. Shane joined me in my laughter, and then, so did Conner.

I had a feeling it was going to be a good day.

Until Griff called me.

Chapter Fifteen

GRIFFIN

My Sunday started out peacefully. I went to my brother's place to talk to him. He lived in this beautiful house at the outskirts of the town—as removed from everything as you could be while still being part of civilization. It sure paid to marry a rich alpha, I thought to myself as I knocked on the door. Only a second later, I found myself face to face with said alpha, carrying a little baby girl in his arms as he opened the door to me.

"Hey, Matt," I greeted my brother-in-law. "Hey, Livvy." I tapped my niece's adorable little nose.

"Hey, Griff. Eli's in the living room," he informed me. "And if you're not careful, Jake's going to barrel into you and force you to play cops and robbers. I've already been shot three times today."

I laughed. "Thanks for the warning." Although I wouldn't have minded playing with my nephew instead of doing what I'd actually come here for. I needed to tell my brother about what a creep Eric had turned out to be. Because I sure as hell wasn't going back to work with him.

I walked into the living room, only a little sad that Jake didn't try to abduct me on my way.

"Oh, hey Griff!" Eli greeted me as I entered. He was sitting on the couch with a heavy book open in his lap. Some textbook for school probably. He was really serious about that, as well he should be. My brother was going to be a veterinarian, finally, and I was proud of him. Not many omegas managed to become doctors. He was a trailblazer, even if he got delayed by a few years.

I sat next to him. "Studying hard?"

"You know it." He put the book aside and stifled a yawn. "Just wish some of these books could be written a little more clearly."

"Maybe you can rewrite them some day."

Eli snorted. "Yeah, right. I want to save animals, not write books. Speaking of animals, isn't today the day Conner's getting his puppy?"

"Yeah." I'd told Eli all about that. Only Jake didn't know, because he would have ruined the surprise. "I hope it goes well. I'm going to go over there later and check."

"Check, right." My brother shot me a knowing look. "What you really want is to play with the puppy."

"Busted." I poked my tongue out of him. "Like you're not becoming a vet to play with dogs all day."

"Please," Eli drawled. "It's serious business." He stretched. "Anyway, you said you had something to talk about?"

"Yeah, actually." I pulled my lower lip between my teeth. How best to approach this subject? "You know the theater teacher? Eric? I think he might have been in your year in school..."

"Yeah, I know him. Of course I do. I'm making some of the costumes, remember?"

Right. "I was at the school Friday night trying to be a good uncle and work on the props, and... well, he was there as well."

Eli's eyes narrowed slightly as he switched into older-brother mode. "Did something happen between you and Eric?"

"Not exactly, but I got the feeling he wanted something to happen, you know? He was really kind of creepy about it. I had to call Dean to pick me up so he would see that I have a boyfriend. Since he didn't want to believe me when I told him. I've never known betas to be so fucking creepy." I shuddered at the memory.

Eli rested a hand on my back, between my shoulder blades. "I'm sorry he was such a creep. I swear he was never like that with me."

"It's alright," I said. "In the end, nothing happened. I'm just not sure I want to go back there. I mean, I still want to help." Especially now that I knew who I was replacing. "But he creeps me out."

"No, I get that." Eli's brows furrowed. "I'll talk to him, tell him to back off if he wants those props done." He took a deep breath. My brother actually sounded pissed, and that didn't happen very often. "You're not going to the school by yourself anymore, either. I'll come with you next time."

"Thank you." I leaned back into the couch, feeling a little better now I had this off my chest and a solution in sight. I glanced at the TV, which wasn't on. "Any good cartoons this morning?"

Eli shook his head. "Like you don't know the TV schedule inside and out."

"Can't fool you, can I?" I reached for the remote—and that was when we first heard the sirens.

Eli and I looked at each other frowning. Nothing much happened in Oceanport. It wasn't often that you heard sirens. This was a call to action for the local fire department.

"Wonder what happened," Eli said, walking to the window to look outside.

"You see anything?"

"Nah. We're too far out."

"Figures. Maybe I'll see something on my way back home later." And that was the extent of my concern at that point, simple curiosity. I didn't know then that the sound of the sirens was connected to someone I knew.

Eli and I didn't find out about that until after we'd watched almost an hour of mindless TV. His phone rang at the end of *Ghostbusters*, and a few seconds after he'd answered, his face went pale.

"I... really? In the hospital?"

Who was in the hospital? I tilted my head, watching my brother grow visibly more uncomfortable with every passing second. What was going on? Eli usually kept a cool head. It wasn't like him to fidget with the hem of his shirt or bite his lip.

"Who was that?" I asked as soon as he'd hung up.

He looked at me, taking a deep breath. "Those sirens... Our parents' house burned."

"Our... what?" I felt my eyes go wide, but this was just... It wasn't possible. Things like that happened to other people. Not to our parents. Even though we hadn't spoken to them since Jake had been born, it was still hard to believe something this terrible could happen to them. Not only had their house burned, but Eli had also said something about a hospital. *Oh God.* "Are they...?"

"Dad's been taken to the hospital. I'm not sure what's wrong. She was hysterical."

"She? Mom?" My voice broke.

Eli looked at me helplessly. I could only imagine what he was feeling. Our parents had kicked him out of the house when he'd gotten pregnant with Jake and there was a lot of hurt still there that would probably never fully heal. I didn't know our mother even had his number, and I wondered about that, but now was not the time to ask. I had a different question instead.

"Do you think we should go?" I asked, drawing my lower lip between my teeth. After all, Dad could be *dying*.

"I don't know." Eli rubbed his face with the heel of his hand and groaned. "Maybe we should. I don't really want to, but..." He shook his head, and then he took a deep breath and straightened, as if he'd come to a decision. "Matt!" he yelled the next moment. His husband appeared in the doorway a minute later.

"Something wrong?"

"Griff and I need to go to the hospital and visit my father," Eli said with surprising calm. It seemed now that he'd made up his mind, he felt better.

Wish I could say the same for myself.

"The hospital?" Matt's eyebrows went up. "Do you need me to find a babysitter?"

"No, you can take care of the kids."

"You don't want me to come with you?"

Eli shook his head. "No, we can't waste time finding someone for the kids, and I'm definitely not taking them. I have Griff, I'll be fine."

"If you're really sure."

"I'll be fine," Eli repeated. He gave his husband a kiss, and then he grabbed the car keys from a bowl near the door and turned to me. "Let's go."

"Okay," I made myself say, even though nothing about this was even remotely okay.

We arrived at the hospital about half an hour later. Since Oceanport wasn't big enough to have a hospital of its own, it was always a bit of a drive, and one that had been spent mostly in silence this time. Eli hadn't really wanted to talk, and I hadn't really been able to think of anything much to say either.

We hadn't always had a bad relationship with our parents, growing up. They'd been… okay. Regular parents with regular ups and downs. There'd been a couple of fights, of course, but I remembered some awesome family holidays as well. Our parents could have been worse. I knew of some omegas who had their mates chosen for them by their families. Our parents never tried *that*, at least.

Things hadn't really gone to shit until Eli came home from school pregnant, pretending not to know who the other father was. They would have been pissed even if he had known, of course, but it was his complete reluctance to even list candidates that drove them completely crazy.

I'd been tempted to tell once or twice, to be honest, but it hadn't been my decision to make. Still, sometimes I wondered if I'd made the right call and if we could still be a family if I'd spoken up. But at the same time, I could never forgive them for kicking Eli out when he'd needed help, no matter the reason.

That didn't mean I wanted either of them to *die*, though.

They were still my parents, and sometimes, *sometimes*, I even missed them. I wondered if Eli felt the same. He never said.

Our walk across the hospital's parking lot was just as quiet as our drive had been, and I suspected that my brother had just as much to think about as I did. It surprised me that he hadn't insisted on having Matt with him somehow. I kind of wanted Dean to be here, and we weren't even married. Approaching the information desk, I resigned myself to calling him later.

My brother looked to me as we stood in front of the lady behind the desk. Okay, apparently I was going to do the talking today.

"Hello," I said. "We're looking for our father? Declan Stephens? He was brought in here this morning."

"Just a moment." She gave me a kind smile. "Mr. Stephens has been brought to room 214 on the second floor. Take the elevator down the hall and turn left when you get off on that floor."

"Thank you."

Eli started walking as soon as we got the room number, and I followed him into the elevator.

"Nervous?" I asked. "Because I kind of am." And this was about as much silence as I could take without crumbling. "How long has it been since we've seen them? Ten years. Must have been almost ten years."

Eli nodded, lips pressed tightly together. I tried not to sigh. Thankfully the elevator was fast; it dinged again after only a few seconds and we were on the second floor.

"It's to the left from here," I said, stepping out first. I found the right room number and then... I didn't know what to do. Knock? Just go in?

I looked to my brother, who seemed to lack my hesitation. He simply put his hand on the door, knocked once, and walked in without waiting for a response.

I entered the room after him.

There they were. Our parents.

My dad lay in the bed, some sort of breathing mask on his face and so pale I hardly recognized him. He was covered in bandages too, and I couldn't tell whether he'd aged a *lot* in the past ten years or whether that was just the hospital effect. His eyes were closed, and so I looked to my mom instead.

The woman who raised me sat in a chair by the bed. She looked up as we came in, and her eyes fixed first on Eli and then on me. And there was so much pain in them. I could hardly stand it. I couldn't deal with people being sad around me.

"Hey, Mom," I said softly, because no one else was speaking and that was something else I couldn't deal with.

"Griffin... You look so grown up."

I had to give her a smile at that, because if there was one thing I hadn't busied myself with over the past ten years, it was growing up. "Looks can be deceiving." I took a step closer and gestured to my father. "How is he?"

"He'll be okay, probably. Smoke inhalation, a broken bone, some burns..." She shook her head. "I'm sorry I worried you. I panicked."

"It's okay." I breathed a sigh of relief. "It must have been scary. I would have been scared." I looked to my brother who still stood by the door. It didn't seem like he wanted to say anything, so I just kept on talking. I was good at that, after all. "What happened?" I asked.

She looked aside. "He fell asleep smoking. It was stupid. The whole smoking thing is stupid. I wish he'd quit, honestly."

"I'm sorry," I said, not knowing what else to say. The dad I remembered hadn't smoked. "What about the house?" I wondered how much damage it had taken.

She only shook her head again.

"That bad?" I asked.

"Let's just say repairs are going to take a while." She sighed.

"But Dad's going to be fine?" Eli suddenly spoke up. He'd crossed his arms in front of his chest, leaning back against the wall next to the door as if taking another step into the room would leave *him* with burn wounds too.

I couldn't blame him for his reservations, not really, but that didn't stop me from wishing things could be different.

"I think so, dear."

Eli's lips curled, as if the endearment insulted him, but he kept his mouth shut. I guess even he knew this wasn't the time or place to start an argument. "I think I'll excuse myself then. Very sorry for the trouble you went through. Give him my best wishes when he wakes up." He looked at me as he pushed himself off the wall. "Griff?"

Obviously, he wanted to know whether I was coming along. He was my ride, after all.

I looked at my dad, then at my mom, who returned my gaze with something nearly pleading in her eyes, as if asking me not to leave so soon. Not now.

I gave a little sigh as I broke. She'd done some bad things, but she was still my mom. "I think I'm going to stay for a little bit."

Eli raised an eyebrow at that, but didn't criticize my decision.

"I'll get a ride from Dean later," I said to reassure him that it was okay for him to go. He probably wanted to be back with his husband and kids to process this. "I'll call you when I'm home."

"Okay." My brother uncrossed his arms and turned to leave.

"Thank you for coming," Mom said before he could close the door behind himself.

"Thank you for calling," he returned, and with that, he was gone, leaving me alone with our parents.

There was another chair by the wall, so I grabbed it and dragged it over to where my mother was sitting. Then I sat, and didn't really know what to say. What did you say to someone you were close to once but hadn't talked to in nearly ten years?

Fortunately, my mom started talking before I had a chance to start my nervous blabbering. “How have you been?” she asked. “Are you still doing photography? You were always so fond of that.” She smiled sadly, as if she regretted the years we’d lost just as much as I did.

“I am,” I said. “That’s how I make my money.”

“Really?” Her smile turned bright. “That’s good. That’s really good.”

“Yeah.” I grinned. I didn’t *need* my mom to be proud of me, but it was still nice to know that she was. Okay, maybe I needed it a little bit. But sitting here and grinning, I almost felt like I was betraying my brother, even though I knew that was ridiculous and that he wasn’t upset with me for staying. He wasn’t, was he?

“How are the children?” my mom asked.

I bit my lower lip.

My mother sighed. “I’m sorry. I guess I really don’t have any right to ask about them, do I? But how long should this silence continue? I’ve tried to apologize a hundred times. Though I know it’s not something that’s easy to forgive.”

“You need to talk to Eli about that.”

“Don’t you think I’ve tried? He won’t listen. Most of the time, he doesn’t even answer the phone anymore.”

“I had no idea you’d tried to contact him. Recently?” I remembered there’d been the occasional call the first one or two years, but they’d stopped eventually and almost faded from memory.

She shook her head, and she looked tired now. “I tried to contact you too.”

I cringed. Vaguely, I remembered letting a call or two go to voice mail and thinking that I might call back at a later time. “I’m sorry.”

"It's alright, dear. At least you came. That means a lot. I'm sure your father would agree."

Glancing at my father's still form, I wondered if that was true. My parents were both betas, but it had always been my dad who called the shots at home. I was pretty sure that kicking Eli out had been his idea as well, even if my mom was just as guilty for going along with it. And I couldn't just forgive her, not like that, not after everything.

"The kids are fine," I said eventually, if only because I needed to say something. "Livvy's super cute and Jake... well, he's Jake," I said as if she would understand, but how could she when she didn't know the boy?

My family was really messed up.

I got up from my chair. "I... uh... need to make a phone call."

My mother nodded. She looked a bit like she was wondering whether I was going to run, but I wasn't running.

I just really, really needed to talk to someone who wasn't related to me.

Chapter Sixteen

DEAN

When I answered the phone, my boyfriend sounded like he was about to cry. His voice was shaky and his breathing shallow and I didn't know at all what was going on.

"Griff? Is everything alright?"

"I'm at the hospital," he said.

At the hospital? My mind immediately jumped to worst case scenarios. "What are you doing there? Are you hurt?"

"No, I'm not hurt. I'm sorry. I didn't want to scare you." He sniffed, and *that* scared me. Not much could bring Griff down, so whatever had happened, it must have been monumental.

"Did someone you know get hurt?" I prodded him along, trying to get the most important facts. I had some experience talking to trauma survivors, and this didn't feel that different—which, honestly, did nothing to reassure me.

"My dad," he said. "There was a fire."

A fire? For a second, my mind went blank, and then it crashed in on itself, burying me under a pile of rubble made from images and memories of the last time I'd had to deal with *a fire*. But I couldn't focus on that, couldn't fall apart when Griff needed my help. *Deep breath,* I told myself. *Talk to him.*

"You're at the hospital right now because your dad was in a fire?"

"Yes."

"I'm sorry. Is it bad?"

"I don't know. Not really? I mean... I don't know. He'll be okay, I think. My mom said so. She said he'll probably be okay."

I had to smile at Griff's babbling, if only because he was moving away from shock and back to coping mechanics that were more characteristic. "That's good," I said.

"I'm just... I don't know... I haven't seen my parents in a really long time."

"I know." Now that he mentioned it, I remembered his family situation. I'd just forgotten about the misery surrounding that at the mention of fire. "Do you want me to come to the hospital?"

"If you could..."

"Okay, just hang tight and I'll be there as fast as I can, alright?"

"Okay. I'm in room number 214. It's on the second floor."

As soon as I was done talking to Griff, I pocketed my phone and let Shane know that I would be taking the car. He didn't seem to mind and he didn't ask why I needed it, which was good because I had no time to explain. I had to get to Griff before my own demons caught up with me.

Luck was with me and I made it to the hospital in record time. Traffic was light that day and I sped right through until I reached the hospital's parking lot. I parked the car and walked in without letting myself think, which honestly wasn't that easy. I'd been hospitalized myself just before coming back to Oceanport, and though this was a different hospital, the memories wanting to bubble to the surface didn't care.

I bit the inside of my lip as I got into the elevator and waited for it to take me up. Once I arrived on the second floor, it took me only a minute to locate the room with the number Griff had given me.

This was it.

I was officially about to meet my boyfriend's parents. In all the rush, this was the first time that occurred to me. Maybe because I wasn't meeting Mr. and Mrs. Stephens for the *very* first time. I had vague recollections of seeing them every now and then when I was a child, but still, this was the first time I was meeting them as the man who wanted to have sex with their son.

Awkward.

But I couldn't let myself linger on that.

I knocked on the door. It only took a few seconds for Griff to open, as if he'd been waiting on hot coals for me to come. I could just picture that he'd jumped from his chair the moment he'd heard knocking.

"You're here!"

I gave him a smile. "Yeah, I am." I leaned in to give him a quick peck on the lips. I wanted to go for a longer kiss, really, because I was so worried about him, but I couldn't quite get myself to do that before I knew how he felt about kissing in front of his mother and his bedridden father.

But as I wanted to draw back, Griff held on to the hem of my sleeve, and pressed our lips together again, opening his mouth to me. Seemed he had no reservations about who was going to see us do this whatsoever. Well, that was a relief. And I shamelessly took him up on his invitation to explore his mouth. He didn't just smell sweet, he tasted sweet as well. I could have lost myself in him.

But this was neither the time nor the place for that.

"Thank you for coming," Griff whispered as we parted. "Thank you so much."

"You don't have to thank me." I kissed him again on the forehead before looking into the room. I spotted Mr. Stephens in the bed, and Griff's mother in a chair in front of it.

"Hello, Mrs. Stephens," I greeted her. "I'm Dean Kramer."

It took her a moment, but then her face lit up in recognition. "You used to be friends with Griffin back in school, didn't you?" She shook her head. "I guess that's not the appropriate term anymore, is it?"

I reached for Griff's hand and held it in my own. "I'm his boyfriend now, and it's a pleasure to meet you again, Mrs. Stephens."

"His boyfriend, I see." She smiled. "I'd been wondering if there was anyone special in my son's life. I'm glad to see he's not alone."

"No, he's not." I smiled back at her, glad that she was taking my role in her son's life so well. Approaching the bed, I glanced at the still form of Mr. Stephens. I'd seen worse cases of fire victims, but I'd also seen better.

"Dean's a firefighter," Griff told his mother with a hint of awe and pride in his voice that made me feel all sorts of things. And not all of them good.

I hadn't been much of a firefighter in a while, and if that was what Griff liked about me, I was going to let him down.

No, you just need to overcome your problems and get your head back in the game.

But the fact that I had no idea how to do that was exactly the reason I'd come to this town in the first place. To run away, like a puppy with his tail between his legs. Fine alpha I was.

Griffin's mother looked at me curiously. "Oh, but you weren't with the nice firemen at our house, were you?" She tilted her head as she scrutinized me.

"No, ma'am. I don't belong to this town's fire department."

"Oh, that's a shame," she said. "They could use more men, and you look capable."

"He does, doesn't he?" Griff said, and then he slapped his hand in front of his mouth as if he'd said too much. He made me smile. The only one who could in moments like this.

"Be that as it may, I'm very glad to see you in relative health after the accident," I said to shift the topic of conversation away from me.

"It was awful," Mrs. Stephens said. "I'll have nightmares for weeks. And the house... oh, the house..." She shook her head.

"It must be bad. I'm sorry."

She only shook her head again. "I don't even know where to stay yet. Maybe I'll just stay here overnight."

"Mom, no. I have so much space, you can stay with me," Griff said. And then he looked surprised at his own words. I was slightly surprised as well, and hoped that he knew what he was doing. From what I'd gathered, he didn't have the best relationship with his parents, but maybe he was right and this was the time to restore some bonds.

"You don't have to do that, Griffin," his mother spoke up, though she was smiling. Then she looked between the two of us. "Are you two living together yet?"

"No!" Griff said quickly as if the thought shocked him. Or maybe it was more the thought of what his mother must be picturing in her head. I hoped for the latter, anyway. "We're not... This is a new thing."

Mrs. Stephens laughed. "I see. But you don't need to act so coy, dear, you know I had two children when I was your age."

Griff's face took on a shade so red it rivaled the stop sign he probably wanted to put to this conversation.

His mother seemed to be amused by it, though. "Are you thinking about having children?" she asked.

"It's a bit too early for that," I cut in before Griff could become the first human to explode from embarrassment.

"Yes, it is!" Griff agreed with me. "We're like... going slow and all, and we're totally not living together so I really have space in my house and all. If you want to stay, I mean. That would be cool. Because you wouldn't be interrupting anything."

"Griff," I said softly to make him aware of his rambling, and he stopped. I kissed his cheek and whispered, "You're adorable when you're nervous," in his ear just to see if he would squirm. He did. Considering the situation, I kept my laughter inside.

"If you really don't mind..." his mother said. "I'd like to see your house." She gave her son a soft smile. "I've always wanted to know what it looks like from the inside."

Griff returned her smile, but his looked rueful, and I could imagine why. The two of them had a lot to discuss, but maybe not right now.

"Shall we go, then?" I asked, still holding Griff's hand firmly in my own to remind him that he had my support in everything he chose to do.

"Yeah, I think we should. I have to call Eli too, when we're home."

I could see on his face that the thought made him slightly uncomfortable. Knowing his family's history, I understood why. If Griff had a difficult relationship with his parents, Eli's was catastrophic. Griff probably feared that his brother was going to be mad at him for taking their mother in, but I couldn't imagine that to be the case. Griff needed to give his brother a little more credit. I squeezed his hand.

"Let's be on our way, then. Are you coming as well?" I asked Mrs. Stephens, because it was entirely possible she wanted to remain at her injured husband's side for a while longer, but she nodded and stood.

"I'm ready," she said with a last look at the man she'd married. "Let's go."

"Good," I said, because I couldn't wait to get out of this hospital and away from all the bad memories it was stirring up inside me. I couldn't unload any of them on Griff, not while he needed me. Maybe not ever.

Chapter Seventeen

GRIFFIN

We passed the ride back to my house in relative quiet—a feat I was proud of, considering how hard it was to keep myself from babbling the whole way. But staying quiet forced me to remain in my own head, to think about all that happened and all that my mother had said. It was obvious that she wanted to make up. Part of me wanted that too, but I couldn't deny that there was also a part of me that was mad at her, still, and I feared it wouldn't go away so easily. And if this was difficult for me, I could only imagine how Eli was feeling.

I looked out the window at the small-town houses passing us by. Oceanport always looked so deceptively peaceful. You wouldn't think that there'd been a fire here today. You wouldn't think that it had almost killed someone. Wouldn't think that it had almost killed my dad before I had a chance to talk to him again after almost ten years of silence.

I took a deep, shaky breath and pinched the bridge of my nose. How was any of this real?

I had to stop thinking. At least I had my mom with me now. I wasn't going to lose *her* after having another conversation and mending this rift somehow. I didn't know *how* yet, but I was going to do it.

We arrived at my house after another few

minutes and got out of the car. I showed my mom in and was extremely grateful that Dean decided to come in with us as well. I wasn't ready for him to leave yet. In fact, I wasn't ready for him to leave *at all*, but could I ask him to stay the night when I had no intention of putting out or was that going to put a strain on our relationship?

I didn't know, and I was tired of thinking about it. Fortunately, Dean offered to make some coffee as soon as we stepped into the house as if sensing my exhaustion somehow.

"Thank you," I said, giving him a quick kiss. "For everything."

"It's fine. Go show your mother where she'll be sleeping."

"Right." I rubbed my face and turned to my mom. "Ready for a tour?" I asked, putting on a smile.

"I would love that." Her smile looked almost as weak as mine, but it had been a trying day for both of us. She'd almost lost her husband.

Don't let your thoughts go there again.

I started my tour off by showing my mom the kitchen, the living room and the downstairs bathroom.

"You used to live here with Eli?" she asked.

"Yes. But he's moved out now to live with his husband, and they bought this house so I could stay here."

She raised an eyebrow. "That's generous. But then, I guess they can afford it."

She wasn't wrong about that. Matt had a lot of money since he'd recently inherited his family's fortune. I couldn't help but wonder though, if our parents would still have kicked Eli out if he'd told them his baby's father was the richest bachelor in town. Would it have made a difference?

But I was the only one Eli had told, and I'd kept his secret, so we were never going to find out now.

"They're not worrying about money," I said eventually and led her up the stairs.

"And how are you doing?" she asked. "Do you have enough money? Do you need help?"

"I'm fine. People pay a lot more for a good graphic designer than you'd think." I was pretty decent, and super glad that I didn't have to ask for help from my parents to pay my bills. It had been difficult for Eli and me in the beginning, but we'd made it work. Just barely, sometimes, but still.

Once we'd made it up the stairs, I opened the first door to the right. "This is where you're going to sleep."

"Oh." She looked inside. It was Jake's old room. I could offer her this or Eli's old room. Both felt wrong, but I felt that Jake wouldn't mind as much, and there wasn't much of his left in here. Only a few drawings still hung on the walls of what was now my guest room. She studied them curiously. "Are these...?"

"Yeah, this was Jake's room." When he'd moved out, I'd asked him why he wasn't taking his drawings, and he'd said that I should have them, so I'd kept them up.

"Oh," my mom said again, and I couldn't quite tell what she thought of this. "They're nice drawings. Very bright and colorful."

I nodded. "He's a bright and colorful boy." *And you'd know that if you hadn't kicked up such a fuss about his existence.*

Yeah, I wasn't going to forgive her tonight, but at least, I managed not to voice those thoughts. She could probably read them on my face anyway, because she grew very quiet.

"Let's head back down," I said. "Coffee should be

ready." It was all I had to say to her at this point, and I still had to call my brother too.

I picked up the phone while Dean was chatting with my mother over coffee. I couldn't tell you how glad I was that he was there and taking her off my back for a few minutes. Going up to my room, I dialed Eli's number.

He picked up the phone after only a few rings. "Griff? Are you back home now?"

"Yeah, we got here a little while ago."

"Did you have Dean pick you up? I'm sorry I left so quickly, but... I just couldn't stay without saying something mean, and I didn't want to do that, considering the situation."

"No, I get it. It's fine. I called Dean and he came and... uh... Now I kind of have our mother staying with me."

"You what?" There was obvious surprise in his voice, but I couldn't tell whether there was also a hint of anger or not.

"She doesn't have anywhere else to stay."

"You know hotels and motels are a thing that exist, right?" Now he sounded more exasperated than anything.

"I know that. But I have all this space that I'm not using, and she's our mother."

"Yeah, but she didn't seem to care much where I was going to be staying when..." Eli trailed off but I knew what he meant, of course.

"I get that," I said softly. "But I'm not like our parents and I can't be like that."

Eli remained silent for a few seconds. "I know,"

he said then. "You're way better than them."

"You're not mad at me?" I asked tentatively.

"Of course I'm not mad at you." He said it like I was stupid to be entertaining such thoughts. "But thank you for warning me."

"Yeah, I didn't want you to come over and suddenly run into her."

Eli laughed softly. "Yeah, that wouldn't have been fun. You're a good person, Griff. Don't let anyone tell you anything else."

"Thank you," I said, relieved that my brother wasn't seeing my need to help as some sort of weakness and that he wasn't going to hold it against me. We'd been through a lot together, and I couldn't imagine not having him around anymore. I'd probably worried needlessly.

"Are you okay, though?" Eli asked next. "Not just with what happened but with having her around as well."

That was a difficult question. Was I okay? Not really, but I wasn't so bad off that my brother needed to worry about me. "I'll be fine," I said. "I can handle her. It's not forever."

"Can you handle what happened to Dad too? I don't like the thought of you taking this all on by yourself. At least I have Matt."

"I have Dean," I said before I could stop myself, comparing my boyfriend with my brother's husband. Not quite the same thing, I knew, but... having him around did help a lot.

"Yeah?" I could hear the smile in Eli's voice. "Is he staying with you?"

"I don't know. I'd like that, to be honest, but I haven't asked yet."

"You should," Eli advised me. "I'm sure he won't

mind, not if he cares about you."

"I know." I sighed. "But he's never stayed the night, and I just feel like... if I ask him then that means... that I should..."

"Stop," my brother cut me off. "It's not about sex, okay? He won't suddenly think that's on the table because you need his support after a rough day, and if he does, he's a scumbag."

"I guess. I just still feel bad about this. It's not like I don't want to touch him, it's just..."

"I know. But don't feel bad, okay? You've talked to him, right? He'll understand."

"Okay. Thank you. I'll call you again tomorrow."

"Take care."

"You too."

I ended the call and put the phone back in my pocket. Then I returned to the kitchen, where my boyfriend and my mother were still sitting with their coffee mugs, though they were empty now and the conversation had quieted down. I guess we were all tired.

"Everything alright with Elias?" my mother asked, looking up when I came in. "That's who you called, isn't it?"

"Yeah." For a second, I wondered how she knew, but then I remembered mentioning that I would call back at the hospital. "He's fine. Do you have everything you need for the night? I'll go put new sheets on the bed. Jake slept in it a little while ago."

"Oh, no, that's fine." She stood. "Don't trouble yourself. All that can wait for tomorrow."

"If you're sure." I really wasn't going to argue with her at this point.

"I'm sure. And I think I'll retire now. Goodnight, Griffin. And you too, Dean. It was lovely seeing you again."

"You too, Mrs. Stephens."

My mother gave him a smile and went up the stairs. I exhaled, watching her go. That was that part of the evening dealt with.

"Tired?" Dean asked me.

"Yeah, kinda," I admitted. It wasn't even that late.

"I can leave," Dean said, but he looked at me as if waiting for an objection.

"You don't have to," I made myself say. "I mean, I would like it if you stayed, I just... That doesn't mean that we..."

"I know. Relax, I'm not expecting anything from you. But if there's anything I can do to make you feel better, I'll do it. You only have to ask." He smiled. "And I don't mean that just for today, either. Anything you need, anytime."

"Thank you." I felt like I was saying that a lot tonight, but he sounded so sincere and I didn't know what else to say, and I wasn't sure how to feel about the fact that he offered me *anything, anytime*, when all I could give him in return was *not yet, maybe someday.* But I was too tired to think too much about that now. "I'll get ready for bed," I said, just hoping that my decision to let him stay really was the right one.

Chapter Eighteen

DEAN

I really, really needed to get my hormones under control. Griff had asked me to stay with him because he'd had a difficult day, because he didn't want to be alone. Yes, we were going to spend the night in one bed, but that didn't mean anything was going to happen. I knew that. So why did the sight of him in his pajamas get me so goddamn horny?

Because you're an alpha and he's the sexiest omega you've ever seen and you're lying in his bed. *You've dreamed about being in this bed.*

I took a deep breath to shake off those thoughts. Personally, I hadn't brought any pajamas, so I was sleeping in a shirt and my boxers... and I'd noticed Griff steal glances as I undressed. He was interested, so that was nice to know, but still, he wanted to take it slow. I could do slow. I could take it *so* slow.

Oh, who are you kidding? You're still staring at his ass.

I rolled on my back and looked at the ceiling instead. Enough staring. I was here to comfort, not to fuck.

"Thank you for staying," Griff said again, as if he hadn't said that like twenty-one times already. And then he climbed into the bed next to me. "I hope this isn't too weird for you."

"It's fine," I insisted for the twenty-second time.

He smiled at me, and that infusion of warmth I got from it made all my struggles worth it.

Turning off the light, he settled on his side of the bed, as far away from me as possible.

I couldn't help but laugh. "I don't bite, you know." What was I here for if not to hold him?

"I know." Slowly, he inched a little closer.

I reached out and pulled him against my chest. "Is this okay?"

He was stiff as a log at first, but then he exhaled and relaxed a little. "Yes." He turned around to face me and his hair tickled my neck and chin. "This is fine."

"Good." I kissed the top of his head. "Try to get some sleep."

"Okay." He settled in, and I gently stroked a finger through the strands of his hair, hoping to soothe him.

But it didn't seem that sleep would come so easily. Griff spoke up again after only a minute. "Dean?" he whispered, as if checking to see whether it was okay to talk to me in the dark. I was oddly reminded of sleepovers we'd had as children, telling each other stories after bedtime in hushed voices. Back before I'd fallen for my friend.

Or was there even a before? I wasn't sure anymore. Looking back, I felt like I'd been lost the moment I first noticed how bright his smile was in elementary school.

And now I was in bed with him, holding him in my arms—if only to comfort him.

"Yeah?" I asked, trying to force my brain back into the present.

"How long are you going to stay in Oceanport?"

Where was that question coming from now? He

hadn't asked me that in a long time, and to be honest, I didn't know the answer. At first, I'd planned to stay for a couple of weeks, and now I'd been here forever. "I'm not sure," I said. "Why do you ask?"

He fidgeted a little. "Just wondering how much time we have."

Oh. I hadn't thought about that. I'd always just figured that I'd go back to Portland eventually, return to my job, and that Griff would just... actually, I hadn't thought about that. Our relationship was too new, and lately, I didn't like to think about the future. But when I forced myself to picture it, I definitely wanted Griff in it. He felt so nice cuddled up against me. A comfortable warm weight at my side. One that I didn't want to lose. "I'm not sure," I said honestly. "I'm kind of getting used to living here, though."

"Really?" Griff's voice sounded hopeful. Of course, if he pictured the same kind of future I did, he wouldn't want me to leave. I didn't have to ask to know that Griff wasn't going to leave this town. He loved his brother and his role as an uncle in the childrens' lives too much. This was his home. I couldn't ask him to abandon ship and come to Portland with me.

"Yeah," I said. "I never meant to stay so long, but I guess I just can't get myself to leave."

Griff played no small part in my reluctance to leave, of course, but it was also because I still couldn't stand the thought of going back to my old job. He didn't have to know that, though. If he never knew how much today's events had shaken me as well, that was for the best.

"Does that mean you're going to stay?" Griff asked, and for the first time that day, his usual cheer seemed to have returned to his voice.

Considering how much I loved hearing it, I really

couldn't say anything but, "Yes."

"Awesome!"

I smiled. Looked like I'd picked the right answer. Griff slung an arm around my back, as if suddenly encouraged to cuddle closer by my response. I pulled him tight against my chest, and then I made the mistake of breathing in his scent and immediately felt punched in the gut in the best way possible.

God, I could have baked three whole batches of cupcakes and their combined smell wouldn't have been as sweet as Griff's. He wasn't simply my boyfriend, he was my *best* friend, and he was temptation made flesh.

And he really needs you to not see him that way right now. You're supposed to sleep next to him, not with *him.*

But knowing that didn't make my arousal disappear, even while I hated what a perv I was.

Griff looked up, his hair tickling my nose. "Dean?" he asked again, his voice just shaky enough to make me wonder what was going through *his* head.

"Yeah?"

"Can I kiss you?" The question seemed to make him feel a bit awkward. "I mean... can I *just* kiss you?"

I understood. He wanted to know if he could kiss me without things escalating. If he could kiss me without me expecting more. But I was going to be true to my word. I was never going to pressure him, no matter how much I wanted him—and *damn*, did I want him. "You can kiss me any time."

Griff didn't have to be told twice. He leaned up and pressed a kiss square on my lips, and his lips felt so nice on mine. All soft and sweet and inviting. And all the while his scent seemed to swirl all around me, tempting me to claim him for my own. I wasn't going to, not yet, but it took every ounce of willpower I had to stick by that decision.

And then Griff completely pulled the rug from under my feet by rolling on his back and pulling me on top of himself. God, what was he *doing*? I groaned. Having him underneath me felt so right in all the ways I couldn't consider now. Did he even know what a tease he was being? Maybe not, because he slung his arms around my neck as if to keep me exactly where I was.

And he was hard.

Damn.

I felt his erection press into my leg, and heard him let out the sweetest little sound when I moved my leg up, effectively rubbing him. I had no idea what had gotten into him so suddenly, but it was sexy as hell.

And then he froze.

I knew that the spell was broken the moment he tensed, and I rolled off him before he could push himself to try to convince me otherwise. "That was nice," I said, pretending like I didn't have a raging boner screaming for attention. Griff had bitten off more than he could chew, and I was sure he already felt bad enough about that without me adding to his misery by demanding things he couldn't give. "Want to sleep now?" I asked.

I waited for a long couple of seconds, but he didn't say anything, still breathing hard.

"Hey," I said, reaching out to stroke his hair. "Don't worry about it, okay? We'll get there." I only wished I knew what exactly he was so scared of. I'd been with virgins before, but none who reacted quite like that.

"I'm sorry," he said eventually, breaking my heart a little with how miserable he sounded.

"Shhh. No need to apologize. Just sleep now. It's been a long day."

He sighed, but he didn't argue. Good boy. I pulled him back into my arms to show him how not-mad I was and held him until he fell asleep finally. I had a lot of questions. There were things that we needed to talk about in the morning, but for now, I was just happy to have him resting. Everything else we could figure out another time. I hoped.

Chapter Nineteen

GRIFFIN

The next morning, I woke up before Dean and carefully peeled myself out of his embrace to leave the bed. I couldn't believe what a total tool I'd been the night before. Just kissing would have been fine. Why did I have to pull Dean on top of me?

Because I'd been so happy at the thought of him staying in Oceanport and instincts had taken over.

And then I hadn't been able to deal with what I'd brought on myself.

Stupid, stupid, stupid.

Berating myself, I got some clothes to change into out of my dresser and walked out of the room, careful not to make any noise that could wake my boyfriend. I needed to take a shower and really wake up before I was ready to face the day—and him. I didn't deserve him, really. He was so kind and gentle and patient. One day soon he would realize that I wasn't worth the trouble, that he could do better—that he could find a boyfriend who actually wanted to have sex with him.

Not that I didn't, I just... had some hang-ups.

In the bathroom, I stepped out of my pajamas and quickly entered the shower and turned on the water. I needed to distract myself from all these thoughts running through my head. They weren't like me. The events of the last day had simply overwhelmed me, and my troubled love life topped it all off.

Why couldn't I just be like all other omegas? I *wanted* Dean. I'd been hard last night. I got hard now, simply thinking about it. Thinking about Dean and the hard planes of his chest, his masculine scent, the weight of his body pressing me into the mattress. Standing under the spray, I sighed and reached for myself, stroking up and down.

If I could just leave my fears behind for a moment, I knew exactly what I wanted to do to Dean, and what I wanted Dean to do to me. I wanted him deep inside of me. I'd never had a dick up my ass, no, but I was no stranger to penetration. I'd experimented. I wasn't scared of it. The stretch felt nice, really, and it wasn't so bad for omegas, or so I heard. I wanted to know what Dean would feel like inside of me.

I jerked myself a bit harder at that thought. God, I wanted that. Wanted him balls deep inside of me, the closest we could be. I wanted him to lose it because of me. I wanted to be the reason he came.

In my dirtiest fantasies, I was on my knees in front of him, his cock in my mouth, my nose pressed into his pubic hair, breathing in the scent of his arousal as my tongue made him lose his mind.

Yes, that was exactly what I wanted. So much so that I came at the thought of it, emptying myself on the shower tiles. I groaned as the hot water washed the evidence away.

Why could I fantasize about fucking Dean, but not *do* it?

"Did you sleep well, dear?" my mother asked me as I walked into the kitchen. Something smelled good, and it looked like she was preparing breakfast. I almost felt like I was twelve again, seeing her like that. Especially since I'd just jerked off in the shower.

"I slept okay." Not the whole truth, but all the information she needed about the night before. "Thank you. How was your night?"

"Oh, it was fine." She turned back to the stove, poking at something in the frying pan. "I'm making pancakes. I hope you still like them the way you used to."

The way I used to meant sugary-sweet and drenched in syrup. Part of me wanted to tell her that I was a grown-up now and I ate grown-up breakfast... but that would have been a lie and I wanted my pancakes.

"Yeah, I do, actually," I admitted.

This earned me a bright smile from my mom, so maybe it wasn't all bad that I hadn't lost my sweet tooth. Sitting at the counter, I watched her whoosh through my kitchen. "Anything I can help you with?"

"No, dear, you just let me do my thing. This is the least I can do to repay you for letting me stay here."

"If you insist." I rubbed my eyes. I didn't have a problem with early mornings, usually, but this morning I was still a little bleary. I felt like I could have slept another day at least, while at the same time being too riled up to find any real rest.

My condition didn't improve when Dean stepped into the kitchen, looking every bit as gorgeous as he had last night, despite his hair sticking out at odd angles from sleep. I wondered if there was anything that could make him less sexy in my mind. I couldn't think of much.

"Good morning," he greeted us.

I gave him a small wave and a grunt, choosing to look at my mother instead of him as memories of last night bubbled to the forefront again.

Dean sat next to me, regardless, and pressed a kiss on my cheek, since my face was turned away from him.

"That smells good," he said to my mother.

"Thank you, hon. I hope you had a good night."

"I did, thank you. But actually, I'm afraid I can't stay for breakfast. I'm running late for work."

"Oh, that's too bad. I could pack you something! Although my son doesn't keep this kitchen too well stocked."

"It's fine. I'll have to drop by home before I go. I'll grab something then. You two enjoy your breakfast." He stood, and addressed me. "Would you like me to come back here after work?"

An innocent question, and yet I didn't know how to respond. Did I want him to come back? Actually yes, but I also didn't want to have the conversation I knew we were going to be having.

"Aren't you busy?" I asked, hoping he would make the decision for me.

"Never too busy for you," he simply said. "Call me later, okay?"

"I will."

He gave me another kiss, this time on the lips, and then he turned to my mother. "Mrs. Stephens, if you need a ride to the hospital..."

"Maybe later, hon, thank you," she waved him off. "They'll call me if anything happens."

"Alright then." Dean excused himself and left.

"I know it's not my place to ask," my mother said when he was gone, "but did you two have a fight or something?"

I felt myself blush as she handed me a plate with pancakes. "What makes you think so?"

"Oh, it's just that the air seemed a bit thick between you. I might not be an omega, but I can sense when my children aren't doing well."

I only looked at her. How could she say that when she'd kicked one of her children out of her house for getting himself in a difficult situation?

She licked her lips. "I know what you must be thinking."

I raised an eyebrow at her. Really?

"I'm sorry for all that happened," she continued, shaking her head. "I regret it all every day, but there's nothing I can do to change the past now. I can only try to be here for you if you need me now. So if there's anything..."

"Thank you, Mom. That means a lot." To me, anyway. I wasn't sure my brother could be placated so easily, but I'd never been as stubborn as he was, and I was sick of the family drama, to be honest. I could never stand any kind of drama. I just wanted everyone to be happy and get along. Was that too much to ask?

"Is anything troubling you?" she asked, taking a seat opposite me. Now I really did feel like I was twelve again, but when I was twelve, Dean and I were only friends and life had been much simpler.

"I'm okay," I said. I appreciated her offer, really, but I wasn't going to discuss my sex life with my mother.

If there was anyone I was going to talk to this about, it was Dean... and Eli. I remembered that my brother was expecting a call from me anyway, so I decided to ring him up after I finished my sickeningly sweet and absolutely awesome pancakes.

Chapter Twenty

DEAN

"You back already?" Shane asked me almost the minute I walked into the door as he wrestled with a little girl who did not want to put her dress on. I'd sent him a text last night, saying that I was staying over at Griff's. "Didn't think I'd see you before work."

"Yeah, well..." I headed past him into the kitchen to get some coffee. I wasn't hungry, but I definitely needed some caffeine after the night I'd had. I'd hardly slept a wink. "Things are complicated."

"More complicated than getting this dress on this girl?" Shane half-shouted from where he was still standing in the hallway.

I had to laugh. "Maybe not!" Coffee mug in hand, I stepped back out into the hallway. "Mary, why do you not want to wear your dress?"

"Want blue dress!" she exclaimed, flailing with her little arms.

"I see." The dress my cousin was currently trying to put on her was pink.

"But you like this dress," Shane said as if to remind her, shooting me a helpless look.

"Want blue!" she insisted.

"Well. At least she knows what she wants. Does she have a blue dress?" I asked Shane.

He scrunched his face up, thinking. "Maybe?" He

sighed, shaking his head just slightly. “Ron would have known.”

I slapped him lightly on the back. “Don’t beat yourself up over it. Let’s just see if we can find a blue dress for the little princess.”

He took a deep breath. “I guess.” He picked Mary up in his arms, and together we walked into the nursery. I marveled at how much progress my cousin had made. A few months ago, a moment like this would have sent Shane spiraling into depression for the rest of the day. Ron had been his whole world, and every reminder that he was gone seemed to break Shane’s heart a little more each day. But he was past that stage now. I wasn’t sure how he’d done it, but it felt like he’d used super glue or something to put the pieces of himself back together so he could be strong for his children.

I only hoped that it would hold up.

I had no idea how I would handle it if anything happened to Griff, and we hadn’t been married for ten years like Shane and Ron. We’d just recently become a couple, but we’d been friends for a long time and I cared about him a lot. We weren’t married, no, but getting completely ahead of myself, I could see that in our future. I didn’t know what I would have done if that had been him in that hospital bed instead of his father. I didn’t even want to consider the possibility.

“Dean? Are you listening? You went all pale there for a second.” Shane poked my shoulder, holding a light blue dress in his other hand.

“Oh, sorry.” I rubbed my face. “Spaced out.”

“What were you thinking about?” he asked as he helped his daughter into the dress of her choice.

“Nothing.”

“Oookay,” Shane said, clearly not believing me. “Are you going to tell me why you’re back so early?

When you texted me where you were staying, I figured you would... you know...” Shane wasn’t shy about this kind of topic. The only reason he didn’t say *I was sure you were gonna bang your boyfriend and drift through the day in happy bliss*, was because his daughter was listening and if Ron had been still alive, that would have netted him a frying pan over the head.

“We’re still taking it slow,” I informed him. “And I wasn’t staying there because we were going to do anything. There was a fire yesterday, did you hear about it?”

Shane nodded absentmindedly as he straightened the dress out once he’d put it on Mary. “Everyone was talking about it.”

“The fire was at his parents’ house.”

“Oh.” Shane’s eyes went wide. “Is everything alright? The gossip varied. You know how it is.”

“It seems alright. I mean, it could have been worse. His dad’s in the hospital, but he’ll recover, and it looks like the house will need some repair work, but that’s all. Griff was pretty upset, though.”

“Yeah, I bet. Good thing he has a strong firefighter boyfriend like you to rely on, huh?”

I grimaced, because I so wasn’t living up to that image, and that needed to change. Griff hadn’t even wanted me around this morning. He hadn’t kicked me out, no, but his reluctance to interact with me in any way hadn’t been super subtle. I could take a hint when it was given to me, and I’d had a bad feeling ever since he’d woken and tip-toed off into the bathroom.

What had happened last night was really weighing on him, and I wasn’t sure how to help him, but I had to think of something.

First though, I had to figure out my own shit. “I think I’m going to call Daniel,” I told my cousin.

"Really?" He raised an eyebrow at me. "Are you thinking about taking that job?"

"Maybe just part-time for now. I know I can't leave you hanging, but I do need to get back into my actual job." Sooner rather than later. I'd thought I could overcome my trauma by waiting it out, but clearly, that wasn't happening. Confronting it head-on was the only thing I had left to try.

"Good for you," Shane said.

"Yeah, good for me." I gave him a smile and hoped he was right.

Chapter Twenty-One

GRIFFIN

Eli suggested that we meet at the school so we could get on with our theater work. He'd told me he'd gotten Eric to unlock the auditorium for us, but no one else would be there. Perfect, really.

"So how is it going with our mother?" he asked as we walked into the auditorium.

"It's not too bad, really. She made me breakfast."

Eli laughed. "Did she?"

"Yeah, pancakes."

"Matt and Jake tried to make me pancakes last Omega Day. It was a disaster." But he was smiling at the memory.

"Yeah? I think I remember you telling me about that." We reached the auditorium and went inside. The school felt weirdly empty at this time, even though I knew it was only because all the students were contained in classrooms. "Mom really seems to be sorry about what happened," I told my brother, just to see how he took it.

"Huh." He didn't give me any visible reaction at all.

"I think she means it too."

"That's nice."

Okay, this was obviously not something Eli wanted to talk about. Message received.

"I'm sorry," Eli said after a moment. "I know you want this to be true, but I also know she's going to change her tune once Dad wakes up."

"Do you really think so?"

He shrugged. "She wouldn't have kicked me out if it wasn't for Dad. But she did go along with it. There's no reason for me to believe things are going to be different now."

"I don't know," I said, preparing my paint. "I guess I just always keep hoping for the best."

"It's what you do." Eli gave me a small smile. Still, it seemed he wanted a change of topic. "You said you had something you needed to talk about? Something other than our parents, I mean?" He pulled up a chair and got his yarn and needles out.

"Yeah, uh... You know I did ask Dean to stay over last night."

"Oh? Good for you! Wait, don't tell me he tried anything."

"Oh no, he didn't. I did," I said with a grimace.

"You did what?" Eli seemed surprised, not that I could blame him.

"It just came over me!" I painted a broad stroke of green on the canvas.

Eli burst out laughing. Well, at least one of us was finding this amusing. I scowled at him, but couldn't keep it up. I had to laugh as well. God, this was ridiculous.

"You're amazing, little brother," Eli said.

I stuck my tongue out at him. "It didn't really go so well."

"No? You can tell me, you know. Not all my sexual encounters have gone well. Did I ever tell you that I made Matt court me for weeks before I let him undress me?"

I shook my head. "No, you didn't really talk much about that. Actually, you only told me about Matt when you were pregnant."

He cringed. "Right. Sorry 'bout that."

I had to laugh again. It was so easy to talk to Eli; I didn't know what I would have done without my big brother. I was so lucky to have him.

"So what happened last night?" Eli asked, getting us back on track.

"Not that much, really," I said. "But I still feel kinda awful about it. I mean we were trying to sleep, you know? Just sleep. Only then I had to ask him how long he was staying in town, because I ended up wondering how long I had to get over my fears..." I bit my lower lip.

"I see. And?"

"He said he might just stay in Oceanport. Said he's getting used to being here."

"But that's great." Eli smiled. "Honestly, I was a little worried you might leave me along with him."

"I was really happy too." Even now I had to grin when I thought of Dean's words. "I guess I was a little too happy. I wanted to kiss him."

"Did you?"

"Yeah. And that would have been fine. We kiss a lot, only something *hit* me when we were lying there, and I... pulled him on top of me. And for like a few seconds, things were really good. Like, *really* good." I shook my head as if to shake myself out of that memory before I could get caught up in it. "And then I realized what I was doing and my fear caught up with me and I froze." I splattered some more paint on the canvas. Felt weird to be painting something so cheerful while I was in this mood. "I feel like I could have pushed through it if I'd been given a chance, maybe."

"What do you mean by that?"

"Just that Dean couldn't get away from me fast enough as soon as I froze." My lips curled downward. I couldn't blame him for considering my feelings, really, but I was still annoyed with the general situation.

"I see." Eli gave me a sympathetic look. "I'm sure he doesn't like the idea of scaring you."

"I know. I just can't help it, and he's gonna get tired of it eventually. And he'll want to talk later, I know it, but I don't know what to tell him."

Eli thought for a moment. "Have you explained to him what exactly it is that scares you?"

"Not in detail. I just said that we needed to take it slow, I guess."

"Maybe you have to give him a little more information so you can come up with a work-around together."

"I don't know. He's not an omega, how would he understand?" This feeling, this all-encompassing need to please that scared me was difficult even for me to make sense of. I couldn't expect Dean to get it when he'd surely never felt it.

"Give him a little more credit," Eli said. "He might not be an omega, but I'm sure he knows what a hormone rush feels like."

"I guess." Maybe Eli was right, but I got tired of talking about this as I worked on the props. "Is Jake still as excited about the play?" I asked, trying for a lighter topic.

Eli smiled softly. "You bet." Then his face fell just a little. "I'm not sure Conner feels the same way, though."

"Conner?" I shot my brother a questioning look. What was wrong with Conner?

"Yeah, I watched him and Jake trying to read

their lines together. I think he's scared."

I grimaced, sympathizing with the shy boy. The only reason he was trying so hard was to make his late father proud, I was sure of that. "Poor kid," I said. "But things will go fine and then he'll feel really good about himself. Maybe it'll give him a boost."

"Yeah, maybe." Eli's lips quirked up as he handled his needles. "Maybe he only needs to face his fears. We all do, don't you think?"

I scoffed. "Subtle." But I got what he was trying to say, and I knew that he was right. If I wanted to keep Dean, I had to face my fears.

But how?

Chapter Twenty-Two

GRIFFIN

I decided to call Dean that evening. It would have been nice to ignore my problem for a while longer, but I knew that was pointless. Besides, I really wanted to see him, and I wanted to make up for being so standoffish in the morning. That wasn't like me, and I didn't want Dean to think that it was.

While my mother was preparing dinner—another chore she insisted on taking on—I went up into my bedroom and dialed Dean's number. He answered his phone quickly, as always.

"Hey," I said softly when I heard him pick up.

"Hey," he returned. "I'm glad you called. Are you feeling better?"

"Well, I haven't freaked out about anything in a couple of hours. Sorry about that, by the way." I tried to play my embarrassment off with a laugh.

"Don't worry about it," Dean said, predictably.

"It's a difficult thing not to worry about," I admitted. "I want this to work. I want *us* to work." I slumped back on my bed. I knew this was only my first relationship and most people went through a couple of them before finding *the one*, but I didn't even want to consider moving on to someone else. I felt like I'd found my number one ages ago; I just hadn't realized it then. And now I only needed to get over myself.

"I want that too," Dean said on a sigh. "And we'll make it work, I know that, but I don't want you to stress yourself now. We have all the time in the world."

"Do we?"

"Yeah, actually. I got really good news, and I was wondering if I could come over to your place to tell you all about it."

I loved how he still managed to sound so happy in spite of everything. I was sure he was smiling on the other end of the line, and I wanted to see that gorgeous smile of his in person. "You can come over anytime."

"Good. I'll be right there, and I'm bringing cupcakes."

"Oh God, I love y—" I cut myself off. "I love cupcakes," I corrected what I was going to say. Way too early to tell him that I loved him, wasn't it? Even if it was true. Yes, it was early, and we hadn't even had sex, but I didn't have to have sex with him to know that I loved him. It was all in the way my heart fluttered in this really happy way when I saw him—even when he wasn't bringing me cupcakes.

He laughed, and he sound reverberated within me and made me feel warm. "I know."

Do you, Dean? Do you?

Dean came over carrying a large box of baked goods for both me and my mother. I took it from him and brought it into the living room while my mom swooped down on Dean and tried to feed him some leftover dinner.

"I've eaten, thank you."

"But a big man like you, I'm sure you could stand to eat some more. I know your mother doesn't live here anymore and you're not married, so who's cooking for you?" She sighed. "And it seems I really failed to impart any culinary skills on my second son. Eli was always good with a kitchen knife, but Griff..."

"Mom!" I protested, dragging Dean away from her. "Dean doesn't need me to cook for him." Honestly, my family was more progressive than others, but my parents still held some pretty old-fashioned beliefs about how alphas and omegas should live.

"I promise I eat enough," Dean said in good humor. "And I have enough cooking skills to keep the both of us from starving." He draped an arm around my shoulders. "I don't mind feeding Griff at all."

I scoffed, but I couldn't deny that he *was* feeding me regularly, and that I didn't mind it. No, I didn't mind at all.

My mom sighed again, but seemed somewhat placated. "Fine. I'll leave you two to it." At least she knew when to make herself scarce.

"Did you two hear anything from the hospital?" Dean asked as we sat down on the couch in the living room.

"Not really," I told him. "Dad seems stable. I tried to talk to my mom about it, but she avoids the topic. I figure she's just not ready to talk yet."

"I guess. It's not too unusual for people to react that way." Dean put his arm around my shoulders again and I let myself sink back into his touch, closing my eyes for a moment as his fingers gently stroked the fine hair above my ear, sending pleasant tingles down my spine.

"Yeah, I guess," I said on an exhale. I liked the way his fingers felt. He had large hands, but they weren't rough, no part of him was. So why was I still scared? Dean would never hurt me or abuse any power he had over me in any way. I was safe with him.

No, it wasn't Dean I was scared of. It was me.

"I'm glad you let me come over today," Dean said. "I do have some news to share."

"Good news?" He'd said something like that on the phone, hadn't he?

His smile fell just a little bit, but not long enough for me to worry. "Really good news, I think."

I looked up at him curiously. "Did you win the lottery or something?"

"Or something." He laughed. "I called the chief of the local fire department earlier today."

"About the fire at my parents' house?"

He shook his head. "No, to ask for a job. Actually, he's been trying to get me on board for a while, so it really wasn't difficult to get in."

"Oooh." I felt my eyes grow wide and a happy, bubbly feeling rising in the pit of my stomach. "You're joining the local fire department?" That meant he would stay, and I know he'd hinted at it before, but now it was like, definite. He didn't need to go back to his old firefighting job if he could do the same in Oceanport.

"Yeah, I guess I am."

Hearing those words, I got the same rush of euphoria I had the night before. And I reacted almost the same way too—I leaned up and kissed him. His lips on mine felt so good that, immediately, I wanted more again. God, I wanted him and everything I'd fantasized about in the shower that morning.

But I made myself stop and draw back, because what I did not want was a repeat of the night before. No, we needed to talk about this shit before going forward.

"I love that you're staying," I told him instead of expressing my feelings with kisses and touches the way I really wanted to.

"Because it means you'll never have to go without cupcakes again?"

I burst out laughing because he managed to look so serious while he asked that. Silly Dean. "No, because it means… that we can be together." That I finally got a shot at getting everything my brother had. That we could be a family someday, maybe, hopefully. The most omega part of me was already picturing babies with Dean's eyes. I wasn't going to tell him that, though. It was way, way too early for us to be having thoughts like that.

"Yeah, I love that too." Dean kissed the side of my face, and it took me a second to remember that he was talking about being together rather than starting a family. Silly me. In any case, I had to get over my sex phobia before I could think about having babies.

Honestly, though, if he was going to be wearing a uniform, that might just make things easier.

"When are you starting this new job?" I asked.

"I'm only on part-time right now, since I still need to help Shane, but I get to take a look around the department tomorrow."

"Are they giving you a uniform?"

He smiled as though he knew exactly where my thoughts were heading. "I imagine so."

"Can you put that on outside of work?"

A chuckle made it past his lips. "I *could*," he said. "Why, would you like that?"

"I might." I kissed the line of his jaw, trying not to imagine *too* hard how he was going to look in his uniform. "What about your cupcake business, though?" I asked.

He laughed. "You know why I made so many cupcakes? It wasn't really because I wanted to open up a bakery."

"No?" I tilted my head at him. That was news to me.

"No." He ran his fingers through my hair, playing with the strands. "Do you know why I even started baking, honestly?" His eyes twinkled.

"Why did you start baking?"

"My mom made me help her bake cookies one day. I wasn't all that interested, really, but then I met you later that day and gave some of the cookies to you, and you ate them looking like the happiest boy in the world."

I blinked. Was he saying the only reason he was baking was to make me happy? "You're too much," I told him, punching his arm and feeling my cheeks heat up. I didn't even remember the day he was talking about, but it must have been important to him.

"I do enjoy baking now, for what it's worth, but seeing the expression on your face when you bite into one of my cupcakes is still my favorite thing."

"Yeah?" I laughed, feeling just a little bit self-conscious, but he seemed happy, so I decided to put on a show by grabbing one of the cupcakes from the box he'd brought and biting into it with the most passionate expression I could muster.

Dean simply stared at me, mouth hanging slightly open as I went to town on the cupcake. I noticed too late that I was basically mimicking orgasmic bliss and that it was definitely having an effect on him.

"Fuck, you're hot," he said under his breath.

I stopped and swallowed. I hadn't meant to rile him up, but damn if his enthusiasm didn't make me feel sexy—and just for the heck of it, I licked my fingers, just to see him twitch. I had no doubt now that he wanted me as much as I wanted him.

Sadly, I had no idea where to go from here.

Next to me, Dean took a deep breath. "Will you tell me what it is that's scaring you?" he asked. "I mean, I know it's sex and that you're a virgin, but I just feel like... that's not all it is, is it?"

"No," I admitted, feeling myself deflate. "But I don't know how to explain."

"Try?" he asked. "And I promise I'll try to understand."

I licked my lips. "It's... kind of an omega thing," I started, lacking better words to put my thoughts into. "There's this rush I get when I'm around an alpha, any alpha, but especially you."

"I think I know what you're talking about. I have a bit of a reaction to the way omegas smell too, although I imagine it's a little different."

"Yeah, probably just a little different." I managed a smile, even though I wasn't sure how. I wondered what exactly Dean felt when he caught the scent of an omega. Arousal, probably, but what else? For me, it was arousal along with a certain eagerness to be taken and thrown on a mattress—or the nearest available flat surface. What was it like for Dean? Did he want to dominate? Did all alphas want that? There was no way for me to find out other than asking him directly, even if that was a bit embarrassing. "When you smell an omega, does that ever make you want to do things?"

His gaze turned dark. "There's a lot of things I want to do to you when I breathe in your scent." The look of lust in his green eyes was so intense that for a moment, I forgot to breathe.

But at least he was taking my question seriously.

"What kinds of things?" I asked, because I needed to know, to prepare myself.

"Well..." His eyes darted to the door as if to make sure no one was listening in before settling on me again.

"All sorts of things, really, but mostly, I want to be in you, I want to claim you, I want to mark your body to let the world know that you're mine." His eyes narrowed. "I can't stand the thought of anyone else touching you. Like that creep from the school."

"You're still thinking about that?" I asked, trying to get my brain to work in spite of the images he'd just put in my head. Not an easy task. Not when such a large part of me wanted everything he talked about to happen in reality.

"Of course I am. That slimebag was trying to get into your pants, and you're..."

"I'm what?"

Dean didn't say anything for a second, as if he knew what he was *about* to say was stupid, but then he let the word escape anyway. "Mine," he growled with a quiet vehemence.

I had to smile at that. "Do you feel like that about every omega whose scent enters your nose?"

He snorted. "No. Not exactly. The need to take is there, to some extent, but never as strongly. With other omegas, it sounds like a good idea, with you, it's an imperative." He looked straight at me as he said this, and I wasn't sure at all how to react.

"That's how you feel?"

"Yes," he confirmed. "I don't think any other omega would interest me at all right now."

I swallowed. He was so open and honest about all of this, and I loved all that he was telling me. But now I had to return the favor, didn't I? Dean still wanted to know what *I* felt when I caught an alpha's scent, when I caught *his* scent. I took a deep breath, getting a whiff of him, as if I needed the reminder.

I wanted to suppress the thrill that ran through me at being this close to Dean, surrounded by his scent.

Instead, I grasped on to it. This was the emotion that I had to communicate to Dean, what I had to put into words in order for him to understand.

I could do it.

Closing my eyes, I opened my mouth. “When I catch your scent, I want to throw myself on the floor in front of you,” I said, trying just to get it all out before I could get cold feet. “I want to wrap my lips around your cock. I want you to use me in whatever way you want. I want to make you come. In my mouth or in my ass, it doesn't matter, just as long as I can get your seed inside of me. Just as long as I can please you. There's moments when that feels like the most important thing in the world, just to be what you need. It's like I exist just to be your fuck toy, and part of me likes that idea way too much.” I pressed my lips together to stop myself from talking, hoping I had said enough. I was positive that my cheeks glowed red, and I couldn't make myself look at Dean. I could hardly even open my eyes. But then I felt Dean's fingers on my chin, tilting my face to him. His touch was gentle, as always.

“Griff...”

I blinked my eyes open, only to gaze into the green pools of his.

“I'm not going to deny that I'm turned on as hell right now,” he said. “But I would never ever treat you like a fuck toy. Do you get that? You're way too good for that and you mean too much to me.”

“Even now that you know what a dirty mind I have?” I tried to crack a joke, even though my voice broke a little, heavy with emotion. Did I really mean so much to him? I hoped so, because he meant the world to me.

He gave me a smile, and it made that uncomfortable, embarrassed feeling go away a little.

"Especially now that I know what a dirty mind you have. Makes us fit together even better!" He leaned in and touched his lips to mine. I ran my fingers into his hair, needing something to hold on to before my emotions could sweep me off my feet. How lucky was I that an alpha as kind as Dean was into me? For the first time, I wondered if letting my instincts take over would really be so terrible.

Maybe with Dean, I could even enjoy it.

"I don't care how long it takes you to get over your fear," Dean said as we broke. "I love you, Griff."

"You..." I looked at him wide-eyed. Had he just said what I thought he'd said?

Dean laughed softly, amused by my shocked expression. "You can't tell me that surprises you."

"But no one's ever said that to me," I got out.

"And that's just my luck," Dean said, kissing my forehead. "But no one's ever confessed to me either. And do you know why?"

I shook my head. I couldn't see how someone like Dean had managed to go through life without omegas throwing themselves at him left and right.

"Because I could never really get interested in the omegas who tried to date me," Dean explained. "Because part of me was always stuck on you."

But how could that be? I tilted my head at Dean, heart threatening to thump out of my chest. "I never knew."

"No." He laughed again. A good-natured sound. "You were always adorably oblivious. Of course, I didn't think it was quite so adorable when I was a teen."

I punched his arm. "You could have said something."

"Nah." He waved me off. "You weren't interested back then and I couldn't stand the thought of losing you."

"I might have been interested!" I just kept myself from pouting. If Dean had confessed to me all those years ago, I would never have made out with that dick Thomas Dayson in high school.

"Might have been?" One of Dean's eyebrows arched up.

I gave him a shrug. "You may have noticed I can be slow about these things, but I can't picture a version of me that could have resisted you at any time. I was heartbroken when you moved." I leaned into Dean's shoulder.

"Were you?" A small smile tugged on Dean's lips. "I used to think it was for the best because I didn't know how much longer I could keep myself from kissing you."

I laughed. Poor Dean. "How about you kiss me now?"

"Good idea."

Our lips met again, lingering on each other just long enough for me to realize how much I loved him too. It could have been perfect if I could only give him everything he needed, everything we both wanted, and as we broke, a plan formed in my mind to do just that.

"I think we should celebrate your new job," I said.

"Yeah? What sort of celebration did you have in mind?"

"I want to cook for you."

Both of his eyebrows shot up. A *bit* unnecessary, if you ask me. "You what? You don't even like cooking."

"But I want to do it for you!" I insisted. After all the things he'd baked for me, it was only fair that I be the perfect omega he deserved *one* night. "Friday night. You come over here, and we'll have a romantic dinner! Come on."

He scratched the back of his head. "That sounds

lovely, but what about your mother?"

"I'll think of something to get her out of the house."

"You're not gonna have her help you cook?"

I whacked the cheeky bastard over the head. "Of course not! I can do this!"

"Okay then." Dean chuckled. "Friday night. It's a date."

"Good." Now I only had to figure out what I was going to make and how to make it. Not that the meal was going to be the main part of the night. No, I was finally going to lose my V-card that night. I was determined. With Dean, it would be okay. It had to be.

Chapter Twenty-Three

DEAN

"Real glad you decided to work with us." Daniel clapped me on the back after showing me around the station.

"Yeah, I think I'm going to settle down in Oceanport," I told him, if only because I wanted to talk about something other than the station and the job. Daniel had been going on about it nonstop for almost an hour and my head was ringing. It was a small station, but he certainly had a lot to say about it.

"Yeah? That's good," he said as he handed me my uniform. "The town could use a few more alphas like you. Thought you were gonna go back to the big city, though. Everyone's saying."

"I was going to, yeah, but..." I shook my head, the uniform weighing heavy in my arms. "I guess I found something worth staying for."

He laughed and clapped my back again. "A sweet little omega, huh? They do that to you."

I wasn't sure that I would describe Griff as 'sweet little omega', but his guess was close enough to the truth, so I simply nodded. "Something like that."

"Good, good." Daniel grinned. "Good to have an omega waiting for you at home. We firefighters, we need something to protect in our lives."

Instinctively, I grimaced, but regained control of

my face again before Daniel could notice. "I guess," I said. I did feel an innate need to protect people, and especially Griff, but after everything that had happened, I wasn't sure anymore that I could do it—and that was a thought I couldn't let myself linger on.

What if something happened and I couldn't protect Griff?

What if instead of his parents' house, it was his house that caught on fire next?

The thought was too horrible to consider. Just the idea of Griff trapped in a sea of flames made me so sick I felt like throwing up before I could catch myself.

I pinched the bridge of my nose.

"Something wrong?" Daniel asked. "You look a bit pale."

"No, nothing wrong, sir."

Get a grip, Dean. Nothing's happening to Griff.

"I heard about that last job you had in the big city," Daniel said. "That's not troubling you, is it?"

I quickly shook my head—almost too quickly. "No. How did you hear about that?" I certainly hadn't told anyone in Oceanport. Shane had heard a bit about it from my parents, but we'd never discussed it.

"What do you think? I googled you. There was a newspaper article about the whole tragedy."

I swallowed. Everyone had called it a tragedy. Me? I called it a failure.

"You don't feel responsible for that, do you?" Daniel asked.

"No," I lied, because I knew what everyone wanted to hear. They wouldn't understand.

"Good," Daniel said. "Sometimes things just go to shit."

I nodded. Things certainly did go to shit. I just had to wrap my head around that and I had to become a functional firefighter again, because I still wanted to protect people. Especially Griff. If anything ever happened to him, I had to be there. Taking this job was going to help me prepare for that and make myself the alpha I needed to be again. I only needed to shove all thoughts of the *tragedy* aside.

When I got back home, I spotted Conner out on the front lawn playing with the puppy. The sight made me smile. It was good for the boy to get some sunlight. He had a piece of rope in his hand that the puppy was trying to tug away from him, yipping excitedly in between his attempts.

"Dean!" Conner called out when he spotted me.

I walked over to him. "Hey, how's it going?"

"Great!" Conner beamed. The expression on his face surprised me a little bit just because of how rare it was. "I've decided on a name for the dog!"

"Yeah?" I knelt down by him and patted the dog, who ignored me in favor of the rope.

"I'm going to call him Max!" he announced.

"That's a good name."

Conner smiled. "After the main character in *Where the Wild Things Are.*"

"You like that book?"

He nodded, and tugged on the rope again. "Can you take me over to Jake's?"

"Have you asked your dad?"

"Yeah. He said to ask you when you're back. He's busy. But Jake and I want to practice for the play."

"Okay, I'll take you."

"Thank you! Can we take Max?"

"You'll have to ask Jake's parents." But knowing Eli, it would probably be fine.

"I'll call." Picking up the dog, he walked into the house. I watched him go, grateful to see the reserved boy open a bit. He still had a way to go, but he was going to get there. I was glad for him and Shane, knowing how much my cousin worried about his kids.

Of course he did. I would worry too, if I had children. And maybe someday I would. Maybe with Griff. The thought made me smile, even if all that was still in the far-off future.

Or so it seemed at the time.

Chapter Twenty-Four

GRIFFIN

I needed advice. On Wednesday, my mother went off to visit my father at the hospital. She told me he was awake most of the time now, and doing well. She asked me if I wanted to come with her and have a talk. I didn't know what to say, but she understood my silence as a no. It wasn't supposed to be that. I just really didn't know. Making up with my mom was one thing, making up with my dad was another thing entirely. I knew my mother wasn't guilt-free, but she hadn't been the driving force behind our family dispute. No, that title went to my father. He wasn't an alpha, but he was damn stubborn, still. I was sure my brother got that from him.

And as soon as my mother was gone, I called my brother. Not only about this. I also needed some advice for what I'd planned for Friday. "Eli?"

"Yeah?" He sounded a little bit stressed.

"Do you have a moment or should I call back later?" I figured maybe his baby daughter had had an emergency or something.

"No, it's fine. Just studying for a test and it's not going great."

"I'm sure you'll ace it." My brother had always been good at the academic stuff, while I'd largely preferred art class. He'd worked his ass off to be able to attend college, while I could never wait to be done with school. Different talents and all that—not that my parents always agreed.

"Maybe," Eli said. "I'm not so sure. But it can wait a little while."

"Okay, if you're sure."

"What did you want to talk about?"

"Mom's gone to the hospital again and she asked if I wanted to go with her to, you know, talk to Dad while he's actually awake."

"Oh." Eli was quiet for a moment as he digested this information. "What did you say?"

"I didn't say anything and then she just went without me."

"I see."

"I don't really feel like that was the right choice," I admitted. "I *am* busy with work and all, but we can't avoid it forever, can we?" I said *we* purposefully because I wanted to know what he intended to do about this situation as well.

"We've managed to avoid it for a pretty long time, though," he said. "And I'm not sure why we should be the ones to take the first step."

"Are we?" I asked. "Because I know Mom's been calling you."

"Yeah, *Mom's* been calling me. Don't think I ever talked to Dad. I doubt he's ready to forgive and forget. Not that I feel a burning need to be forgiven. Wait, I need to go somewhere the kids won't hear me."

"Okay." I heard some rustling on the other end of the line as well as a door opening and closing. "You don't think Dad's ever going to change his mind?" I asked.

"I don't know," Eli said. "Maybe yes, maybe no. I try not to think about it."

"I'm sorry. I just want—"

"I know you want everyone to get along." He sighed. "I'll talk to him if he talks to me first. Is that a deal you can live with?"

"Yes, thank you." That was enough. It had to be. Maybe next time my Mom went to the hospital I'd go with her and see if there was anything to be done.

"I owe you a lot, Griff. If there's anything I can do to make you feel better..."

"Well, actually..."

"What?"

"There is something else," I said, remembering the other reason I'd called. "Don't worry, though. It's got nothing to do with our parents."

"Well, that's good." He breathed an audible sigh of relief, as if I was being especially taxing this morning.

"I might need your help this Friday, if you can make it."

"What's happening this Friday?" A note of curiosity seeped into Eli's voice.

"Dean and I have reason to celebrate, so I decided to make him dinner."

"I don't know what to be more suspicious of," Eli said after a moment. "Whatever your reason to celebrate is or that you want to cook."

I found myself wishing that I'd gone over to have this conversation in person so I could give him a not-so-light pat on the back of his head now. "Dean's decided to take a job with the local fire department. That's what we're celebrating, not whatever you might think. And I can totally prepare a meal." *Totally!*

"Yeah, right." He laughed a little, the bastard. "Still, that's great. But what do you need me for? To do the actual cooking?"

"I can cook!" I insisted again. "I just need you to um... help me pick out an outfit. Something that'll help me... uh... *progress* our relationship."

"Ohhh. My little brother wants to get laid!"

"Eli!"

"Well, it's true, isn't it?" His voice turned a little more serious again. "Do you think you're ready?"

"Yeah." I wanted to be, at least. "I trust him."

"I'm glad. I'll come over on Friday if you need me."

"Around six? I'll make sure Mom's gone before you show up."

"Thank you, but that's not necessary. I can handle her."

"If you're sure."

"I'm sure," he said. "See you Friday."

"See you," I returned, hanging up. Whatever was going to happen Friday, it was going to be an interesting day for sure.

Thursday evening, after several failed attempts to create anything edible at all in the kitchen, I broke down and asked for help. "Mom?" I stuck my head into the living room, where she was watching some show on TV. It was still weird to see her sitting there so normally, as if we hadn't spent years not talking to each other.

She looked up at me. "Yes, dear?"

"You remember how you tried to teach me how to cook?"

She raised an eyebrow. "I do." She shook her head. "How could I ever forget? It was a disaster."

I forced a grin on my face. "Yeah, uh, fun, wasn't it?"

"You nearly set the kitchen on fire more than once!" For a second, she seemed as if she was going to start laughing, but then the mention of fire and all its recent implications silenced her. Mom never wanted to talk about it, and so we didn't, but I suspected she wasn't fully over the shock yet.

"I've gotten a little better at it," I said. "No damage to the kitchen, I promise." That was something, right? "So I was wondering, if, uh... maybe we could try again."

"You want me to teach you again?"

I didn't *want* that, not especially, no, but I needed to prepare something for Dean to eat, and this was my best bet, short of ordering take-out and parading it as my own food. "Maybe something simple?" I asked. "Something simple but delicious?" That would be perfect.

She turned the TV off. "And where does this sudden enthusiasm come from?"

"Nowhere." I shrugged. "I just uh... figured it was time for me to learn?"

"You're not fooling me, dear. You want to cook for your man, don't you?"

I grew bright red before I could stop myself.

My mom shook her head. "You should know that I don't mind. There's no better reason to cook, really. Certainly no better motivation." She gave me a soft smile. "Well, other than to feed your children, anyway. But I hope that's not going to happen for you for a little while, at least."

"No." I wanted children, yeah, but even I knew it was too early for that.

"Good." She stood and opened her mouth as if to say something more, but closed it again. I knew what she'd been *about* to say, though. What I'd been told all my life. *An omega needs to be married before having children.*

It was one of her core beliefs, and part of what had driven Eli out of the house when he had Jake. I suspected that was why she wasn't saying it now, even if she still believed it. She didn't want me to make my brother's *mistake*, but she wasn't going to say it out loud to keep the peace.

I was a fan of peace myself, so I didn't call her out on it. After all, I still hoped that my family could be mended with a bit of time and understanding on all sides.

My mother walked past me into the kitchen. "Let's see what we have to work with. I'll help you feed your man. Dean's a good alpha. You should hold on to him."

I guess that was as close to approval of my plans as I was going to get. Still, I wondered what she might have said if I'd told her that I wanted to get rid of my virginity.

Use protection, probably.

Chapter Twenty-Five

GRIFFIN

By the time Friday night rolled around, I had learned to make a simple pork roast without setting the kitchen on fire. It wasn't much, but it wasn't going to give Dean food poisoning, and at this point, that was the best I could hope for. I had severely overestimated my omega abilities when I offered to cook for him.

I'd arranged for my mother to stay at the only bed & breakfast in town, which was going to raise suspicions of course, but I didn't care. I'd been through far worse gossip than that I might be sleeping with the hottest alpha in town. What I did care about was that I couldn't get my mother to leave before my brother showed up. She dilly-dallied the whole time, and I suspected she did it on purpose. In hindsight, maybe I shouldn't have told her that Eli was coming over, but there was nothing I could do about that now, short of throwing my mom out of the house.

In all my life, I'd never seen my mother run, but when Eli knocked on the door, she very nearly did.

"Elias!" she said when she was face to face with him. "It's so good to see you!"

My brother stood in front of her and obviously had no idea what to say. He'd said he knew how to handle her, but maybe not. "Hi, Mom," he got out in the end, before his eyes searched for me and he met my gaze with an awkward smile.

"Mom was just about to leave for the bed & breakfast," I said, trying to help him out.

"Oh, I was," she said, never looking away from Eli. "But I have a few minutes if you'd like to chat."

Eli glanced at me again, biting his lip.

I shrugged. *Sorry, you're on your own, bro. Your decision to make.*

"I guess a few minutes won't hurt," he said eventually.

Yes! A step forward. I tried to keep from smiling. "I have a few preparations to make in the kitchen," I excused myself, because I figured it was best to give the two of them some privacy, no matter how badly I wanted to listen in on their conversation.

In reality, I was done with everything I had to do in the kitchen, so I just sat with a coffee and waited. And maybe I spiked my coffee with a little extra because my nerves could really use it that day.

My mom and my brother had gone to the living room, so I couldn't really hear them aside from muffled voices. At least they weren't raised. If they could talk for five minutes without fighting, that would be awesome, especially since I got the feeling that Eli was making an effort on my behalf, and I didn't want to drag him into anything too uncomfortable.

But this drama couldn't continue forever. What if the next time tragedy struck someone actually died?

I didn't even want to think about that, so I just sipped my coffee and waited.

It couldn't have taken longer than ten minutes before I heard the front door open and a few seconds later, my brother stepped into the kitchen.

"You got any more of that coffee?" he asked.

"Sure." I got up to pour him some. "You didn't

fight, did you?" I asked because I couldn't contain the questions any longer. I'd given him a few minutes of privacy; that was all he could ask.

"No." He shook his head. "No fighting. She really just wanted to chat." Accepting a mug of coffee from me, he sat at the counter. "It seems she genuinely wants to make up."

"That's good, though, right?"

"I guess. Maybe. I got the feeling she wants to see the kids." He stirred some sugar into his coffee. Not as much as I took with mine, but still a good amount.

"Does that surprise you?"

"Not really. Just don't know how to feel about it." He raised the mug to his lips. "Guess I'll have to figure it out."

"Guess so, yeah."

He gave me a small smile. "Let's just move on to the fun part of the evening, okay? Let's get you ready for your date."

"Okay," I said, pretending like that thought didn't freak me out a little.

Dean rang my door bell at 7pm sharp carrying a bottle of wine, and I opened the door in an old-fashioned pink apron, immediately getting a laugh out of him. So far so good.

"What's that?" he asked, pointing at it after giving me a quick kiss.

"You don't like it?" I feigned disappointment. "I thought I'd dress like a good house-husband for you."

He shook his head. "I'm sorry, but it doesn't suit you."

I sighed and took it off. "Okay then. No apron. No

good docile omega. Your loss."

"My gain," he disagreed. "You look stunning under that thing."

I grinned to myself, because yeah, Eli and I had spent some time picking out my outfit. I'd put on all my best clothes to get Dean out of his. "Do I?" I walked in the direction of the kitchen, turning my back to him and making sure to wiggle it just a little in my tight pants.

"You're devious."

I laughed, but my hands still shook a bit as I grabbed the pot on the stove. I couldn't completely calm my nerves. Dean looked great tonight too. More edible than what I'd cooked up, really. I couldn't wait to move on to the after-dinner activities of this evening, but at the same time, I was also terrified of it. Dean had told me not to worry, but what if I froze up again? I couldn't keep disappointing him.

"Where's your mom tonight?" Dean asked.

"At the bed & breakfast," I told him.

"So she'll be gone all night?"

I had to give Dean credit for trying to sound casual while asking, even if he didn't quite manage.

"Yeah," I said. "We have the house to ourselves. All night." My lips quirked up, and so did his.

"All night, huh?"

"Yup." I took his hand. "Now please come have dinner with me. I've prepared a table for two in the most exclusive place in town. Only you and me here."

"I like that guest list."

"I put it together myself," I said with a grin as I led him to the table, which I'd decorated with a nice red tablecloth and a single long candle in the middle. It was perfect, or at least I hoped so.

"Looks good," Dean said, and to my relief, he was still smiling when I brought the food in. He ate it too, without cringing. At some points, he even managed to look like he enjoyed it. That was more than I could say for myself, really. I would have preferred to eat *anything* I hadn't created. The roast wasn't super bad, but it sure as hell wasn't praise-worthy either.

Dean tried anyway. "You did a really good job," he said, while I refilled my wine.

"You don't even want to know how much time it took me to create something you wouldn't spit out in disgust."

He chuckled. "I would never do that."

"Then you're a braver man than I." I sipped my wine, starting to feel a pleasant buzz. I wasn't going to drink much more, but for now, the liquor was helping me keep my nerves at bay.

"It can't have been that bad," he insisted.

"Oh, you have no idea. One day I'll make you eat something I made as a test of courage. I swear, I fail so hard at being an omega it's not even funny." I said it jokingly, but Dean still felt the need to reach across the table and touch my cheek.

"You don't fail at anything. You're kind and sweet and funny, and I can't think of a single omega I'd rather be with tonight. Or any night."

Heat crept across my cheek, and I couldn't tell whether it was caused by his touch or his words. Maybe a combination of the two; it didn't matter. What mattered was that a fire started burning inside of me, slowly but insistently. I had to get up from this table and take Dean into the bedroom with me.

I glanced at his plate. He was nearly done anyway. I grabbed the hand that was touching my cheek and took it in my own. "Want to go upstairs?"

Dean licked his lips in a way that let me know just how much he wanted that. But still, he hesitated. "You know I'd love to, but are you sure you want to do that?"

I took a deep breath, almost wishing he wouldn't give me time to think about this and let the doubt creep in. I needed to keep this fire burning, stoke the flames. "Yeah," I said. "I'm sure. I just need to work through this, and you have to promise me that you won't stop unless I tell you to. I mean, I might tense up or something, but I don't want you to abort mission because of that again. I'm gonna be nervous, I can't help that, but I trust you. I want this to happen, okay? Can we just get through with it?" And I was babbling again, of course.

"I don't want you to just get through it. If we do this, I want you to enjoy it."

I gave him my best smile and stood from the table. "I'm sure I will."

"Okay, then." Dean stood as well. His hand was still in mine, and I kept holding on to it all the way up the stairs and into my bedroom, my heart thundering in my chest.

We were really going to do this.

Breathe, Griff, it's going to be fine.

As it turned out, breathing was exactly the right thing to do—more specifically, leaning into Dean once we were in my room and breathing in his scent. It was so strong now, because he was aroused, and that did a number on my brain. It was as if I could actually scent Dean's desire for me in the air and that was incredibly intoxicating—and it wasn't the only way I could feel his desire. It was in the way he kissed me too, his fingers in my hair and his tongue exploring every corner of my mouth, our bodies pressed close together, until I felt another piece of evidence of his arousal against my thigh.

One of his large hands roamed down my body to

my ass, and the heat of his touch seemed to flow into my veins. I was both nervous and excited, but for the moment, more excited than nervous. The fine stubble of Dean's beard scratched my cheek as his lips moved on mine, and the sensation shot straight to my groin. It didn't even bother me that the taste of our meal lingered on his tongue. Suddenly it tasted much better than it had before.

I put my arms around his back to pull him closer and his thigh rubbed my groin, just like that one time we'd been in bed together—only this time the spark of need that went through me at the touch didn't make me freeze up. If anything, it made me feel even hotter. I wanted more of that. Wanted *him*.

And as if to state my intentions, I dug my fingers into his ass. That got me a low rumble from him, and slowly, he raised his hand to slide underneath my shirt, making goose bumps break out on my skin while his lips left mine to speak into my ear. "God, I love you so much."

"You can call me Griff," I quipped, even while my voice came out breathless.

He chuckled, still so close to me that I felt his chest vibrate. "I love you, *Griff*."

And how lucky did that make me? "I love you too," I responded, before I could chicken out, because it was the truth. I loved this alpha, and I wanted him. No, that wasn't it. I didn't simply want him. This went deeper. I *needed* him.

And as soon as I accepted that, I felt a rush so intense I couldn't even put it into words. It was what I felt every time I breathed in Dean's scent—multiplied by a hundred, and without the added fear factor that usually kept me from acting. No, that was gone, and all that was left was fire burning through my veins, and an overwhelming desire to get this alpha inside of me. It was all that I could think about, all that mattered. “Lose your clothes,” I muttered, my hands already fiddling with Dean’s belt.

“Whoa, slow down.”

“Not gonna happen,” I muttered as I opened his belt and fly in record time to stick my hand down his pants. I nearly hissed as my fingers brushed his hot flesh. Oooh, yes, he was hard.

“Shit, Griff,” He groaned, and then he pulled his shirt off over his head as if finally believing that I was serious. About time! I wrapped my hand around his cock to spur him on, loving the weight of it. He was an alpha—and definitely hung like one. God, I couldn’t wait to feel that cock inside of me. Every part of my body ached for it, and involuntarily, I shuddered. I’d always had dirty thoughts, but I’d never come so close to *living* them.

After a moment, I let go of Dean’s cock, but only to pull his pants and boxers all the way down, revealing his strong thighs and calves. I was proud of myself for not salivating at the sight even as the fire inside of me seemed to burn even hotter. He was so freaking gorgeous. Lightly tanned skin, beautifully defined muscles, and my favorite part—that sexy smile on his lips as he looked at me with a hunger in his eyes that mirrored my own.

I realized he wanted me to undress as well, but I didn’t want to take my clothes off. No, I wanted him to do that for me. “You can take my clothes off if you want to,” I said, beckoning him closer. *Come take me.*

To his credit, he took me up on the invitation without a moment’s hesitation, peeling me out of the clothes I’d picked out so carefully earlier that day as if unwrapping a present. I’d never felt so fucking hot as I did the moment he kissed my neck and pulled my pants down.

Even though it was summer, the air in the room made me shiver as it hit my skin. Not because I was cold, though, but just because it reminded me how exposed I was. It wasn't a bad feeling. It was just intense. Dean undressed me piece by piece, and heat blazed through me when he finally took my underwear off with a low, possessive growl.

"Like what you see?" I asked.

He smashed our lips together in response, effectively silencing all the questions in my head. What remained was my burning need for him, and so I took him by the arm and dragged him to the bed with me, where I tumbled onto the sheets with him on top of me.

I exhaled, lying beneath him and feeling his weight on top of me. No other place on earth had ever felt so right for me to be. I was painfully hard now, all thoughts of fearing this feeling forgotten. My nerves were nothing more than a distant memory at the edge of my mind. This moment, all I knew was that I was going to go up in flames if I didn't get him inside me soon.

Oblivious to my thoughts, Dean didn't proceed to that part of the action, though. He kissed me instead. First my lips, then my chin, then my jaw, moving down my body at a torturously slow pace, grinding our hips together in a way that made both of us gasp and strain for more.

Some other night I might have enjoyed that, but right then, I had zero patience. What he was doing felt really fucking good, but it wasn't what I wanted—what I *needed.*

"Fuck me," I said on a sharp exhale.

Dean stopped moving, both of his eyebrows raised. "Really?" Dean asked. He *sounded* eager enough, if apprehensive.

“Please.” I bucked my hips to nudge him along. *Please*. How could he not see how desperate I was?

He still hesitated, so I rolled us over until I was on top. That didn’t feel quite as nice, but at least I could now grab the lube out of my dresser drawer to get this party started. Omegas had an easy time with penetration, but even through the haze in my mind, I realized that this *was* my first time taking a cock up my ass, so getting Dean slicked up wouldn’t hurt. Or at least I hoped so.

Dean stared at me as I squirted some lubricant on my hand, and then the look on his face changed to one of bliss as I wrapped that hand around his hard cock. He was so damn hot like that, the sight mesmerized me for a moment. I gave him a stroke, just to see what would happen, and enjoyed the low rumbling sound he made in the back of his throat.

I focused my attention back on the cock in my hand, my whole body burning for it. I knew there was something I was forgetting, something that nagged me like a buzzing fly in the back of mind, but I shoved the feeling aside as I guided that beautiful cock into myself. I went slow, because the stretch was unlike anything I’d ever experienced, but it was, so, so good.

God, why had I waited so long to experience this?

“Griff…” Dean groaned, his voice strained. He sounded a little like he had something else to say, but he didn’t, not when I kept lowering myself on him. I grinned, brain doused in endorphins. Being on top wasn’t so bad. Not exactly what I wanted, but not bad. But nothing could really feel bad while I was fucking Dean.

I couldn’t believe I was really fucking Dean, but I was totally doing it. He was fully sheathed in me now, and goose bumps had spread all over my skin, my insides burning and tingling in the best way. I leaned forward to kiss Dean, and by the way he responded to the touch, I knew I wasn't the only one consumed by fire. This was just as intense for him as it was for me, and just knowing that made the whole experience even better, if that was even possible.

I was so glad my first time was with Dean. I couldn't think of any other alpha I could have trusted with this, but Dean made it perfect.

Especially when he rolled us around again so he was back on top.

"God," he rumbled. "I can't even tell you how much I've wanted this."

He kissed me again before I could respond, but that was okay because I was out of words anyway. He'd started to move his hips and that slow in-out motion eradicated all coherent thought from my mind. It was all colors and explosions behind my eyelids. My whole world centered around the need in my groin, the fire burning in my veins, the feeling of him inside of me and the sparks of desire running up and down my spine.

If you'd asked me, I couldn't have told you my name.

Not that my name was particularly important. Dean sure wasn't asking any questions now. Neither of us was quiet, though. Thank God I'd sent my mother away. We were *loud.* Groaning, moaning, gasping out incoherent words. Especially when Dean upped the pace. *Jesus fucking Christ.*

I'd always been a bit awkward about all of this, but in the heat of the moment, I knew no shame. I was a changed omega.

And I was loving it.

Maybe a bit too much. Because once Dean got a

hand on me, I tumbled over the edge at breakneck speed. There was no slow build-up. My orgasm came over me like an explosion with no regard for casualties, leaving me panting for breath and struggling not to black-out.

Dean didn't hold on much longer than me. He came gasping, fingers digging into my hips.

He was beautiful. It was all I could think. Covered in sweat, face contorting in absolute bliss. He was beautiful like that, and it was me who'd made him look that way.

Maybe I wasn't a total failure of an omega.

That was the last thought on my mind before I dozed off.

Chapter Twenty-Six

DEAN

Smoke entered my lungs through my nose, and I felt it scratch and sting in my throat. When I looked around myself, it was everywhere, hanging thickly in the air, threatening to black out the whole building. I needed to get out of here, but I didn't even know which way I'd come in, and there was that woman, lying right in front of me. I had to get to her and get her out. But as soon as I took just a step forward, the floor gave way underneath my feet. With a crash, I went down.

And with a start, I woke up.

My heart raced. My eyes searched the room. Griff's room. I was still at Griff's.

Deep breaths, Dean. It was just another dream.

These had been happening far too often lately. I suspected that my decision to join the local fire department had something to do with their increased frequency, but I hadn't had *one* restful night of sleep this week.

At least I didn't wake up screaming.

Griff was snoring softly beside me, still asleep. He hadn't noticed a thing. Good, because I had no idea what I would tell him. I didn't want to worry him, and I sure as hell didn't want him to see me as weak. A grown alpha struggling with nightmares. Really? The idea was ridiculous.

I swung my legs out of bed and got up. Part of me wanted to cuddle up to the warmth that Griff generated, but I knew I had to get moving to burn off the adrenaline still coursing through my veins, so I threw on the clothes I'd discarded the night before and went down to the kitchen. Once there, I got the coffee machine going and searched through Griff's fridge for something I could turn into breakfast for the two of us. He had pancake batter, so I decided on a sweet breakfast for my sugar addict.

As I moved about the kitchen, taking in the morning sun shining through the window, the nightmare I'd had slowly faded from my mind to be replaced with memories of the night before.

Griff had been *amazing*. I had no idea what had gotten into him, but could it please happen again? Even just the memory sent a pleasant tingle down my spine. I loved Griff, with or without sex, but I definitely wouldn't say no to a repeat of last night. I might, in fact, have started humming while pouring the pancake batter in the skillet. Yeah, I was in a good mood. The nightmares would go away over time, and when they left, I would still have Griff. I was sure of that, because now that I had him back in my life, I was never going to let go of him again.

When I was done cooking, I divided the pancakes on two plates, grabbed a bottle of syrup, some cutlery, put it all on a tray along with two cups of coffee—one prepared with copious amounts of sugar—and carried it up to Griff's room.

My love was still asleep, clutching a pillow to himself and managing to look absolutely adorable even while dead to the world. I set the tray down on the bedside table and climbed onto the mattress beside him. Gently, I kissed the top of his head, his forehead, his eyelids, the bridge of his nose and then his lips, until he started to stir and come to.

"Morning, sugar."

He blinked at me, still half-asleep. "Sugar?"

"Can you think of a better pet name for an addict?"

"I'm not an addict," he mumbled on a yawn. "Maybe just a little." He sniffed the air. "Is that coffee?"

"It is, indeed. With lots of sugar, just the way you like it. Unless you'd rather drink it black?" I sat up and reached for the cup to hand it to him.

"Ew, no. Black coffee is poison." Quickly, he grabbed the coffee from me before I could exchange it for something toxic. "Still not an addict," he muttered under his breath.

"Fine. I'll try to come up with a better pet name. How would you like *my sweet red velvet cupcake* or *snuggy-bear*?" Both things I'd heard my sister call her boyfriend at one point.

He made a face, and I had the hardest time keeping my own expression neutral. "Sugar is fine."

"Thought so." I placed a kiss on the side of his face and caught a whiff of his scent again. He wasn't made of sugar, but he smelled just as sweet.

"You made pancakes?" he asked, peering at the tray on the bedside table. "How long have you been up?" He glanced at the alarm clock. "It's not that late."

"I'm used to getting up very early," I lied, handing him the tray so he could eat. He started by pouring a generous amount of syrup on his pancakes, of course.

"I could get used to breakfast in bed," he said. "Are you going to treat me like this every morning or only when I put out?"

"I think I'll reserve this for special occasions," I said, chuckling because he managed to look so serious while asking that question.

"Special occasions?" He had to laugh too.

"I don't know about you, but I think last night was pretty special."

A faint red colored his cheeks. He couldn't claim virgin status anymore, but I figured a part of him would always remain innocent. "Was it?" he asked. "I have nothing to compare it to."

"Did you enjoy it?" I asked. "Because I did. It was amazing." He needed to know that. He had every reason to be proud of last night's performance. I'd never expected all that from him.

"I enjoyed it," he mumbled into his coffee. "We should do that again sometime."

I had to laugh again and give him a kiss. "Yeah, we definitely should." I couldn't wait.

Griff looked tempted too, licking his lips as he looked at me. But then he said, "My mom could be back any second." He glanced down at the tray, as if the pancakes were being particularly interesting. "Actually I'm probably going to the hospital with her today."

"To visit your dad?"

"Yeah." He cut into his pancakes with a little less gusto than before. He was clearly nervous about this, but I wasn't sure how to help him. "My mom's practically been begging me," he said. "And I think, I don't know. It might be good? I mean, I visited him in the hospital before, but it's not like it really counts because he wasn't awake, so if he got into another accident next week, it'll still feel like I never visited. And..." he stopped himself. "Sorry, I'm rambling again."

"Don't worry about it. I don't mind. I think it's kind of cute, actually."

He raised an eyebrow at me, the disbelief obvious in his expression.

"I'm not just saying that!" I ruffled his hair. "You're super cute. Especially when you're rambling, so don't apologize for that. It's just how you process things. You're nervous about seeing your dad. I get that." I wasn't super close with my own parents, but at least we were still on speaking terms and got together for all the big holidays. I couldn't imagine it being any other way, really. "If I was in your position, I'd be nervous too."

"Really?"

"Of course." I kissed his hair. "You'll be fine, though. Your dad is the one who messed up here. He has no right to judge you."

"No... I know. I just... want to make up, I guess. I want things to go back to normal. Maybe that's stupid. I don't know..."

"It's not stupid." But it was very like Griff to wish for peace. I wanted that for him too. There wasn't a vengeful bone in his body. I was pretty sure he'd never wished for bad things to happen to anyone. It just sucked that they still happened to him. I wanted to wrap him in my arms and hide him away from everyone who wasn't as innocent as him. "It might not be easy, but maybe it's doable. I guess you have to go talk to him to see if there's any chance..."

"Yeah, I know."

"Would you like me to come with you?"

He looked up at that. Then he shook his head. "No, I don't think that's a good idea. I don't want to introduce you to both my parents in the hospital. And he would ask all sorts of stupid questions. It would be awkward as hell. It'll probably be easier if I go by myself."

"I see. But call me when you're done, okay? I want to know how it went."

"I'll do that." He leaned up to give me a kiss.

"Thank you."

"Nothing to thank me for. I want you to be happy."

He showed me a soft smile and leaned his head on my shoulder. "I am."

I couldn't help but smile myself, wishing we could stay like this forever.

Chapter Twenty-Seven

GRIFFIN

My mother and I left for the hospital almost as soon as she got back from the bed & breakfast. I thought I'd be nervous the whole drive, but for the most part, she distracted me. My mom could talk like a waterfall. I figured I got that trait from her, even if I didn't do it all the time. But maybe she was nervous too. If she really wanted us to be a family again, and I thought she did, she had every reason to be nervous about this meeting.

That wasn't what she was talking about, though, no, she decided to pry for information about my date instead.

"How did it go last night?" she started innocently enough. But a simple *fine* wasn't enough of a response. "No, I mean, did he like the food?"

I grimaced. "Well, he ate it. But he was probably just being polite." And I wasn't going to put him through that again. No more last minute cooking lessons from me. From now on, I was going to stick to what I was good at, which was... Well, I was going to figure that out.

"Still, that's an important trait in a partner," my mom pointed out. "And it sounds like he really likes you. I'm glad."

"Me too." I gave her a small smile. At least she approved of my choice in partner. Not that it would have mattered either way. I wanted to make peace with her, yes, but not enough to give her a say in who I dated. Involuntarily, I tightened my grip on the stirring wheel. It was Dean or nobody else for me, I knew that.

"Did he stay the night?" she asked without warning and I almost drove us into a ditch.

"Mom!"

"What? Can't I ask?" She laughed, as if she'd inquired about the weather. I could only shake my head at her. "I'm not judging you if you let him stay," she continued. "He's damn fine."

I bit my teeth together, trying to keep the blush from spreading on my face. Nothing I could do about it, though. I blushed too freaking easily. "He left this morning," I muttered.

"Good, good." She smiled. "I only hope you used protection."

I swallowed. "Mom..."

"Just saying! But I know you're old enough to be responsible."

I only shook my head again and let her interpret the gesture as annoyance. In reality, though, I wasn't annoyed. I was *terrified*. I got the creeping realization, that no, we *hadn't* used protection. *I hadn't used protection.*

Oh my God.

I'd completely forgotten about it. How had that happened to me? Going back over the last night in my head, I could even pinpoint the exact moment I'd *almost* thought of it, but then hadn't, as if part of me had really, really wanted to go without. I swallowed again, knowing exactly what part of me that was.

Maybe I shouldn't have let my instincts dictate *all* the action.

Too late for regrets now, though. Now I could

only hope that my stupidity hadn't doomed me. It wasn't like I never wanted to get pregnant, but I didn't want to get pregnant now. I wanted to get pregnant some far off point in the future when I was ready to be a full-time adult and parent. For now, I liked being the goofy uncle much better, even if I loved Jake and Livvy like my own. The level of responsibility was just different.

But I'd only had sex one time, and how many people got pregnant their first try? Sure, omegas were super fertile, but it was still a long shot, right? Right?

Don't panic, Griff. Nothing's confirmed yet.

And I was going to have to wait at least two weeks before I could take a test. Two freaking weeks! Might as well be *forever*.

I took a deep breath and tried to focus on the road again. Panicking now wouldn't help. I probably wasn't even pregnant.

Right?

My dad was sitting up in his bed when we entered the room.

"Griffin." His eyes widened when they fell on me. "I wasn't expecting to see you."

I glanced at my mother, but couldn't read her face. Apparently she hadn't told Dad that I was coming. Great. This was already awkward. "I thought I'd drop by to see how you're doing," I said while my mom pulled up chairs for both of us.

"That's... nice of you." He reached for a glass of water that stood on his bedside table. "It's been long enough since you've shown your face, after all."

I grimaced. "What did you expect after throwing

us out? That I'd be over for Sunday dinner?" This was ridiculous.

"I didn't throw you out. Your brother decided to leave and you decided to go with him." My father looked hospital-pale, but his face still had all the same hard lines it had had years ago.

"Eli left because you told him he had to if he wanted to raise Jake." I'd been there for that conversation. He couldn't confuse me now.

"He wanted to throw away his future and his reputation to raise a child at nineteen when he didn't even know who the father was. I did what I could to make him see reason."

I groaned. How could I have thought that my father's bullheadedness might have changed over the past years?

"Boys, please," my mother cut in. "Declan," she addressed my father. "You told me you were ready to let this go, or I wouldn't have brought Griffin to see you. Our sons did a very good job living their lives without us, and don't think they won't keep doing that if we can't admit to our mistakes. Is that what you want?"

"No," my dad grumbled in a low voice.

I looked at my mother, both eyebrows raised. All my life, I'd never heard her talk to my dad like that. A small part of me was also pleased to hear that she thought Eli and I had done a good job as well. But this wasn't the time to preen.

My mother gestured to one of the chairs and I took a seat.

"You've been doing well, huh?" my father addressed me.

"Can't complain, really."

"He's working as a photographer, as I told you," my mother chimed in, sitting next to me. "He's also seeing a very handsome alpha."

"Mom!" My eyes snapped to her. Did she really have to bring that up now? As if this meeting wasn't awkward enough already!

She patted my shoulder as if brushing off dust. "Dear, dear. You have nothing to be ashamed of now, do you?"

Not exactly, but that didn't mean I wanted to discuss my love life with my parents. It was bad enough that my mom was living with me while I tried to get closer to Dean.

"He treating you right?" my dad asked in a gruff voice and I just about wanted to die on the spot. My family was progressive, insofar as my parents hadn't tried to find mates for us, but they'd never made a secret of the fact that they wanted to see us married and taken care of. *A good life for an omega*, in their eyes.

"We've only been seeing each other for a little while."

"But you've known him forever!" my mom interjected. "It's that boy who used to come over to our house sometimes. Dean Kramer. You remember him, don't you?"

My dad pondered this for a moment before shaking his head. "I don't recall. But it doesn't matter, as long as you're making good choices."

I grimaced, because who was he to judge whether my choices were good or not? And also because I'd definitely made a poor choice last night, but he didn't have to know that. Oh God. I hoped neither of them ever needed to know. "I'm doing my best," I said.

He nodded. "Good. Good."

"Tell him about your job, Griff!" my mom encouraged me, and I was more than happy to move on to a topic that didn't concern my relationship with

Dean. My parents might not know yet how hard I might have fucked up, but it was constantly on my mind.

I'd thought about calling my brother at the end of my hospital visit, but I didn't. Instead, I went straight over to his house after dropping our mother off at mine.

"Griff? I didn't know you were going to come over?" Eli said as he opened the door to me, carrying his daughter in his arms.

"Yeah, I was going to call, but I didn't want to talk about this on the phone."

Eli's brow furrowed in an expression of concern. "Did something happen?"

I shrugged helplessly and looked at my niece, who was staring back at me with her big blue baby eyes. Was I going to have a baby like her soon? That couldn't be. I couldn't be a parent yet.

"Griff?"

I shook myself out of my stupor. "I'm not sure we should be talking about this in front of your girl." How much did they understand at that age? Probably not too much, but I wasn't going to risk it.

"Okay," Eli said slowly. "Well, come inside."

I took my shoes off and followed him inside the living room.

"Matt's out grocery shopping with Jake," he told me. "But I assure you Livvy won't share your secrets with anyone. She won't even say *dada*." He glanced down at his little one. "I'm sure you could, but you don't want to, do you?"

Livvy babbled something in response that was incoherent, but made her daddy smile anyway.

Maybe it wouldn't be so bad if I was pregnant.

Jesus, what was I thinking?

I sat on the couch with my brother and ran a hand through my hair. "I'm an idiot."

"I don't necessarily want to disagree with you there, but tell me what happened first."

Could I really? I took a deep breath. This was my brother, who had come to me when *he'd* screwed up—and he'd screwed up *twice* by now. I could admit one mistake to him. "Dean and I had sex last night," I started, surprised that I got the words past my lips.

"You did? Awesome!" Eli grinned and patted me on the back. "I knew you could do it."

"Yeah, well..." I exhaled. "I don't know what happened, really."

"Did something go wrong?"

I bit my lower lip. "I don't know. Something just came over me. I mean, at first I was nervous, as usual, and then... I guess I decided to trust my instincts? And they completely took over. I wasn't myself." I shook my head, looking back on it. If I'd been in full control of my brain, I'd never have been so stupid as to forget a condom. I might have acted like I was twelve sometimes, but I wasn't. I knew better than most people what happened when you got careless in bed.

"I don't want to say this," Eli started. "But it sounds like you went into heat."

"Only teenagers go into heat." I waved him off.

"That's why I didn't want to say it. I was just thinking, maybe... if you never actually *had* one as a teen... Or never acted on one..."

"You think I delayed it and now it's come to bite me in the ass?"

"Kinda, yeah. I remember my own and it's a bit like what you describe. Seriously, how do you think Jake came to be?"

"I try not to think about that," I said, but it made sense, of course. When we were younger I'd always wondered how my brother had screwed up like that. Having sex without protection with his secret lover wasn't like him. But now it made sense. If he'd felt the way I'd felt last night...

"Feels good, though, doesn't it?" Eli elbowed my arm with a dirty grin. "Sometimes I wish I could be a teen again, but honestly, when you find the right partner the hormone rush can totally feel like being in heat. Maybe it was just that for you."

"I don't know." I shrugged. I'd never gone into heat as a teen, so I had nothing to compare last night's experience to. "It doesn't really matter what it was, I guess. Just that I did something really stupid."

Eli raised an eyebrow at me. "What did you do?"

"Kind of the same thing you did to have Jake?" I tried.

"Oh." My brother grimaced. "No condom, huh?"

I buried my head in my hands. "It didn't seem important at the time."

"Yeah, it never does, does it?" Eli rubbed my back. "Never seems like there's enough time to put one on. And then nine months later..." He stopped. "I don't want to scare you. We don't even know yet whether anything really happened."

"But what if it did?" I didn't dare look up. "What if I'm pregnant? What do I do then?"

"We'll figure that out when we get there," Eli said. "But you'll be fine, even if you are. Look at me. I've messed up twice and I'm alright."

"Yeah, but you're a lot more responsible than me. I'm not really an adult. If I could, I'd sit around in my boxers all day and watch cartoons while eating candy bars." Sometimes I even did that when I had a day off.

"Don't talk like that. You've helped me so much with Jake. You know a lot more about babies than I did when I first became a parent. You would make a great dad, I know that. My kids love you. Here, hold Livvy."

I had to sit up straight when Eli handed his daughter to me. She'd fallen asleep while we were talking and I was careful not to wake the little darling. She was so cute when she was asleep. And when she was awake. Basically, she was always cute.

Not that I was biased or anything.

"You can't feel sad with a warm and happy baby in your arms, can you?" my brother asked in a low voice.

"No," I agreed, studying my niece's sleeping face with her tiny little nose. "I do want to have a baby." I really did. "Just maybe not so soon."

"I know, but we'll figure it out, if you really are pregnant. You might not be."

"Yeah," I said, and something was wrong with me because, despite all reason, a part of my heart hoped that I was. I sighed. How was I going to make it two weeks without knowing? I had to come up with lots of good distractions. Starting now. "I went to the hospital today," I told my brother.

"Did you?" His face didn't betray his emotion, but his body tensed. "How did it go? Did you get to talk to Dad?"

"Yeah. It was a bit awkward because Mom wanted me to tell him about Dean."

Eli snorted. "Oh, that's just like her."

"Yeah, but something weird happened today too. Mom actually told Dad off when he wanted to lay into me for leaving."

"Really?" Both of my brother's eyebrows shot up. "I don't think I've ever heard her criticize him."

"Right? I was surprised too. Maybe she's really

changed."

"Yeah... maybe." A thoughtful look crossed Eli's face. "I've been thinking about inviting her to come see the play."

"Jake's play?"

"Yeah. I know she really wants to see the kids, and this way she could see Jake without the two of them actually interacting. I don't want to introduce Jake to her now and then have her do a 180 when Dad's released from the hospital, you know?"

I nodded, knowing how protective my brother was of his children. Even inviting our mom to the play would be a huge step for him. "I think that's a great idea."

"Really?"

"Yeah. She's going to love Jake. Everybody does."

Eli gave me a smile at that. "True. He's the best, and super pumped about this play."

"I'm sure it'll be great."

"I hope so."

I returned my brother's smile. Maybe everything would turn out for the best somehow. Or it wouldn't, and I was doomed. Anyhow, nothing to do now but wait.

Chapter Twenty-Eight

DEAN

I couldn't sleep. The whole week after Griff and I had first had sex, I got maybe two to three hours a night at most. Either I couldn't get my mind to shut off enough to doze, or I was engulfed by flames in my dreams and woke with a racing heart. I didn't blame Griff for that, of course. No, the hours I spent with him were the only time I felt truly at peace with myself. It was simply impossible for me to beat myself up when I was around him. His laughter had always been infectious. It was one of those little things I loved about him that hadn't changed since our childhood.

But he wasn't with me this night. No, I was lying in my bed at my cousin's house, staring at the ceiling at 2am, willing myself to fall asleep and dream of something nicer than that goddamn accident. I had to get this under control if I wanted to function in my job. Hell, I had to get this under control if I wanted to be an alpha worth dating. Worth marrying, perhaps, someday. But I was getting ahead of myself, and I wasn't going to fall asleep.

With a sigh, I decided to get up and grab a glass of water.

When I went down the stairs, I saw that the light was on in the living room. I figured maybe Shane had forgotten to switch it off when he went to bed, but as I stepped into the room to do it myself, I spotted my cousin sitting on the couch with a glass of something that looked like liquor in his hand.

What was he doing up and drinking in the middle of the night? We both had work in the morning.

"Shane?"

My cousin startled a bit when he heard me speak. "Oh, it's just you," he said, looking at me.

"What are you doing down here?"

He shrugged, and I noticed the bottle of whiskey on the coffee table beside him. It looked like he'd already consumed a considerable amount of it too.

I sat with him. "Is something wrong?"

"Nothing," he said, half-heartedly. "Couldn't sleep." Well, that made two of us, but I hadn't been aware that anything was troubling Shane. Anything beyond the usual, anyway. And it didn't seem like he wanted to share. It was a stupid alpha trait really, never wanting to share your worries. Not that I was one to talk.

I grabbed the glass from him. "You realized that we have work tomorrow, right?" I asked because I knew the seniors meant a lot to Shane, simply because they had meant a lot to Ron.

"I know that." He snatched the glass back from me. "Do you, though?"

"What do you mean?"

"I know you haven't been sleeping, man, look at those bags under your eyes. You can't judge me."

I scratched the back of my head. Was it that obvious? Come to think of it, Griff had asked whether anything was bothering me too, but how could I tell him that I felt like I was suffocating on smoke every time I tried to sleep?

How was I even going to start talking about that?

I had no idea. Once or twice now I'd caught Griff looking at me with such open admiration that it felt impossible to let him down now.

"I just have a lot on my mind," I told Shane.

The way he looked at me told me he didn't believe me, but he wasn't going to get anything more.

"This isn't like you," I said, gesturing at the bottle of whiskey.

He shrugged. "I have a lot on my mind too."

I grimaced. He obviously wasn't going to share if I wasn't. "I'm having a hard time going back to my old job," I said, putting it as harmlessly as possible.

"Really?" he looked up at me. "You've only been once or twice. Did anything happen?"

"No, nothing special." Not yet, anyway. I shuddered to think of the first time there would actually be a fire in town. "It just still brings back memories of the accident," I said.

Shane let himself sink back into the couch and stared at the ceiling. "You know that wasn't your fault, right?" He snorted as if he'd had some funny thought, and I guessed the alcohol was taking effect. "I always knew you were gonna go back to being a firefighter someday, but I still hate it."

"You hate it?" That was news to me.

"I hate that I have to find a replacement for you."

Ah. Now we were getting closer to the heart of the issue. "I'm not going to leave you hanging, I told you that."

"Yeah, you're a part time firefighter now." He laughed as if the idea was ridiculous. "You're going to want to go full time sooner rather than later. I know you. You don't fuck around like that." He took a sip of the whiskey. "So I'm starting to look for someone to help me so you can move on. You've helped me a lot,

Dean. I'm not gonna keep relying on you forever, man."

While that was a nice sentiment, I really didn't *want* to go full time in the near future. But Shane wasn't going to believe that unless I told him a lot more than I was comfortable sharing.

"You've already started looking?" I asked, because I'd had no idea.

"Had a few interviews today, in fact." He set the glass down on the coffee table.

"Is that why you're drinking?" Did it go that badly?

He laughed again, although there wasn't a hint of amusement to be found in his voice. "Kinda," he admitted. "They're all awful. I don't want to work with any of them." He sighed, and I got the feeling that something heavy was weighing on his mind. Something that went beyond the simple prospect of awful coworkers.

"What was wrong with them?" I asked.

He licked his lips. "They're all... I don't know. They're not... They're all omegas, of course, but they're not..."

"They're not Ron?" I asked. And by the silence that followed my words, I assumed that I'd guessed correctly. Offering private senior care had been Ron's brainchild, first and foremost. I could see why Shane felt uneasy at the idea of replacing him. When I'd come here, I'd jumped in without asking and he'd mostly been to numb back then to protest. And my stay here was always supposed to be temporary.

"I don't want to do this without him," Shane admitted. "I thought I could, but... It just doesn't feel right."

I nodded. "Have you thought about selling?"

He shook his head. "I know I could, but that

doesn't feel right either. He would never have sold."

"Perhaps not," I agreed, "but he would have wanted you to be happy. There's no point in holding on to a job that makes you miserable."

"I guess." He took a deep breath and exhaled, running his hands through his ginger hair. "You make it sound simple, but it's really not."

"I just think that selling is an option you need to consider. Find a job that makes you happy."

He gave me a grim smile. "This job used to make me happy."

I wasn't sure what to tell him. *Things change?* That sounded so crude. "I know," I said instead. "Maybe it's just time to move on."

"The way you're moving on from your job?" he shot back.

Touché. "We're not talking about me."

"Maybe we should be."

I scoffed. "No way. I'm way too sober to get into that." Joining him, I let myself sink back into the leather of the couch as well. Maybe I did need to talk to someone, but if so, it should be Griff. Lately though, whenever I went by his place, his mom hovered around us. As much as I wanted Griff to reconnect with his parents, the fact that his mother was always around was really inconvenient. It had been a week, and we hadn't had a chance to get intimate again after that first time—which was a shame really. I couldn't wait to have Griff to myself again, find out more about his body, what made him gasp, what made him moan...

"What are you thinking about?" Shane asked, as if cluing in to the way my thoughts went off track.

"I think we need to get out."

"Out?"

"Yeah." I hadn't really thought about it before

speaking, but as soon as the words were out of my mouth, I knew that I was on to something. “We need to break the routine.” It might just help us get a fresh perspective, and we could sure use a few hours of fun.

Shane regarded me curiously. “What do you have in mind?”

I stared up at the ceiling. What did I have in mind? What could you do for fun in Oceanport? The town had a small movie theater, but aside from that, there wasn’t much. As a teen, I’d spent a lot of time either hanging around the harbor or hiking in the woods. The weather had been good lately, so maybe… “How do you feel about camping?”

“Camping?” Shane looked at me as if I had gone insane.

“Yeah, you know, sleeping in tents, roasting marshmallows over a fire… the works.”

“You’re serious?” Shane paused. “I should have a tent in the attic. Maybe even two. Haven’t used them in forever, though.” His expression turned thoughtful. “We should take Conner, and I’m sure my mom would be delighted to have Mary for the weekend.”

I grinned. “Two tents are perfect. You can share with Conner, and I’ll take the other one.”

Shane snorted and boxed my arm. “You and who else?”

“Do you even need to ask?”

“Don’t do anything inappropriate with my boy around.”

“Wouldn’t dream of it.” But maybe sharing a tent with Griff I could finally sleep through a night. And maybe we could stay a night longer than Shane and Conner, to do all the things we couldn’t with Griff’s mother around.

Chapter Twenty-Nine

GRIFFIN

Dean looked like shit when he surprised me with a visit Thursday afternoon, when I'd been just about to run to the drug store. Not that he knew anything about my needs for a pregnancy test. Yeah, he'd been there when we had unprotected sex, but we'd never discussed it after. And honestly, he always seemed so exhausted lately that I never wanted to bring it up. He had such deep lines under his eyes that he couldn't be getting much sleep. But whenever I asked, he pretended like he didn't know what I was talking about.

"Am I interrupting anything?" he asked, after I'd opened the door and given him a quick kiss.

I tilted my head and shot him a questioning look.

"You've got your wallet in your hand," he pointed out. "Looks like you were going somewhere."

"Oh, uh..." I glanced at the offending item in my hand. "No, I was just about to... order pizza?" Ugh, why did I make that sound like a question? I was such a horrible liar. This was the reason why, every year, Jake pestered me about what he was getting for Christmas—and why Eli had stopped telling me.

"You don't sound too sure about that." He smiled. "Maybe I should take you out for dinner."

"Nah." I took his arm and dragged him inside the house with me. "We can order in. My mom's napping." I waggled my eyebrows to entice him into staying. The way he looked he had no business taking part in any activities that didn't mainly consist of sleeping or snuggling. At least he didn't argue. "What kind of pizza do you want? I was thinking Hawaiian."

That seemed to amuse him. "Figured you'd go for the sweet option."

I stuck my tongue out at him. He kissed me, and I forgot why I was pretending to be mad at him. God, there was nothing better in the world than kissing him. The way his lips felt on mine almost distracted me from the outstanding pregnancy test. Almost. I sighed as we broke.

"I think I'll go for Hawaiian as well," he said.

"Oh, really?"

He shrugged, eyes twinkling. "Let's just say I got a craving for something sweet."

"Oh, you." I shot him a look, and picked the phone up to order food. Not that easy, really, with a hot alpha kissing my neck while I tried to have a conversation. I choked on my words when he nibbled on my ear lobe and let out a not so subtle gasp.

"What was that, sir?" the pizza guy asked me on the other end of the line.

I blushed and tried to come up with something intelligent to say because Oceanport had only one pizza delivery service and I couldn't even contemplate the tragedy of having to avoid them in the future. "N-nothing," I stuttered when Dean sneaked his hand underneath my shirt. I should have pushed him away while I was on the phone, but damn. Never having pizza again sounded more acceptable than breaking from Dean's touch just then.

We really didn't have enough time to ourselves!

"Is everything alright over there?"

"Yes, everything's fine!" I got out in one breath. "We'll have an extra-large Hawaiian pizza." Behind me, Dean chuckled. Asshole. Not that I could really stay mad at him when his fingers trailed up my chest, raising goose bumps in their wake until they found one of my nipples.

"Your address, sir?"

My... what? Oh, I was still on the phone.

Fortunately, Dean took it from me and completed the order in a few short sentences. Then he laid the phone aside and dragged me onto the couch with him.

"Couldn't wait for dinner, could you?" I asked in between kisses. His hardness pressed into my thigh and made it difficult for me to focus, but I still wanted to tease him.

"Nope." He grinned against my lips. "Needed to satisfy my craving now. What can I say? You're hard to resist."

"I see." And that was all the patience I had for talking, because he was equally as hard to resist. A small part of me still remembered being scared, but I could push that aside more easily now. Dean was never going to hurt me. With him, I could let myself be the omega I was born to be. Without shame and without any genuine fear.

But, apparently, not without parental interference.

The sound of footsteps in the hall registered in my brain only seconds before I spotted my mom standing in the door way of the living room, looking at me as I lay on the couch with Dean draped all over me.

Shit.

My mom knew that we were dating of course, but her seeing us act like animals was still embarrassing as hell.

"Dean!" I hissed, because he hadn't seen her yet. He shot me a questioning look as I shoved him off me, but then his eyes grew wide as they fell on my mother.

"Oh," he mouthed.

I forced a smile. "I didn't know you were up," I said, facing my mother, because I really didn't know what else to say, cheeks burning up.

"I didn't mean to disturb you..." She said on a laugh. "Don't mind me, boys." She left the room again.

Clearing my throat, I looked at Dean. "Uh, sorry about that. I really thought she was out." And honestly, while Dean was on top of me, I forgot about her existence altogether.

Dean shook his head. "It's fine." He sat on the couch beside me. "But this reminds me what I came here to talk to you about."

"What's that?" My mother's sudden arrival had quenched my arousal, and slowly, my ability to think returned. "Was there something you wanted? I mean, aside from the obvious."

"I'm hoping it'll lead to the obvious," he admitted.

"Oh? You have my full attention."

He grabbed my hand and ran his thumb across my fingers, making some of my blood flow south again. He *definitely* had my attention.

"Shane and I were talking, and we were thinking it might be fun to go camping."

"Camping?"

"Yeah, out in the woods. He and Conner would be coming, but we'd have our own tent, and we could stay a night longer. Think about it. Just you and me, and nothing but the wilderness. No one to run into us..." Dean gazed at me intently, painting all sorts of pictures in my mind of what we would be doing in that tent.

"I like that idea." I liked it a lot.

"Great." He gave me a smile, and a kiss. "Then it's settled. How do you feel about going this weekend?"

"This weekend is great." I swallowed, wondering if I might have any news to share with him by then.

The next day, I texted my brother to come by and bring a pregnancy test. I didn't like the thought of Dean running into me again on the way to the drugstore—or, hell, *at* the drugstore—and I'd bought his last time he got himself knocked up, so he owed me.

Like the great big brother he was, he obliged, showing up at my door just an hour after I'd first texted him. Thank God our mother was at the hospital with our dad. It seemed he was going to be released soon, and they had to discuss what they were going to do about their living situation then.

But I couldn't think about all that now.

My pregnancy test came in a brown paper bag, which Eli held out to me without comment.

I accepted it grimacing. This was it. The time had come to find out whether I was going to be a dad or not. I took a deep breath, contemplating that.

"What are we hoping for?" Eli asked.

I had to laugh, because that was the exact same thing I'd asked *him* the last time he'd taken a test. He hadn't been able to give me an answer, and now I understood why. This was so complicated. Ups and downs to every possible outcome.

"I get it," he said, laying a hand on my shoulder when I didn't respond. "I'll wait in the living room until you're done."

I nodded, willing my hand to stop shaking. There was too much nervous energy cursing through my body.

Just get it over with, I told myself, and then I made my way to the bathroom to find out what the future held for me.

For a second or two, I wondered whether I should have told Dean that I was taking a pregnancy test, whether it would have been nice to have him here with me for this, but I didn't want to excite or worry him unnecessarily, and I had Eli. I was alright. I just had to go through with this.

Deciding to rip the proverbial Band-Aid off, I closed the bathroom door behind me, got the test out of its packaging and went to business.

It said that I had to wait for two minutes.

Impossibly long.

Instead of standing around and waiting, I pulled my pants up, washed my hands, grabbed the test stick and took it into the living room with me.

"All done?" Eli asked. He sat on the couch and looked up as I came in.

"Kind of." I shook the stick in my hand. "I don't have the result yet." Although, if I looked now, I'd probably know.

Eli stood. "Want me to tell you?"

Wordlessly, I held the stick out to him.

He took it and looked. He smiled, but I didn't know what that meant.

"So?" I made myself ask.

His smile grew wider, as if he just couldn't help himself. And then he said the words that sealed my fate. "Looks like it's my turn to become an uncle."

My mind blanked. There was a little life growing inside of me. I was going to have a baby. I was *actually* going to have a baby. A baby for my firefighter!

I nearly giggled, I couldn't help myself. The part of my heart that had wished for this felt like it was going to flow over with joy. I hugged my brother.

"Congratulations!" he said.

"Thank you!" I responded, trying not to sniffle. Even though I was happy, it was a huge thing to process.

And I had no idea how Dean was going to react to this news. I was going to find out soon, though. This weekend, during the camping trip. I would tell him then.

Chapter Thirty

GRIFFIN

When we set out for the camping trip, part of me was excited, and part of me was scared. I had such big news to share with Dean over the weekend, and no idea how he was going to take it. I could only hope for the best. Things started out well enough. Sunny weather had been forecast for the whole weekend and as we set out into the forest, the sky above us was a cloudless blue. The mountain air mixed with the smell of the sea carried to us by a summer breeze, and nothing at all indicated that this wasn't going to be a super fun weekend.

Even if Conner didn't look super enthusiastic. His backpack seemed heavy, and I wondered whether he'd stacked it full of books.

But I'd brought a secret weapon to distract him; I'd brought Jake, who was already trying his best to lighten the mood.

"What do you have in there?" he asked, curiosity lighting up his features.

"Books," Conner mumbled, confirming my suspicions.

"Cool. Do you have any comic books?"

"Uh... no." Conner shook his head and pressed his lips together as if slightly embarrassed.

"You need to read some! They're really cool. I'll

lend you my newest. It's about people with all sorts of superpowers." Jake grinned and spread his arms wide. "What would you pick if you could have a superpower?"

"I don't know..."

"Maybe you should pick being able to breathe underwater. Then you wouldn't have to learn how to swim!" Jake laughed.

Watching him and Conner chat reminded me of when Dean and I had been their age, bantering and teasing each other about silly things. The memory made me smile.

"You look like you're in a good mood," Dean commented.

"I am!" I said, grinning. "Remember that camping trip the school sent us on that one time? I was thinking about that."

"Was that the one where Dean was caught skinny-dipping?" Shane chimed in.

"Oh, that wasn't me, cousin." Dean patted him on the back. "That was you."

"Oh, right!" Shane grinned. "Good times!"

I shook my head at the two.

"What's skinny-dipping?" Jake asked.

"Something you won't be doing," I replied. "You promised your daddy you were going to behave."

Jake tilted his head and feigned innocence. "How do I keep from doing it if I don't know what it is?"

Clever little—

"Skinny-dipping is swimming naked in a lake," Conner said, surprising me. How did he know that? I glanced at Shane, who just held his hands up and shrugged as if to say he was wondering the same thing.

"I read it in a book," Conner clarified when he noticed our confusion.

"Totally naked?" Jake asked before any of us

adults could ask what books Conner was reading.

Conner blushed a little, and I decided to save him from answering by quickly changing the topic.

"That spot up ahead looks like a good place to set up tent, doesn't it?" We'd reached the small valley we were heading for. I'd discovered it on a photo-taking trip recently, and it was perfect for our purposes.

"Looks great," Dean agreed.

I smiled at him and set my backpack on the ground. "Ooof. That was heavy."

Dean raised an eyebrow at me. He'd offered to carry my stuff earlier, but I'd declined. He and Shane were carrying the tents and our sleeping bags, and that was enough. "What did you bring?" he asked.

"Oh, only my most essential equipment." I grinned. Just because it was the weekend didn't mean I couldn't sneak some work in. Who knew what great shots I might be able to take at this outing! A few of nature, and a few candid shots of my travel mates. My fingers itched to take a few good pictures of Dean. Maybe in the light of the setting sun with the red and gold mountain sky in the background...

"Why are you smiling like that?" he asked.

"No reason! C'mon, let's set up the tents."

When the day was nearing its end, the alphas started to set up a campfire so we could roast some marshmallows. No camping trip was complete without roasted marshmallows, after all. Shane and Dean were doing the bulk of the work, but Jake, and eventually even Conner, had enthusiastically helped gathering firewood.

I took the opportunity to pick up my camera. It was still light enough to get a few shots, and I couldn't think of anything I'd rather photograph than my alpha building a fire. All my caveman instincts adored the image in front of me, and since I'd decided not to argue with my instincts anymore, I might as well indulge them, right?

"Are you taking pictures?" Dean asked when he noticed me with the camera.

"No better motive than an alpha who knows how to handle a fire." I grinned, but Dean's face fell. The expression lasted only a fraction of a second, but I noticed. I had no idea what caused it, though. Had I said something wrong?

"Don't you wanna help?" Shane asked, distracting me.

"Nah, you got it." I fiddled with my focus and looked at the alphas through the camera, waiting for that perfect moment to click the shutter.

Dean got some sparks going and I pressed my finger down.

Click.

"This is so cool!" Jake nearly shouted, watching Dean in awe.

I grinned. Coming here had been such a great idea. I was having so much fun.

Smoke started rising from the wood, and I took another picture of Dean.

I was so focused on watching his every move and all the fine details of his face that I immediately noticed when a shadow fell over his features. I hadn't imagined it earlier; something wasn't right. He was staring at our little campfire as if it had just burned his grandmother on her birthday.

What was up with that?

I put the camera down and approached him. "Dean?"

His eyes snapped to me. He was pale, his body stiff,

as if it was taking all his willpower not to shake. No one but me was looking at him, though, and I didn't want them to, either. I had the feeling he wouldn't want to be in the spotlight right now, so I took his arm and gently led him away from the fire and toward the woods.

"Where are you going?" Shane called after us.

"We'll be back in a minute." I forced a laugh. Let Shane think I was up to something naughty. At least that didn't invite questions.

Shane groaned. "Really? Don't take too long!"

"Right!" This wouldn't take long, would it? I just needed to know what was going through my boyfriend's head. He kept saying that everything was fine, but I wasn't buying it. I'd never believed it, and I wasn't going to keep pretending that I did. It was obvious now that something big was bothering him, and we needed to talk about that. We couldn't have any monumental secrets between us when we were about to have a child together.

Oh God, we're going to have a child together.

I hadn't told him that yet, but I was going to. Tomorrow when we were alone. I took a deep breath.

Focus on the here and now.

Here and now, my alpha needed me. He'd relaxed a bit since we'd left the others, but he was still pale. I could see that even in the low evening light. I touched the side of his face to make him look at me, loving the feel of his stubble underneath my fingertips. "What's wrong?" I asked, not willing to give him a chance to pretend like nothing was.

He swallowed and licked his lips. "It's…"

"Don't say that it's nothing," I warned. "I'm not stupid."

"I don't think you're stupid. It's just…" He took a deep breath. "Difficult to say."

I gave him a sympathetic smile. "I promise I won't

tell? Pinky swear?"

That got a little laugh out of him, even if it was short-lived. "I'm not worried that you might tell." He ran a hand through his hair. "I'm worried what you're going to think of me."

I creased my forehead. How could he worry what I was going to think of him? Didn't he know that I loved him? He was the only one I'd ever dated. The only one who'd ever broken through my barriers. He was *the one.* Whatever he was about to tell me wasn't going to change that. "You don't need to worry about that," I told him, kissing the corner of his lips. "You're my boyfriend *and* my best friend. I love you. Who could you tell if not me?"

He exhaled. "I don't want you to see me as weak."

I stroked a hand through his hair and kissed the tip of his noise, breathing in his alpha scent. "I could never see you as weak, but I don't think anyone can be strong *all* the time. You know, my brother and I had to rely on one another all the time. Those first few years weren't easy, but we made it through, because we had each other. I know I can rely on you like that too, and I want you to be able to rely on me as well."

Screw alpha and omega roles. I could be there for my man. I wanted to be. Wasn't that kind of the omega's job, anyway? To pick up the pieces when the alpha crashed?

I could do that.

"Okay," Dean said eventually, kissing my forehead. "I guess I need to tell you what this is all about." He rubbed his face.

"Go on." I took his hands in mine to show support.

"You remember why I came to Oceanport?"

"Because your cousin needed help." It had impressed me a bit, how he'd left everything behind to help Shane out.

He grimaced. "That's not the full truth."

"No?" Had something happened to him before coming here?

He licked his lips again. "There was a fire before I left. A bad one." He shook his head. "The house belonged to an old lady." There was so much pain in his voice that I wanted to hug him, but it was probably better if I let him finish his story first.

"What happened?" I asked to prod him along.

"I tried to get her out. I could see her, but before I could get to her, the floor gave way beneath my feet. I broke in and I was trapped by rubble." He took another deep breath, and I squeezed his hands. I couldn't even imagine going through all that. It must have been horrible, being trapped like that. I got the feeling, though, that for Dean, not being able to save that old lady had been the worst part.

"A colleague got me out eventually," he continued. "My injuries weren't too bad, but I still asked for a break from work when I was released from the hospital." He let out a breath, shaking his head. "I can't get the memory of her out of my head."

Of course he couldn't. If Dean thought he was the reason this woman had died before her time, it would haunt him forever. No wonder the campfire had made him look like that, if this was the memory it called up.

"I'm so sorry that happened to you," I said, letting go of his hands just so I could circle my arms around his back and rest my forehead on his chest, tucked under his chin, burrowing close. "You can't blame yourself, though. I'm sure you did everything you could. I'm proud of you, no matter what. It takes a lot of courage to run into a burning building."

Dean chuckled softly. "I don't know about that. One time when we were called to a house fire, we had to stop a frat guy from running in to save a case of beer."

I had to suppress a laugh at the image. "Okay," I said. "It takes a *sane* person a lot of courage to run into a fire."

"I know." Dean sighed. "I just always feel like there's something more I should have done."

"I understand," I reassured him, feeling him embrace me. "But it's not true."

"How can you know that?"

I looked up at him. "Because I know you." From the time we were young, my friend had always looked out for everyone. If there was anything he could have done, he would have done it. He just cared that much. Of course, it was that same caring that was eating him up inside now. "Is this why you haven't been sleeping?"

He sighed. "Yeah," he finally admitted.

"Because you took that job at the fire department?" That was when this had started, wasn't it?

"Kind of?"

He really didn't like to talk about this, did he? "Maybe you need to put that job on hold for a while."

He shook his head. "I've already let enough time pass. Going on a break didn't help, so I figured I'd take it head-on."

"But that's not working so well either, is it?"

"I guess not."

I could tell that it was not easy for him to share this with me, but I loved that he did anyway. "Maybe it's time for a career change," I suggested. Hadn't he saved enough people? I would sleep easier too, if I knew he never had to enter another burning building.

"I can't just stop being a firefighter," he said. "It's who I am. I don't know what else I would even do."

"Open a bakery?"

He laughed, as if I'd meant it as a joke. I hadn't, but

for the time being, I was just glad to hear him laugh. "And bake for someone other than you? Wouldn't you feel betrayed?"

"You bake for the seniors all the time, and I cope," I reminded him.

"I guess you're just awesome like that." He kissed the top of my head.

"I guess I am." I grinned. "Are you ready to go back to the others? Should we just hide in our tent instead?" Absentmindedly, I played with the hem of his shirt. I couldn't wait to be in a tent with him to show him just how much I loved him still—and always.

"I think I can manage the fire if I can hold on to you."

I leaned up to kiss him. "You can hold on to me any time."

"I'll take you up on that promise," he said, tightening his hold on me for a moment before letting go so we could walk back to the fire.

When we got there, Shane had already gotten the marshmallow roasting started with Jake and Conner. "Took you two long enough!" he greeted us.

I gave him a sheepish smile. "We had important things to discuss," I said, knowing he wouldn't believe me anyway.

"Yeah right." He turned back to the fire.

I exhaled quietly and grabbed one of the twigs we'd prepared earlier, speared some marshmallows on it and started to roast them. Dean put his arms around my waist from behind. I leaned back into him, hoping my presence could chase the demons from his mind just for a little while.

Chapter Thirty-One

DEAN

We withdrew from the fire after a little bit. I told Shane that I wasn't feeling well, but he probably thought I was making shit up so I could be alone with Griff. I didn't blame him; I *did* want to be alone with Griff.

My omega was amazing. He kept surprising me with his love and kindness in ways that made me want to squeeze him close to myself and never let go. Every time I got to hold him in my arms and breathe in his scent, I felt lucky.

And I wanted him to get lucky tonight. Screw being within earshot of the others, we could do this quietly. I just needed to feel him right now, to hold him as close as possible, and to know that I was giving him pleasure.

He hissed my name when I pulled his back against my chest, kissed his neck and cupped him through the fabric of his jeans. "We shouldn't be doing this right now," he said.

"Don't worry, we'll be decent. No loss of clothing required." I could totally make him come in his pants.

"They'll hear us."

"No, they won't." I smiled at him in the glow of the flashlight we'd brought into the tent with us—and then I turned it off and turned Griff around in my arms to kiss him. He hesitated for only a second before kissing me back. Couldn't resist, could he?

Not that I was one to talk. Sharing this small space with him was driving me crazy. Especially after all this time we'd spent getting interrupted any time we wanted to get intimate. I needed to touch more of him, feel more of him—and judging by the desperate way Griff's breath hitched when I lowered us unto the ground, me on top of him, he felt the same way.

To keep him from making any further noise, I simply sealed his lips with my own. There was no better place for my mouth anyway—aside from maybe his cock, but I wasn't going to go there tonight. Someday I would, and I was looking forward to it, but right now, Griff wanted me to keep him quiet and decent, so that had to wait for another time.

I would never do anything Griff wasn't cool with, but I didn't hear him utter complaints when I lined our groins up until I could feel the hardness in his jeans pressing against my own. The small sound he did make was muffled, but it sounded like approval. And there was definite approval in the way he dug his fingers into my back. Yeah, this would work. Not exactly textbook sex, but that didn't matter as long as I could be with Griff, taste the sweetness of his lips, feel his warmth in my arms and draw his scent into my nose. The fact that I could also feel him buck up against me in search of friction only added to the experience.

Heat blazing through me, I dug my hands under his ass to keep him in place as I ground into him, our cocks sliding against fabric and each other. I swallowed a moan before it could escape me. Trying to get off like this was such delicious torture—and something I hadn't done since my teenage years.

It seemed fitting, though, to do this with Griff

now. He'd been the star of all my teenage dreams after all, and those dreams hadn't lost their intensity even now. I still wanted him just as much as my horny teenage self had wanted him, only now I got to live those fantasies, and it was every bit as good as I'd imagined. Better, even. Dreams couldn't come close to actually smelling the sweat build on Griff's skin as he squirmed against me, trying to relieve the ache in his pants.

Not that I was faring much better. I wanted to moan, but I kept kissing him instead, even though he sounded breathless as well. We couldn't make too much noise, though. Shane already suspected what we were doing, and I didn't want to give him more evidence. I sure as hell didn't want him to have to explain to the kids. Griff would kill me in the morning.

It wasn't easy to keep that in mind as the need in my groin built, though. Something about our breathless kisses spiraled it even higher, as though my brain knew I was going to asphyxiate if this didn't end soon. I'd rather stop breathing than stop kissing my omega.

"Dean," Griff gasped between kisses, voice shaky. "Dean, I'm gonna..."

I captured his lips again to keep him from speaking as he tightened his grip on me, his whole body going tense and his hips jerking against me as he came.

I followed soon after. No way could I keep my cool after feeling Griff come unraveled because of me. There was nothing sexier than feeling him cling on to me, body shaking with pleasure.

"Wow," he uttered once we were both sticky.

I smiled at him in the darkness of the tent. "Told you we could do this."

He laughed softly. "Thank you."

"I'm the one who needs to say thank you," I told

him honestly. I still couldn't get over how wonderfully he'd handled my earlier confession.

"You don't have to thank me for anything," he insisted. "I only want you to feel better."

"I will," I promised. I wasn't quite sure yet what to do about my problem, but I knew I was going to figure something out. Nothing could really scare me as long as I had Griff by my side.

When I woke up the next morning after a blissfully nightmare-free night, Griff wasn't in the tent with me. I looked around groggily, but he was nowhere to be found. There were sounds coming from outside, though, so I opened the tent flap. It was awfully light. The sun stood high in the sky already, raining heat down on the forest and making me wonder just how late it was.

"You're up!" I heard Griff say and found him sitting where we'd made our fire yesterday. He was on the phone, but ended the call when he saw me.

"Who was that?" I asked. "What time is it?" I ran a hand over my face and through my unruly hair, trying to wake up properly.

"Just Eli. I swear he calls me only to make sure I have my phone with me. I told him he doesn't need to worry because Jake's headed home already."

"Is he?" I looked around, only to notice that the second tent was gone. "They left already?"

"Dude, you slept forever. Shane took the boys to the lake this morning and then they packed up so they could get fast food in town." Griff shook his head as if disapproving of this decision, but I could only laugh.

"Sounds like a fun day."

"I guess." Griff gave me a small smile.

I crawled back into the tent and looked for my own phone to check the time. 2pm. Jesus Christ, why had no one woken me?

"Are you going to come out of there?" Griff asked. "I have breakfast. If you can call it breakfast anyway." He laughed. "I missed a perfect photo opportunity because of you, you know? Didn't want to leave here until you woke up."

I climbed out of the tent and stretched. "You could have woken me."

"Nah." Griff waved me off. "You needed it. And I still got some good pics of the sunrise. I love taking pictures out here. It's so relaxing." He let himself fall back into the grass and stared up at the sky.

"Didn't know you were such a child of nature," I teased.

He peered at me from his position in the grass. "I'm not really. Not long-term. Not unless nature comes with cupcakes and chocolate bars."

"I see." I walked over to him and sat in the grass beside him. "What's this breakfast you speak of?"

He laughed again. "Cookies, mostly. Why do you think the others went into town to eat?"

"You seriously brought cookies for your breakfast?

He shrugged. "There's also granola bars, beef jerky, apples and bananas. But the cookies are the best."

"I see."

"Help yourself." He pointed at his backpack. "I'm not super hungry today."

"No?" I walked over to his bag and dug through it. I found an apple that looked good and took it, but not before finding something else that stirred my interest. "You brought a bottle of soap bubbles?"

He sat up and directed his brightest smile at me. "I walked by the toy store and saw them on sale and thought it might be fun! For old time's sake. You can't feel bad while blowing soap bubbles. It's impossible."

"Why would you be feeling bad?" I asked, taking the bottle in hand.

"Oh, not me." He stood. "Truth is, I have something to tell you, and I'm not sure how you're going to take it."

I raised an eyebrow at him. How was I going to take what? "You can tell me anything, I promise." It was the least I could do after the events of last night.

His smile turned soft. "It's good news, actually. At least, I think it's good news. I don't feel bad about this."

What was he talking about? I tilted my head. "Why don't you tell me what's going on?" I put both the apple and the soap bubbles down on the grass and sat beside my love.

He took the soap bubbles up and opened the bottle. Without saying anything, he blew into the stick and stared after the colorful bubbles it produced as they floated away on the mountain air.

I gave him time. Whatever he needed to say seemed important enough to warrant that. I was curious as hell, yeah, but if Griff needed me to be patient, I would be.

"You remember the night we first had sex?" he asked eventually.

Silly question. "How could I forget?" Griff had blown my mind that night.

He gave me a shy smile. God, he was so adorable I wanted to wrap him in my arms. But I also wanted him to finish speaking before we did anything else.

"Do you also remember how we... kind of sort of didn't use a condom?"

I blinked. We hadn't, had we? In the heat of the moment I hadn't really paid it any mind, but sitting here with Griff, a cool breeze caressing my skin, the full weight of our actions finally hit me.

Griff needed to tell me something. And it was related to the fact that we hadn't bothered to use a condom.

I swallowed.

"What are you trying to say?"

I knew, of course, but I couldn't believe it.

Griff licked his lips. "I'm pregnant," he said, and then, in true Griff fashion, he rambled on. "Like I said, that's good news to me, but I wasn't sure how you were going to feel about it. We're going to be parents! That's big! But I know that we can do it! Probably. I think."

"You're pregnant?" That one sentence played in my mind on repeat. It was going to take me another minute or two to move on from it, even as Griff rambled. There were so many different emotions wrestling for attention inside of me. I wanted to hug Griff, and the whole world! But at the same time, I also wanted to throw up a little bit. I felt like the ground was slowly dissolving underneath my feet.

Something else that Griff had said stuck with me.

We were going to be parents, Griff and I. Together. *Oh God.* We were going to be parents.

"Dean?"

I snapped back to reality when Griff blew some bubbles into my face. That little...! I grabbed the bottle from him and tried to blow some bubbles at *him* too. But the wind worked against me and threw them back in my face.

Griff burst out laughing, and I couldn't help myself either. We were going to have a baby! How could we, when we hardly qualified as grown-ups ourselves?

But somehow, I knew that we were going to be fine. I was going to do the best I could to protect Griff and the baby to the end of the world.

"How long have you known?" I asked. "Have you told anyone else?"

"I've known for a few days. Not long. I've only told Eli."

A smile found its way onto my lips. Of course he'd told Eli. It was good that Griff could rely on his family, though. Even if it was only part of his family.

"This is so exciting." I took a deep breath.

"It is, isn't it?" Griff's voice sounded hopeful.

"Yeah." I drew him into my arms, where he fit like he was made for me, and kissed him. "I've always wanted to have a child someday, and I couldn't imagine anyone better to have it with." Besides, the thought that Griff was carrying my child appealed to my alpha instincts in a big way. I'd put my seed into him and he was mine now. Truly mine. What could be better? His belly was going to grow, and I couldn't wait to see him heavy with child. That image excited me more than I wanted to admit.

"Good." Griff laughed against my neck, blowing warm breath on my skin. "Now we only have to tell my parents."

I kissed the top of his head. "Sure thing."

I wasn't scared of his parents. What could they do?

Chapter Thirty-Two

DEAN

I was going to be a dad. The news still made my head spin when I got home late the next day and Conner's puppy greeted me at the door. A baby dog. I was going to have a baby human soon. I couldn't stop thinking about it. Griff was having my baby. I wish I could say that I'd gotten used to the idea at least a little, but it was still novel and exciting and a little bit overwhelming.

"You really milked every last minute you could stay in the woods, didn't you?" My cousin turned to me when I picked the puppy up and walked into the living room.

"Gotta make use of the time we got," I replied without shame. It had been good to be away from watchful eyes and out of earshot. Griff said his parents were probably going to move into an aunt's summer cottage when his dad was released from the hospital, so we'd have Griff's place to ourselves in a little while. Not soon enough, though. I didn't mind Griff's mother, but her son got very shy when she was around, and I'd waited long enough to be with him. Even my patience knew ends.

"I get you." Shane grinned. "I just like to tease."

I flopped on the couch beside him, my expression mirroring his. "It was a good trip." Even if that first night had very nearly turned into a disaster.

"Yeah, it was a good idea to get out," Shane agreed. "Really gave me room to breathe and to think about a few things. Like whether it actually matters how I make my money when I have the kids to focus on. It was so good to see Conner laugh this morning, you know? I want to take him out more often. Maybe a less demanding job would give me more time for that."

"So, you're going to sell?" I asked.

"I'm thinking about it, at least."

"That's good. I mean, I'm sure you'll do what's right."

"Yeah." He leaned back. "And if I do sell you can go back to being a firefighter full time, too."

I swallowed. "Yeah, I'm not so sure about that..." I stopped because even though I'd told Griff, I wasn't sure I was ready to tell anyone else. I was a firefighter. That was how people saw me. It was how I saw myself as well. For the longest part of my life, it was all I'd wanted to be. But how could I be a firefighter now when I didn't feel like I could protect anyone anymore? I knew in reality I'd only failed to save *one* person, but it was hard to live with the certainty that no matter how hard I tried, I couldn't save everyone every time. I'd always known that, of course, but *experiencing* it changed what I was willing to accept.

"What do you mean?" Shane prompted, looking at me curiously.

"Nothing," I said, and then I changed the topic to throw him off. "I have some big news, though."

"Yeah? Good news?"

The question made the corner of my lips tug up. Griff had called it good news, and I thought so too. "Yeah, it's good." I let the smile take over my face. "Griff's pregnant."

Shane's eyes went wide. "Griff's what? When did

that happen?"

"Do you really want all the details of when and how it happened?"

"Oh, I guess not." He made a face. "Spare me."

"You got it."

Shane was quiet for a moment, probably churning this new information over in his head. "So you're going to be a dad, huh?"

"Yup."

"How do you feel about that?"

"Honestly?" I looked at him. "It's pretty amazing."

"That it is!" Shane's lips broke into a grin. "I still remember when Conner was born like it was yesterday. And Mary." A hint of pain flashed over his features, probably because the memory included Ron, but it was gone again before it could take hold. This grief would stay with him forever, but he was learning to get a hold on it.

"I'm looking forward to the birth," I said, but I was also kind of glad that it was still a few months off. Griff and I needed time to prepare, both practically and mentally.

"Are you two going to move in together?" Shane asked.

Were we? "Probably? We haven't talked about it. This is all still so new."

"Yeah, I guess. Not that I want to kick you out or anything, but you should probably think about living together if you're going to be raising a kid."

Shane was right; I really needed to be thinking about that, didn't I? About Griff and me and our kid, and the future we were going to have together. I wanted Griff like I had never wanted another omega. The thought of moving in with him didn't scare me. The opposite, really, it excited me. I wanted Griff to be mine in every way possible. I looked forward to raising our child together, maybe even our children.

But it wasn't just our combined future that I needed to think about. I needed to think about my personal, professional future as well. Griff had suggested that I run away from my problems by resigning from my firefighting career. Could I really do that now that we were going to be parents?

If there'd ever been a time in my life that I needed to be a strong alpha, it was now.

“Dude, you look so serious,” Shane said. “What are you thinking about?”

I shook my head. “Just something I should have figured out a long time ago.” He couldn't help me with this. This was something I needed to figure out for myself.

Chapter Thirty-Three

GRIFFIN

Please, everyone just get along.

The weekend after our camping trip, my father was finally ready to be released from the hospital. Eli, my mother and I drove up to the hospital with his car. From there we were going to collect Dad and take our parents to our aunt's cottage a short drive outside of the town. She'd promised that it was well stocked and they would find everything they needed there. I only hoped that was true. As much as I enjoyed this chance to reconnect with my parents, things were still tense. Especially when my brother was around.

Honestly, it surprised me that he'd decided to come with us today.

"I want to be a better person than they were," he'd said simply when I asked him about it.

Still, the air in the car was thick, no matter how much my mom tried to lighten the mood with her chattering about whatever went through her mind as we drove.

Part of me was glad to reach the hospital. Part of me knew things weren't going to get better once we added my Dad to the mix.

My fears were confirmed once we stepped into his room. He'd expected me and Mom to show up, but Eli was a surprise to him, and it clearly showed on his features. For the first minute or two, nobody said anything while the two of them stared at each other, and I was frantically searching my mind for things to say to break the silence.

My mom was faster than me, though. It was her I got my tendency to talk like a waterfall from, and she was still better at it than me. “Aren't you glad to get out of here today, dear? Look who's come to celebrate the special occasion! Say hi to our sons. Wasn't it nice of them to come today? They're going to drive us to the cottage.” She whirled around the room collecting Dad's things as if we were any other regular family and this meeting wasn't tense whatsoever.

“Very nice,” Dad mumbled finally. “Hello, Griffin. Elias. You look like you've been doing well.”

Eli opened his mouth, then closed it again, as if swallowing some sort of insult that lay on the tip of his tongue. “Thank you,” he said instead. He was really trying to keep things civil, if not friendly. I was grateful for that. “I'm doing okay.”

“Your mother tells me you're married now?”

“I am,” Eli confirmed, absentmindedly playing with the ring on his finger.

“Good, good.” Our father nodded, then he laughed gruffly. “It's almost like you're doing what I've been telling you to do all along. Marry the father of your children. It's only good sense, really. I don't know why this caused all this family drama.”

Ouch. Couldn't he have kept that thought to himself?

Eli's lips turned into a thin line. “I married him because I love him, not because he got me pregnant ten years ago. And not because anyone told me to, either.”

My dad waved his hand. “Things turned out the way they were supposed to. We should just be happy for that instead of arguing. And now you're pursuing a degree too. That's good, really good, even if you were delayed for a few years."

Eli took a deep breath. "It is good."

I admired the patience my brother displayed that day, but I also knew that it wasn't going to last much longer if this line of conversation kept up.

"Now, now, Declan." My mother approached my father. "What have we been talking about?"

My father took a deep breath and turned to Eli again. "I am very sorry for all the misunderstandings we had."

Misunderstandings? It seemed Eli took offense to that word too.

"What are you talking about?" he burst out, his veneer of calm finally dissolving. "We didn't have misunderstandings. You threw me out."

"I didn't throw you out. I gave you a choice."

Eli shook his head, a look of disbelief on his face. "That wasn't any kind of choice. You wanted me to give up Jake."

"*Or* tell us who his father was so we could approach the guy. Was that so unreasonable? I don't think so, but no, you decided to pack your bags and leave like the stubborn child you've always been."

"It was you who said not to come back if I was leaving," Eli said, his voice taking on a bitter sound. "I couldn't give up Jake, and I couldn't tell you who his father was. Not back then."

I watched the two of them anxiously. Part of me wanted to interfere in this conversation. Part of me thought maybe it needed to be had. After all these years, didn't they need to talk this out?

My mother looked as if the same thoughts were going through her head as well, and she kept her mouth shut the same as me.

“Why couldn't you tell us?” My father asked. “You see, that's the part I don't get. We're family. You should be able to tell us.”

Eli sneered. “You say the word family like it means something, but I told you about my pregnancy and look how that turned out for me.”

Dad looked him up and down. “Seems to me you turned out all right. You're a strong omega, just the way we raised you to be. You have two children, a good man and good career prospects. I only feel you could have had all of that a lot earlier if you'd listened to us.”

“Perhaps... but you couldn't know that. You should have simply trusted my judgment and supported me when I needed your help. That's what I'm going to do for my children when they come to me with their problems. That's what I would have wished for from you.”

Our father sighed. “Maybe you're not the only member of this family who's too damn stubborn for his own good.”

I felt my eyebrows go up, knowing this was as close as our dad was going to get to an honest apology. And maybe Eli realized it as well, because he backed off.

“Let’s just get you out of here and to the cottage,” he said.

“Great idea!” Our mother jumped on the change of topic immediately. We helped her pack everything up and carry it to the car while she supported Dad on his crutches, since he refused to be wheeled around. He really *was* stubborn.

Still...

“That was big of you,” I told my brother in a hushed voice as we walked to the car. “Letting it go.”

He gave me a half-shrug. “Honestly, I think I’m

too happy with my life right now to stay bitter for long. Just doesn't seem worth it. I want to get this over with so I can return to my husband."

His words made me smile. I was so happy for the way things had worked out for him. I was even happier now that I knew there was going to be a little ray of sunshine in my future as well. And as if reading my thoughts, Eli asked, "Are you going to tell them?"

And just like that, my good mood took a hit. "Not today." Yeah, I'd joked to Dean that we needed to tell my parents, but not yet. Not when things were finally going well. I didn't want to drop this bomb on this family right now. No, my parents would only lay into me about how I needed to get married to Dean like... yesterday!

I loved him, but we hadn't talked about that yet, and this was really something I needed to discuss with my boyfriend before inviting my parents to the conversation. Our new-found family peace was so fragile. I didn't want to do anything that could hurt it.

Chapter Thirty-Four

GRIFFIN

"Are you really going to eat that?" Dean asked, a look somewhere between awe and disgust on his face as he watched me shove the pickles-and-mayonnaise-and-ham sandwich he'd just prepared for me into my mouth.

"Deliciousss," I said, drawing out the "s" sound for emphasis. On a rational level I understood his disgust, but my cravings didn't care about that. This baby had weird taste, and all I could do to stay sane was satisfy it. "I don't think this baby is mine, you know," I said, munching on my sandwich. "Could it have been switched before birth?"

"What makes you think that?" Dean asked, sitting beside me at the counter.

"It doesn't like chocolate. I mean, what's up with that? How can any child of mine not like chocolate? It's simply not possible." And yet the smell of a Mars bar had nearly made me throw up last night. I'd been relatively lucky in that I was now at the start of my second trimester and I hadn't experienced any morning sickness, but the food aversions I got were fierce.

"Really? No chocolate?" Dean mimicked shock. He hadn't been here the night before. We'd talked about moving in together when the baby was born, but hadn't done so yet. He spent most of his free time at my place, and yet, something was still holding us back from taking that last step. I couldn't quite put my finger on *what*, though. "I guess I'll have to stop baking for you then," Dean said.

I made a thoughtful noise and rested my head on his shoulder. "You'll have to bake a huge amount and save it all up so I can eat nothing but cupcakes for a month after the birth."

"A month? Don't you think that's a bit drastic?"

"Please, it's as if you don't understand my situation. I depend on those cupcakes! They're my life blood! And now I might not be able to eat them for nine full months! If I don't binge eat on cupcakes after the birth, I might die!" I spread my arms wide. "Do you want me to die? Is that it? I thought you loved me." I pretended to be close to crying, taking a huge, sobbing breath.

Dean laughed, not buying the show I put on at all. "It's a good thing you chose to be a photographer rather than an actor," he said.

I boxed his arm. "Meanie. I still want those cupcakes."

"Okay, okay." He leaned in to kiss my cheek. "You can have your cupcakes."

"Yay!"

"I just hope your nephew is a better actor than you are."

I stuck my tongue out at him. The play Jake and Conner were acting in was just a month from now. I'd gotten all the prop work done, and I knew Eli was finishing up the costumes too. They'd turned out so well. We'd both done our parts, now it was up to the kids to do theirs. I knew from Dean that Conner was still a bit scared, but that was just normal, I assumed. He was going to get through it. With Jake's moral support, if nothing else. I smiled to myself, wondering what my kid was going to be like when he or she was born. I wouldn't mind having my child be as strong-willed as Jake. God knew that was a good quality to have in the world we lived in. “I want to be mad at you, but I can't,” I told Dean. “I'm too happy.” In fact, I couldn't help but keep smiling at him. Somehow, I was in a good mood. But I'd been having a lot of mood swings lately, so I was going to enjoy this while it lasted. “I'm looking forward to the play,” I said.

“Yeah? Me too.” Dean grinned. “But speaking of the play... your parents are going to show up for that, won't they?”

“Yeah... so?” I asked, wondering what exactly Dean was getting at. We hadn't seen much of my parents since they'd moved into my aunt's cottage, but Eli had invited them to come see the play, which I thought was a great idea. I liked the thought of attending it as a family.

“Shouldn't we maybe tell them about our situation before that time?” Dean asked.

“What situation?” I pretended like I had no idea what he was talking about, if only because I didn't want to talk about it.

“Uh...” He pointedly looked at my belly. My still flat belly.

“We can tell them after.” I waved him off, feeling my good mood evaporating. “Not like the baby is going to be born tomorrow.” And I didn’t want to have some sort of family fight before the play.

“There’s a chance that they’ll know what’s up just by looking at you.”

“What do you mean?” I asked, staring at him indignantly. “Are you saying that because you think I'm going to be fat or something?” Yeah, my good mood had vanished just as fast as it had come.

“I'm not saying you're going to be fat,” he said. “I'm saying you're going to have a cute little baby bump. I mean, it's already starting.” He reached out for my belly and I jumped from the stool to evade him.

"Don't touch me when you think I'm fat!"

One of Dean's eyebrows shot up. "That's not what I'm saying, sugar."

"Ugh, don't talk about sugar." I held a hand in front of my mouth.

"This pregnancy is going to last for another half year, isn't it?" Dean asked and I thought he suppressed a sigh.

"Yeah, why?"

"Oh, no reason."

I glared at him, but he only smiled in response. I was lucky to be with the most patient alpha on the planet.

He tried to state his point again. "I was just thinking that maybe your parents might even be happy about this pregnancy. We'll never know unless we tell them."

"Yeah, that's not going to happen, just believe me. They'll hear about the baby and then they'll start making all sorts of demands." I'd seen it happen before. My parents seemed sorry for what had happened with Eli, yes, but only because they'd been given enough time to feel the consequences. If I sprung this pregnancy on them, there was no guarantee that they wouldn't flip again. My mother liked Dean, yeah, but she'd still want us to live a certain way. She and dad would both want us to get married right away. We didn't need that kind of pressure right now. I pouted.

"Okay, okay. I believe you." Dean stood and embraced me from behind. This time, I let him. I even leaned in to him a little bit.

"I'm sorry for being so moody," I said, suddenly feeling just incredibly sad about the state I was in.

"It's fine." He kissed my neck. Then he laughed a little, bless him. "I know this isn't going to last forever, after all. We can talk about something else if you don't want to talk about your parents."

"Yeah? Like what?"

"Like baby names?" Dean suggested. "Have you thought about any yet?"

"I'm not sure," I admitted. "I think I'd like to wait until we find out the sex. That might make things easier."

Dean nodded. "You know one of the old ladies I work with keeps insisting that we call our first child after her, since she brought us together."

I had to laugh at that. "Is that Mrs. Rosewood? How does she think she brought us together?"

"Oh, she thinks it was all her positive influence and moral support. And she taste-tested all those cupcakes for me. You know, to make sure they were good enough for you."

I shook my head, amusement taking the sadness away. "She's a sweet old lady, but she has some weird ideas."

"She does."

"Wait," I said, turning my face to look at Dean. "Did you tell her about the pregnancy?"

"Nope." He kissed my hair. "She just assumed. I wouldn't tell anyone without your permission."

"You better not!" Although I knew he wanted to. It was really unfair of me to keep this under such a tight lid, wasn't it? I sighed. Sooner or later we would have to let the cat out of the bag, but I'd rather that moment be later than sooner. "I'm sorry," I said. "I know you really want to tell your coworkers." Dean still went to do his job at the fire department two times a week. He also had nightmares two times a week, but he insisted he was fine, he would get over it. I only hoped that was true. He was stubborn as well as patient. But at least he told me about his problems now, even if there wasn't much I could do to help.

"Don't worry about it." He tightened his grip on me a bit and I took a deep breath, inhaling his scent. I could hardly believe now that it had scared me once, when all it made me feel these days was comfort and safety—and an ever present under-current of arousal. There was no better smell in the world. Not anywhere. “I care a lot more about making you happy then I care about telling my coworkers,” Dean tried to reassure me. “I can wait a little while longer.”

“Thank you.” I didn't like to make him wait, but rumors spread like wildfire in this place. If he told anyone at the department, it would be all over town the next day. And it wouldn't take long to reach my parents after that.

“What do you say we just watch a few episodes of anime on Netflix and forget about all this?” Dean asked.

“That sounds perfect! *You’re* perfect!”

Dean chuckled. “I’m at your service.”

“Does that mean I get another sandwich?”

“Depends. Do you want it to have pickles and ham again?”

“Nah, just ham this time.” I paused to think about it for a moment. “Ham and mustard.”

“Ugh. You’re disgusting,” Dean said lightly.

I boxed him with my elbow. “It’s your child demanding these things! So get to it!”

“Right.” He broke away from me and walked into the kitchen to do my bidding. I watched him, smiling. He really was perfect, and I knew he would stick by me whatever my parents said.

So why was I still afraid to tell them?

Chapter Thirty-Five

GRIFFIN

When the day of the play finally arrived, we met my parents in front of the school. Eli was already inside and so was Shane, as the two of them had needed to drop their kids off early and Eli had also wanted to make sure that there were no issues with the costumes. But this meant that Dean and I were alone with my parents.

I'd put on my most baggy clothing for this night, but yeah, I was seventeen weeks along, and I definitely had the belly to show for it. Still, I hoped I had managed to obscure it well enough that there wouldn't be questions.

Tomorrow. I'll tell them tomorrow. Just not tonight, please.

I wanted this to be a fun night. Dean took my hand and squeezed it as we greeted my parents. He knew how important it was to me that this evening go well. It would be the first time in ten years that my family had fun as a family.

"Hello Griff, Dean. So good to see you." My mother hugged me, and I put my arms around her back tentatively. Was she feeling my belly underneath the clothes? She seemed to still for a moment, but then she broke away without saying anything. She did look at me a bit oddly, though.

But maybe that was all in my mind?

"I'm glad that you could come," Dean said, distracting me. "I'm sure the play is going to be a lot of fun."

"Yeah," I chimed in. "I've seen the costumes, and they're adorable."

"Eli made them, didn't he?" my mother asked. Then she turned to my father. "Isn't that great?"

My father made himself smile. "Yes, great." He hadn't brought his crutches tonight, which was nice to see. Looked like he was really getting better, and soon enough, that fire would be nothing more than a dark spot in our memories. A dark spot that had brought us back together, though. I didn't know whether to be grateful or not.

"Shall we go inside?" Dean asked.

"Yeah, let's," I said before anyone could say anything else and keep us standing here talking. The light would be low inside the auditorium. I kind of counted on that to obscure my belly for a little longer.

"Alright then," my mother agreed and we entered the school, which was already filling up with parents and siblings of all ages. I spotted Eli, Matt, and Shane sitting in the front row, waving at us. "Over here!" Eli called out.

I exhaled as I flopped in the seat next to him. "Going well so far?" Eli whispered as our parents sat down.

"So far, no one's said anything," I gave back.

"Good. The kids are excited. Jake's been running in circles around me and Matt all day."

"I hope he burns all that energy off in the play," Matt remarked, holding Livvy, who marveled at the stage lights and the toddler in Shane's lap.

"I wish Conner was that excited," Shane chimed in, worry lines creasing his forehead. "I mean, he is, but not in a good way. He wouldn't eat all day, really."

And almost as soon as he said it, a small child came running to us. Conner. He came straight for his dad.

"Aren't you supposed to be back-stage?" Shane asked.

"I want to go home."

"Really? But then they'd be short one dwarf."

"I've thought about it. Snow White can have six dwarfs. That's okay. It's a new adaptation, an original re-telling."

This kid...

Shane stood and handed Mary to Dean. "Watch her for a minute?"

"Sure."

Shane nodded to him, then took Conner by the arm. "Why don't we step out for a minute?" He led his son off. I looked after them, wondering how Shane was going to solve this. I felt for Conner. The limelight was definitely not his favorite position, and not everyone could be like Jake.

But then I was thrown off by a weird comment my mother made.

"You look good with a toddler in your arms," she told Dean.

What was that supposed to mean? *Was* it supposed to mean anything? I knew my mom just said whatever came to mind, but still... Her words made me paranoid.

"That's because little Mary is the cutest," Dean said. "She makes anyone look good. Don't you, sweetie?" He kissed the little girl's cheek. She laughed.

"I wear pretty dress," she said.

"Yes, very pretty," my mom agreed. "You know I'm almost a little sad I only had boys. I never got to buy cute little dresses! Don't you think having a little girl would be marvelous?"

Okay, this was definitely more than my own paranoia, wasn't it? She was not so subtly trying to make Dean slip up and tell her something incriminating.

Dean was too glib for her, though. "I think little girls are the greatest," he said. "But boys can be fun too. My mother always said she was happy to have both boys and girls."

"That's nice. Which would you like?" my mom asked, but Eli spoke over her.

"Having one of each really is great. Don't you think so, Matt?"

"Oh, I don't know," he said, rocking Livvy. "I wouldn't mind having more than one of each."

"That's just because our children are the best." Eli gave him a kiss. Then he turned to our parents again. "Have you gotten a good look at Livvy? I think she has your lips."

Wow, Eli was really going far to throw her off my track, but it worked. Once given the chance, our mom was cooing over Livvy like she was the most wondrous thing in the universe.

Crisis averted. For now, anyway.

And it seemed Shane had mastered his own crisis as well. He came back with Conner after another minute, and the boy seemed a bit calmer than he had before as he went backstage again. "How did you manage that?" Dean asked as soon as the boy was gone.

Shane smiled sadly. "Told him his daddy was watching him." By the way he said it, I knew he wasn't talking of himself.

There was a small pause as none of us knew how to respond.

"Let's hope his daddy is gonna see a great play,"

Eli said then, and we all agreed.

"Wasn't Jake just the cutest in his little dwarf costume?" my mother asked after the play was over and we were done clapping.

"Oh, totally," I responded, just glad that she was too distracted by her existing grandchildren to think about the possibility of future ones. There were no more weird looks. Indeed just a few minutes after our exchange, she was completely enraptured with Jake, who came bounding off the stage to talk to his parents.

"How was I?" he asked, staring up at them with big eyes and a wide grin.

"Absolutely amazing," Matt said. "You're a little star."

Jake's grin threatened to split his face apart. Conner walked over as well. He looked relieved most of all. I patted him on the back as he passed me. "Good job!"

He gave me a smile. "Thank you."

"Jake," Eli stood and addressed his son. "These are your grandparents. I told you they were coming to see the play tonight."

Jake turned to them and gave the pair a curious glance. "Thanks for coming! Did you like it?"

"It was lovely," my mother said. "You're the cutest dwarf I've ever seen."

"You did a good job, kid," my father added.

Jake beamed. "My daddy made the costume!" he said in his proudest voice, instantly capturing my mother's heart and making her forget all about my existence.

Thank God I had such an adorable nephew.

"That went well, didn't it?" I later said to Dean when we were emerging from the school.

"Better than expected," Dean agreed. "Somehow I feel like we were let off the hook too easy. I was *sure* your mother had noticed something."

I shrugged and gave him a kiss, joy bubbling up in me now that this evening was nearing its end and I could spend the rest of it with my alpha. "Let's just be happy she didn't dig any deeper."

But she did, of course. The very next day.

I'd barely gotten out of bed when the doorbell rang and I found my mother standing in front of the house. *Jesus Christ*, I thought, seeing her. I was still in my pajamas and Dean hadn't even woken up yet. The only reason *I* was awake was that I liked to catch the early morning cartoons with a bowl of Cheerios.

"Mom?" I muttered, trying to get my brain to work in spite of the early hour. "What are you doing here?"

"I want you to tell me what's going on with that bump of yours," she said, matter-of-factly.

Bump? I looked down on myself. *Oh no.* I'd opened the door for her in my pajamas, and now that I wasn't wearing the baggy clothing I'd had on yesterday, my condition was pretty obvious. "You noticed, huh?" I tried a joke.

She wouldn't be distracted, though. "Are you pregnant?" She didn't put her hands on her hips, but I could tell she was close to it. I felt transported back to my childhood, to days I'd been caught with my hand in the cookie jar. Something that had happened way too often, by the way. My mother had an uncanny ability to sense when I was up to no good. But perhaps all mothers did.

"Did you really come all the way out here this early in the morning just to ask that?"

"It's no small question, is it?" She walked past me into the house.

I closed the door, probably to the disappointment of at least one neighbor. "No, I guess not," I said.

"Do you have coffee?" my mother asked, making her way into the kitchen. I followed.

"There on the counter," I pointed at the nearly full pot I'd just made for Dean and me.

"Good, good." She took it and poured herself a cup, and that was all the respite I got before she laid into me again. "You know you shouldn't be drinking too much coffee if you're pregnant."

"I know. I only have the one cup to wake up," I defended myself. "I'm not stupid, Mom."

"But you are pregnant?"

Damn, I'd admitted it, hadn't I? Still, at this point, I'd lost the battle anyway. She'd known the day before and seeing my baby bump now only confirmed her suspicions. "I am," I said. *So, what now?*

"Is it Dean's?" she asked without further ado. I couldn't read from her expression how she felt about any of this.

"It is." No reason to hide that.

She smiled, but only for a brief moment. Then she sighed, seeming tired even with the coffee in her hand. "I just don't understand why you wouldn't tell us about this."

"I was going to tell you," I said quickly.

She only raised an eyebrow at me. Yeah, I wouldn't have believed me either. I'd screwed this up, hadn't I?

I should have listened to Dean.

"Were you going to tell us before or after the birth?" she asked.

Her question hit me like a knife twisting in my heart. Did she really think so little of me now that we were finally starting to feel like a family again? "Before! I promise!" I tried to convince her, but then my mood shifted the other direction and I felt myself get angry.

What business of hers was my pregnancy anyway? After the way she'd treated my brother, how did she expect me to trust her with news like this?

"I just hate the thought that you're still trying to shut me out of your life," my mother said as if I'd hurt her in some deep way by waiting to tell her about this pregnancy.

"I'm not trying to shut you out of my life. These past months I've been trying my hardest to make this family a family again!" I burst out. How couldn't she see that? The only reason I hadn't told her about my pregnancy was because I was scared it would lead to arguments that would tear us apart all over again.

I just couldn't stand that thought, and I couldn't stand to argue with my mother now either. I was so tired of it.

"We're not going to be a family by keeping secrets like that," my mom pointed out. "Are you unhappy with your pregnancy? Is that why you didn't say anything? Because it *should* be good news. Especially when it's Dean's baby you're carrying." She tried to give me a smile.

And I exploded.

"Oh, *my* pregnancy is a good thing, is it?" I went off on her. "Because it's Dean's baby? Fuck that. You should be happy about any baby I'm carrying. Any baby Eli and I are bringing into this world, they're all your grandchildren! You should love them no matter what! No matter if we have partners or not or if we plan to marry them or not!"

My mom's eyes grew wide, but I wasn't done yet.

"You're proud of Eli now that he's married and he's about to become a vet, but you should have been even prouder of him when he was a single dad. He worked so hard." I stopped to take a breath because I felt myself choking up. Damn pregnancy hormones.

My mother looked like she was close to crying too, and that made it even harder for me to keep my emotions in check. "Maybe we should talk at another time," she muttered.

"Yeah, maybe that would be best," I replied, trying to keep my voice calm.

And then, just as quickly as she'd come, she left, and I found myself standing in the kitchen by myself, wondering how I was going to fix this and if I even wanted to. I honestly couldn't say. My emotions were a mess.

Times like this, there was really only one thing that calmed me down. Taking a deep breath, I went into the living room and picked up the clothes I'd discarded by the couch last night when Dean and I hadn't quite made it to the bedroom before getting down to business. The memory made me smile even now, but I didn't linger on it. Instead, I wrote a short note for Dean.

Had to go out and get some fresh air.
See you later.

Love,
Griff.

I paused for a moment, then picked up the pen

again.

PS: You can have the last bowl of Cheerios, but don't touch the pickles.

With that important note added, I got dressed, picked up my photography gear and headed out.

Chapter Thirty-Six

DEAN

When I woke to find Griff gone, I wasn't immediately worried. No, I got up, found the note in the living room, and figured he'd be back any minute while I ate my breakfast, which consisted of yes, a bowl of Cheerios and no pickles.

Seriously, only someone pregnant could worry about having their pickles stolen.

When Griff was still not back by the time I finished eating, I started wondering where he might have gone, and how long ago. I liked to sleep in late on the weekends when I could, while Griff often got up quite a bit earlier. He said he did it to catch the cartoons on TV, but I knew that he was just really in love with the morning sky. Not that he would ever tell you that.

After another hour passed without a peep from him, I looked around the living room. It was nearing noon now, and I couldn't help but wonder what he was doing outside for so long. Like a detective, I looked for clues. Griff had evidently dressed in his clothes from yesterday—probably so he wouldn't wake me. His camera was gone as well. I concluded that he must have gone out to take some pictures. If he'd decided to go all the way out into the woods for that—which I knew he loved to do—it wasn't odd that he wasn't back yet.

Still, worry grew in the back of my mind. It wasn't

like him to just up and leave like that. Not for so long. Normally, he would have at least waited until I was up to tell me if he was going to be gone for hours.

I decided to call him on his cell phone, since there was no reason for me to pace the living room and worry needlessly when I could just ask him what he was doing.

But only a moment after I'd dialed his number I heard his ring tone coming from the bedroom.

Of course.

He hadn't taken his phone. I sighed. One day I was going to have to glue the phone to his hand or something. Or put a tracker on him. His brother joked about doing that sometimes. I didn't find it so funny anymore.

Calm down, Dean. You have no reason to worry. Griff is going to waltz in through the door any minute and you're going to feel silly.

I stroked some hair back from my face. The voice inside my head was right. My boyfriend was a grown man, and he didn't need me to worry about him when he'd simply gone out to take some photographs.

Trying to take my mind off the issue, I turned on the TV. It couldn't hold my attention. Still, I kept my eyes glued to the screen. I wasn't going to leave this house before Griff came back and I could hold him safe in my arms again.

I held out for exactly thirty minutes before I decided to call Eli. I didn't have his number, but it was on Griff's phone, and maybe my boyfriend had decided to hang out at his brother's after taking a stroll in the woods. It was possible, right?

Eli answered his phone after a few rings. "Hi. What's up?"

"Hey, it's Dean. I was just wondering if you'd heard from Griff today."

"Oh, hi, Dean. No, I haven't heard from Griff. Don't tell me he forgot to take his phone again." Eli's irritation was apparent in his voice, though it was still light-hearted.

"I'm afraid he has."

"I see. I'm sorry I can't help you. I haven't heard from him," he said again, then he paused. "I've heard *about* him, though."

I frowned. "What do you mean?"

"Our mother came by here earlier, totally out of the blue and crying."

"Your mother?" What was *she* up to now?

"Yeah, I was shocked too." Eli gave a little laugh before turning serious again. "She said she'd been in a fight with Griff and wanted to tell me how much she loved me." I heard the frown in his tone. "She was really upset."

"She and Griff had a fight?" I licked my lips. If this fight had left his mother at the point of tears, it must have devastated Griff as well. He was such a sensitive soul. Especially now that his hormones were out of whack. "Did she say what they were fighting about?"

"She wasn't really coherent, honestly. She babbled on about babies, though, so I'm pretty sure it had something to do with that."

I groaned. "She must have confronted him about the pregnancy."

"I guess so, yeah." Eli sounded less than happy himself. "I was afraid there was going to be a fight about that sooner or later."

I couldn't argue with him there. I'd seen it coming too. I just hadn't done enough to prevent it, or maybe it couldn't have been prevented. I wasn't sure. That didn't matter now, though. What mattered was finding out where Griff had gone. Damn it, why couldn't I have woken up early? "When did your mother show up at your place?"

"Uh… a few hours ago while I was making breakfast for the kids. It was early. Around eight?"

"Eight…" I sighed. Griff must have left here earlier than that. "That means he's been gone for almost five hours. If he left right after the fight, anyway." But something told me that he had. It was the kind of thing he would do. If he'd taken the time to calm down first, he would have woken me, or waited until I woke up by myself. No, this had been a spur-of-the-moment decision brought on by his argument with his mom.

"Five hours? Where did he go?"

"I don't know. He took his camera, but not his phone." And wherever he'd gone, he wasn't coming back. Anxiously, I stared at the front door, but nothing happened. Where *was* he?

"Sounds like he needed to blow off some steam," Eli said, but I could tell that he was starting to worry as well. The two of them were close, and Eli had to know this wasn't normal behavior for his little brother.

"I figure he's probably gone into the woods," I said.

"Yeah, that's possible. You want to go have a look? See if we can find him?"

I exhaled. "Yes. I'm gonna go. I'm tired of waiting."

We decided on where to meet up and ended the call. As soon as I was done talking to Eli, I headed out the house, bent on finding the man I loved and bringing him home.

Chapter Thirty-Seven

GRIFFIN

I was absolutely fucked. Like, seriously. Trying not to let the rising panic in my gut swallow me whole, I stared up the walls of the ravine I'd tumbled down. It was still every bit as steep as it had been for the past hour. At least I *thought* I'd been stuck down here for at least an hour. Since, idiot that I was, I hadn't brought my phone, I had no real way of telling. I liked to fool myself into thinking that I could tell the passage of time by the way the sun moved in the sky overhead, but in all honesty, I had no idea. I'd never been a Boy Scout or anything. I was just a photographer who liked to take a few pretty shots of wildlife.

And I couldn't even do *that* now because the fall had scratched up my camera lens. God, that was going to be expensive to replace.

If I ever got out of here.

I swallowed. People were going to come looking for me, right? Even if I didn't have my phone.

Normally, I would have been able to climb back up where I'd fallen, but I did something to my hand when I tumbled to the ground, and I could hardly move it now without tears stinging my eyes. It *hurt,* even when I was holding it still. I must have broken my wrist or something, and of course, I'd also twisted my ankle because I was just that freaking unlucky.

So climbing was out of the question.

On the other side of the insurmountable ravine, I was faced with a creek. Dean and I had come here as teens sometimes. It was off the beaten path. A good hang-out spot, if you were a teen and all your limbs had full functionality. Now it was just a spot that I could neither swim nor climb out of.

Originally, I'd wanted to come here to think. I had *not* planned on going down into the ravine—I'd misstepped. At least now it seemed I had all the time in the world to think.

Lucky me.

It could be worse, though. It was still early in the day, which meant I had a couple hours of sunlight left. Time to think of a way to get out of here before it grew dark because I really, really did not want to spend the night here.

Just the thought alone made me shudder as the wind dragged some colored leaves into the ravine and blew them into my face.

At least it wasn't winter yet. The weather had cooled down a bit over the past few days, but we hadn't yet reached freezing temperatures. The night would be cold, though.

You're going to get out of here before then.

Right, I just had to keep believing that.

Taking another look around, I had no idea *how* I was going to be gone by nightfall, though.

I didn't want to admit it, but I really needed a knight in shining armor to get me out of here.

Why, oh why, had I forgotten to take my cell phone? All those times Eli had bitched at me over it and I'd shrugged him off. I should have listened.

That realization came a bit late, of course. I would do better next time, but there was nothing I could do about the situation now.

Even without the phone, though, people would notice that I was gone, right?

The note I'd left for Dean wouldn't keep him from worrying if I was gone all day. I hoped.

But would he think to look for me *here*?

He might not. Even if he figured that I'd gone into the woods, he could search all day without finding me. That was the problem with preferring places *off the beaten path.*

Sighing, I rubbed my belly as I felt a small fluttering within. The little one was getting restless, just like me. Probably hungry too. I knew I was.

"Hang in there, baby," I muttered. "Daddy's gonna come for us, you know?"

I couldn't help but think back to that evening I'd crashed Dean's date and he'd kissed me. I'd told him I was so embarrassed I wanted to hide in the forest.

I would have found you, he'd said.

Please, was all I thought now.

Chapter Thirty-Eight

DEAN

Eli and I decided to split up at the entrance to the forest.

"We'll cover more ground that way," he said, and I agreed. I was all for anything that would help me find Griff faster. By this point, I was honestly worried. Before coming here, I'd left a note at Griff's place, telling him to call me immediately if he came home, but so far, I had gotten nothing. More and more I was starting to fear that he wasn't going to come home unless I *brought* him home.

And that was exactly what I was going to do. I didn't care how long I would have to search the woods for him—if he was here, I *would* find him.

First, I decided to head for the spot where we'd gone camping. The hill overlooking the valley where we'd set up our tents had a great view, and I figured maybe he'd gone there to take a couple pictures.

No luck, though. When I got there, the valley as well as the hill were deserted with no signs of anyone having been there.

Gotta press on.

Heart pounding in my ears, I racked my brain for where else he could have gone.

The lake, maybe. It wasn't warm enough to swim anymore, but we'd had a lot of fun there and maybe he just wanted to reminisce? The scenery probably made for a few good snapshots too.

Mind made up, I made my way to the lake where we'd taken Jake and Conner swimming at the start of summer, shortly before we'd become an item.

There were some teens there, trying to skip stones, but neither of them had seen a man fitting Griff's description come by. I thanked them anyway, and took a deep breath, adrenaline pumping through me as I started to run out of ideas.

Where are you, Griff?

I checked my cell phone, but I had no missed calls or messages. Of course not. It didn't look like I was going to wake up from this nightmare any time soon, and what a nightmare it was! Certainly worse than the ones I had at night. They couldn't even compete, really.

Nothing could be worse than losing Griff.

But I couldn't think like that.

Calm down, you're not *losing him.*

If only because I simply refused to let that happen. I was an alpha and I could be damn stubborn if I wanted to.

But I couldn't just run blindly through the forest, either. I had to think, even if I felt like I was wasting daylight just standing here and breathing in the mountain air.

As soon as I was home, I was going to kill Griff's mother for upsetting him.

But that was not a productive thought, either.

Think, Dean.

Griff and I had met up out here a lot as teens. There really wasn't much else you could do, growing up in Oceanport. There was the harbor, the one movie theater and the woods. And I was pretty sure Griff was neither at the harbor nor at the movies. He'd never been much of a fan of either. No, we'd come here. And we'd gone...

There were certain spots we'd visited more than others, but it was all so long ago and I hadn't thought about this in years.

I remembered the creek, because it was there I'd told Griff about my family's plans to move. He'd looked so sad that day I'd almost kissed him. Almost.

In hindsight, I guess I really should have.

No use in lingering on that now, though. The only thing that mattered was whether Griff might have gone there.

Maybe yes, maybe no, but since the creek was all I could come up with, I decided to go check it out. The need to do something, *anything*, urged me on.

The day was starting to grow cold by the time I reached the ravine with the creek. I wasn't holding much hope when I peeked down, but... I spotted a piece of fabric hanging off one of the roots sticking out of the wall of the ravine. It was the same color as Griff's shirt!

Could it be?

Please!

"Griff?" I called out.

No response came, but I figured I had to try my luck anyway, and slowly, I climbed down into the ravine. I wanted to hurry, but I couldn't help anyone with a broken leg.

Once I reached the bottom, I looked at the creek, lying silent in front of me. Had Griff swum to the other side? No, he wouldn't have. It was too cold. He could have gone left or right from here, but to the right, the path seemed narrower. Wetter.

To the left, then.

Please let me be right.

Biting my lower lip, I sped up my pace. Could

Griff be down here? If so, what was he doing?

I had to walk for about fifteen minutes before I spotted a silhouette up ahead, outlined against the light of the setting sun.

"Griff!" I called out again, hoping that my guess was correct.

Startled, he turned around to me. "Dean? Oh my God, you really came!"

I exhaled. There were so many questions in my head, but for now, they were all swept away by the wave of relief that washed over me. I'd found him. Everything else was secondary. "Of course I came!" I muttered, before I sprinted up to him so I could pull him into my arms and kiss him to quiet the storm raging in my heart.

But as relieved as I was, I couldn't help but notice that he favored one foot over the other.

"What happened?" I asked, still holding him close. For one because he seemed to be needing the support, but also because a huge part of me never wanted to let go again. "What are you doing out here?"

"I just wanted... I didn't mean to be gone for so long. I'm sorry." He sniffed.

"Shhh, it's fine." His skin felt cold, so I put my jacket around his shoulders, wondering just how long he'd been down here. "Did you fall?" I asked.

"I was stupid," he said. "I didn't even want to climb down. I misstepped and lost my balance."

I looked him over. "Why didn't you climb back up?" I asked, because it was obvious he hadn't stayed voluntarily.

"I can't move my wrist," he said, holding his left hand out to me. It looked swollen, and I cringed. "And I think maybe I twisted my ankle."

Well, that explained why he'd decided to sit it out, but the thought still made me shiver. How long would he have been stuck here if I hadn't found him? If I hadn't thought to look for him here?

"What about the baby?" I asked.

"I think it's fine. I mean, I can still feel it and all. But I think it's hungry."

"Yeah, I bet you both are." I kissed the top of his head, breathing in his scent. God, was I ever glad to have him back. "You are never allowed out of the house without your cell phone again."

Griff chuckled, tucking his head under my chin. "Yeah, I don't think I'm going to forget it again."

"I'll buy you a second one just to make sure," I said, absolutely serious.

"Yeah?" Griff asked. "I'm sorry I scared you. I really only planned to be gone for two hours, tops."

"You scared the shit out of me," I admitted. "What if I hadn't—"

"I knew you'd find me," Griff cut me off.

"You weren't scared even a little bit?"

He shook his head, his hair tickling my skin. "Of course I was. But I knew you'd find me," he insisted.

"I wish I was as optimistic as you are."

He gave me his brightest smile, and I was momentarily stunned by how beautiful he was. Even after a day spent lost in the woods, my omega had lost none of the spirit that had attracted me to him in the first place. "It's easy to be optimistic when your boyfriend is a hero," he said.

"I'm hardly a hero," I argued. "I still struggle with my job and I—"

"But that doesn't matter," he cut me off. I got the feeling that if he hadn't twisted his ankle, he might have stomped his foot on the forest floor. "You'll always be *my* hero." And before I could protest again, he pressed his lips to mine.

For the first time, I got the feeling that maybe, he was right. Even if the only people I could protect were him and our baby, maybe that was enough. Maybe it truly *was* all that mattered.

Chapter Thirty-Nine

GRIFFIN

Two weeks after Dean had rescued me from the woods, my mother came by with a gift basket. This visit was just as unexpected as the last one had been—Dean and I had just come back from the doctor's office, really—but she seemed a lot friendlier than she had the morning after the play.

"Dean told me what happened," she said with a glance at my hand, which was wrapped in a cast. As it had turned out, my ankle was only strained, but my wrist was broken. Still, nothing that wouldn't heal, even if it sucked for now.

I let my mother into the house and she set the gift basket full of fruit down on the kitchen table.

"Dean talked to you?" I asked, addressing her but looking at my boyfriend, who chose to examine the basket instead of joining the conversation.

"Yes," my mother confirmed. Then a small smile crossed her features. "It seems your boyfriend likes to look out for you. Honestly I'm glad to know you're in safe hands."

I blushed. "Mom..."

She shook her head. "I should be allowed to say that. Although maybe I shouldn't have said some other things." Her voice turned soft. "I came to apologize to you. You were right. You had every reason to be reluctant to tell me about your pregnancy. I promise you I'm not here to tell you how to live your life. Your father and I would be *delighted* if the two of you married, but we won't *ask* that of you."

Behind me, Dean coughed. Right, I hadn't told him how crazy my parents were about marriage. Well, now he knew.

"I'm glad to hear that," I said, focusing on my mom instead of Dean. Him I'd talk to later. "Dean and I are super excited about the birth and we'd hate if you couldn't be around for that!" I said completely truthfully. "I wouldn't have kept it a secret *that* long, you know?"

"I guess." A smile found its way onto her lips. "Do you know anything yet?" she asked, clearly burning with a need to know everything there was to know. "How far along are you? When's your due date?"

"Not for a while yet," I said laughing. "But I'm almost twenty weeks along so... halfway there? And I got something to show you. Wait a minute. We had an appointment today, just before you came." I went into the living room to fetch one of my newest, yet most precious, possessions. A picture more beautiful than any I could ever take, because it was of the child inside of me. Every time I looked at it, I felt awed.

And now I showed it to my mother and the expression on her face mirrored my own.

"That's your newest grandson," I told her proudly.

"Really? You're having a little boy?" Her eyes seemed to mist over. I gave her a hug. It was a little awkward with the cast—I couldn't wait for that thing to come off—but I made it work.

"Yes, we're having a little boy!"

"That's amazing," she said. "I'm so happy for you

two! Have you thought of a name yet? You need to give him a strong name. But not something too..." She stopped herself, probably realizing that she was falling back into old habits of wanting to meddle again. "I'm sure you will think of something good."

"Yeah, I think so too." I shared a glance and a smile with Dean. "We haven't really talked about it yet." But we *had* decided that we weren't going to tell anyone whatever name we settled on before the birth. Mostly to annoy my brother, if I was being honest. He'd never shared his kids' names with me before birth, either. Everything else, but not that. Now he was gonna have to wait too.

When my mom was gone, Dean and I retreated to the living room.

"What's all this about marrying?" he asked almost as soon as we were alone.

"Oh, don't worry about that," I waved him off. "Just one of the things my parents badgered Eli about when he told them that he was pregnant. They couldn't cope with the idea that he was going to have a baby without marrying anyone. I was kind of scared they'd try to pull the same kind of shit again. I know it's silly because I'm an adult and all... I guess I just don't often feel like one." I laughed weakly. "How am I gonna raise a kid?"

"You'll do fine," Dean reassured me, stepping close. Gently, he rested his hands on my belly. "We'll figure this out together."

I leaned up to touch my lips to his just as I felt the baby kick. Seemed our little boy agreed with that.

Chapter Forty

GRIFFIN

The day my cast came off, my alpha had a surprise for me. He wouldn't tell me what exactly it was, though. He just told me to wait in the bedroom, so that was what I did. I waited on the bed while he finished preparing whatever he had in store for me.

I honestly had no idea.

Until he walked into the room in his firefighter uniform and my jaw nearly dropped. Dear God, he was hot. I licked my lips. Why couldn't he wear that uniform every day?

Probably because random omegas would throw themselves at him in the streets. Now that was a thought I did *not* like. Other omegas had no business throwing themselves at Dean. He was *mine*.

Dean smiled at me. "Just asked Daniel to give me full-time hours today."

I jumped up from the bed and embraced him. "That's awesome!" I hadn't been sure whether Dean would continue his job at the fire department. I would have supported him if he'd decided to quit, of course, but I got the feeling that wouldn't have made *him* happy, and I really wanted him to be happy. He'd said his nightmares had gotten better over the past few weeks too. Partly because he'd regained some of his confidence after that day I'd gotten stuck in the woods, and partly because he'd started seeing a therapist about his issues shortly after that, saying he didn't feel the need to be 'strong' about his trauma anymore. "I'm sure you're going to be the best firefighter in town," I told him.

"Yeah?" He closed his arms around me. "I don't know about that, but I don't need to be the best. It's just a job. It's not who I am. Not anymore."

"No?" I kissed his neck and breathed in his scent. "I gotta say I like you as a firefighter, though."

He chuckled, the sound a low rumble that made his chest vibrate. "You weren't kidding when you said uniforms were hot, were you?"

"I thought that was the whole reason you put it on now," I gave back, sliding my hands down to his ass. "Isn't this my surprise?"

"Oh, it totally is."

I grinned with my lips against his skin. "Guess I should unpack my present, shouldn't I?"

"If that's what you want..."

I didn't respond, not in words. Instead, I went on my knees in front of him. I'd dreamed of doing this, sucking him off in his firefighter uniform. But he'd never been too comfortable wearing it and I'd had my own hang-ups. None of that now, though. My heart was so filled with love for Dean that fear found no space in it anymore. I wanted to do this and I was damn well going to.

Dean still seemed a bit unsure about all of this, though. "Griff... do you really want to do this?"

I grinned up at him. "Yeah, absolutely."

"I don't know, with you being pregnant and all, I feel like—"

"I'm pregnant, not dying, okay?"

That made him shut up, and I could finally set out to do what I'd been wanting to do for so long. Slowly, I opened Dean's fly and breathed in his scent. That moment, Dean smelled so alpha it made my head spin—in the best way possible. I nuzzled his thigh with my nose, taking in as much of that smell as I could, feeling almost overpowered with desire.

How could I ever have been scared of this? Right here on my knees in front of Dean, this was where I belonged. How could things be any different?

I exhaled on a sigh as Dean ran a hand into my hair, playing with the strands. I could have started to purr, really, but that wasn't what I was kneeling here for. No, I wanted to make *Dean* purr, or at least make him moan. With all my heart, I wanted to please him, and the need to do just that was intense. It didn't inspire fear in me anymore because I knew my alpha cared for me the same way.

What could be better?

Not much, I decided while pulling Dean's pants down a bit and freeing his cock of its confines. He was so big and beautiful. This wasn't the first time I saw his cock, of course, but the sight still made me lick my lips each and every time. There wasn't an alpha on Earth more gorgeous than mine.

I wrapped my hand around the base, feeling him grow harder between my fingers. I let myself revel in that feeling for only a moment before I stuck my tongue out to lick at him, making him twitch.

"Griff..."

"Yeah?" I licked him again, more slowly this time, giving him a good swipe of the tongue. I loved the way it made his breath hitch. I wanted to please him yes, but that didn't mean I couldn't have some fun while doing so.

"I should have known you'd be a tease."

I laughed. "Just enjoying myself. But I guess I can enjoy myself in other ways too," I said, and then I took him into my mouth, finally living my fantasy.

And it felt so good. Just feeling the weight of him on my tongue, the heat of his flesh, the salty taste of his skin.

Yeah, I could definitely enjoy myself like this. Already, I was getting all hot inside, the hormonal rush flooding my brain and turning my thoughts hazy.

Having Dean's cock in my mouth was even better than stuffing it with cupcakes, and I'd never thought anything could be better than stuffing my mouth with cupcakes.

I took him a little deeper, running my tongue along the underside and savoring the taste. I couldn't take him all the way, he was too big for that, but I tried to get as much of him into my mouth as I could, and he didn't complain. Nope, he was too busy breathing hard, and I was loving it. Right then, right there, nothing mattered more to me than making him lose his shit.

Every little appreciative noise Dean made seemed to vibrate through me and travel straight to my groin to make my own cock strain against the fabric of my pants. My arousal turned into a pleasant buzz in the back of my head, drowning out everything but my need to get Dean off and taste his semen on my tongue.

Just the thought alone made me shudder.

Dean tightened his grip on my hair a little bit, but not to the point of hurting. No, he was restraining himself, I could tell. I loved it, though. Loved feeling my alpha's strength. I rested one hand on his thigh just to feel the way his muscles bunched. His strength made me feel safe—and impossibly aroused.

A surge of lust made me redouble my efforts, sucking on the hard flesh in my mouth. I knew Dean was getting close when I tasted his precum on my tongue. The sensation made me moan around his cock, I couldn't help it. I was too turned on. Too high on endorphins.

"Damn, Griff." Dean groaned. "You feel so good." He twisted his hands in my hair, taking shallow breaths.

I peered up at my firefighter. His eyes were closed,

lips slightly parted, head tipped back. He looked like he was about to become unraveled, all because of me. God, could there be a hotter sight in the world?

My musings were interrupted when the first hot drop of semen hit the roof of my mouth. I swallowed all my alpha's seed down greedily as he moaned my name. Even though I was in a submissive position, I'd never felt as powerful as I did then, wrenching sounds of absolute pleasure from Dean.

And I was happy to lick him clean until Dean pulled me up. Rising to my feet, I kissed my lover to share the taste of him between us.

And then I gasped as Dean reached down to open my fly and his hand found its way inside my loose-fitting paternity pants. I came embarrassingly fast—within seconds of feeling Dean's large hand around me, really. There was nothing at all I could do to stave off the orgasm crashing into me and taking my breath away. I might have been ashamed, if it hadn't felt so damn good.

"God, that was amazing," I mumbled, resting my head on Dean's shoulder.

He chuckled, his voice just a bit hoarse. "Yeah, it was."

"I'm so glad you came back to Oceanport." And so glad I managed to face down my demons and get over myself.

"I'm glad too," he said, holding me tighter. "This place is home after all."

"Because home is where the heart is?" I teased.

He simply smiled. "Exactly," he said, and then he kissed me again.

Chapter Forty-One

DEAN

When Griff's pregnancy neared its end, I thought I was prepared for everything. I'd read all the books, and Shane and I had had all the conversations about what was going to happen during childbirth. I was confident in my knowledge. I was set.

Until the day things actually got real.

I'd just moved all my things in with Griff a few days before, and Eli had come over with cake to congratulate us on starting our life together. He'd also brought his dog, and Griff was cuddling with the dog when the Labrador suddenly gave a surprised bark.

I glanced over at the pair, because Fiona never usually made a sound.

"I... think my water just broke," Griff said, staring at me.

Within an instant, I felt all color drain from my face. "Your water broke?" I repeated intelligently. Everything I'd read about what to do in this instance, all the knowledge I'd gathered, it was gone from my brain as if it had never existed in the first place. All I could think was *oh my God, oh my God, oh my God.*

Not super productive, I admit.

It was a good thing Eli was there with us. He had a handle on things.

"Awesome!" he said with a huge grin on his face.

"Looks like today is the day I get to meet my nephew!"

Griff looked to his brother and smiled as well. "Yeah, I guess we're going to meet this little guy today."

Meanwhile, I was still racking my brain for anything to say.

Eli glanced at me and laughed. "No need to panic yet. It'll probably be a few hours before the kid gets here."

A few hours. I was going to be a parent in a few hours. How was I supposed to keep calm knowing that?

"I'm going to take Fiona home," Eli said. "And then I'll meet you guys at the hospital." He shot me another look. "Are you okay to drive?"

Was I okay to drive? Of course I was! I shook myself out of my stupor. I could get my pregnant mate to the hospital. It wasn't like I'd never been around women and omegas in labor on the job.

Still, this was different. This was Griff, and that was my child he was about to give birth to.

Just get him to the hospital for now.

Right. "Guess we should get in the car, huh?" I asked Griff, trying to sound calm and collective and not the least bit panicky.

"Yeah, but we should also take the bag. We packed one, remember? For when my water breaks."

"Yes, of course." I'd completely forgotten about that. Damn, when had Griff turned into the more responsible one of us? I really had to get a grip. As Eli had said, it could take hours before the baby would be here, and I couldn't act like an idiot for all that time. What if my baby's first impression of me was that I couldn't be trusted with adult tasks?

That was a silly thought, but still...

Giving it my best effort, I somehow managed to get Griff and myself into the car and drive us to the hospital.

There, Griff was wheeled into a room to wait for his contractions to get stronger. No one at the hospital seemed panicked, and the general calm let me breathe a little easier as well. We were going to be fine, weren't we?

"Should we call your parents?" I asked, kissing Griff's forehead after the initial check-up.

"Nah, the doctor said it would be a while yet, and I don't want my mother running circles around me all the time up to the delivery."

The image made me laugh. "Guess you're right. She would do that." I straightened. "Do you think we should talk about names again?" Because we hadn't really settled. I took a deep breath. "I can't believe we're going to be the parents of a baby boy in a few hours."

Griff smiled. "Maybe you could believe it if you'd spend the last nine months getting fatter and fatter."

"You're not fat," I protested. "You're beautiful. But good point." I had to chuckle. God, how lucky was I to be with an omega who could make me laugh even when I felt so out of my element. Hospitals always threw me off. I liked to take action to help people, but here, I had to leave it all up to the doctors and nurses. All I could do for Griff now was provide moral support.

"I think we're going to see what name fits best when the little one is born," he said, playing with a corner of the bed sheets.

"Maybe you're right... or you're speculating that I'll be so distracted by the miracle of birth that you get to decide by yourself." After all, there were two names we were considering, and each of us liked one of them a little better than the other.

Griff tilted his head. "Oh, that's a good idea."

Darn, I'd given him a plan he'd never have come

up with on his own. Still, I didn't mind so much. Griff had done the most work in creating our child, carrying it close to his heart for nine months. If he wanted to be the one to give our son his name, that was fine with me. I wasn't the kind of old-school alpha who needed control over everything. I just wanted my little family to be happy.

"I'm sure you'll make the right choice," I said, leaning down to kiss him.

We'd come this far, nothing was going to go wrong at this point. At least that was what I thought until about an hour later when his contractions started coming more rapidly.

I looked to Griff's brother, who had entered the room about twenty minutes ago. "It's fine," he said with a small smile. "Just means we're getting there."

Getting there, right.

"You don't have to worry so much," Griff agreed.

Eli laughed softly. "Alphas are always like that."

I huffed, but couldn't really protest. I *was* acting ridiculous. Griff was going to be fine, I knew that. I just didn't like watching him suffer when the contractions hit harder and he got all red in the face. That was when it started to dawn on me how exhausting it really was to give birth.

I hated seeing my love like this. Especially when there was nothing I could do to help him or make him feel better. Ultimately, I could only hold his hand as they rolled him into the delivery room.

"Not long now," I told him, trying not to panic myself. Not long now and the two of us would be parents.

Deep breaths.

I couldn't freak out when Griff looked so calm. Sure, he was red in the face and the contractions were taxing him, but in spite of all that, he didn't seem like he was the least bit worried.

"I can't wait to meet this little one," he said in between breaths when the doctor asked him to push. He was optimistic. That was what I loved about him. He wasn't going to let negative thoughts or panic or worry cloud the birth of our child, so neither could I.

He gripped my hand tightly and I squeezed his. It didn't matter whether I was scared or not. What mattered was that we were together in this. And together we would raise this child, in the good times and the bad times. We might not be married, but we absolutely made that commitment to each other. I knew that I could count on him, just the same as he could count on me. No matter what happened, we would be there for our child and each other.

All in all, the birth didn't take long once we'd entered the delivery room and really got things started, even though it felt that way. Time seemed to stretch out forever when I had to watch Griff suffer—and when I was pretty sure that he was about to break the bones in my hand. I was actually starting to wonder if I could reuse his cast if that happened.

But then, when I was almost sure it was never going to end, I heard the doctor say that we were almost there.

Thank God.

Now there was a chance that I wouldn't someday have to tell my kid the story of how I fainted in the delivery room during his birth.

Griff cried during the last push, and then soon after, I heard a different cry—this one much louder. Our little boy had great lungs on him!

After all the panic of the day, a huge smile broke out on my face.

The doctor was holding our child. And he was perfect. I knew that before I could even get a closer look at him. He had two arms and two legs and everything.

It was *amazing*.

We'd made that.

Griff looked just as fascinated as I did when a nurse finally handed him our son after wrapping him in a tiny blanket. But fascination wasn't the only emotion apparent on Griff's face. I also saw awe and adoration and the kind of love that went deeper than anything else. I knew exactly how he felt because I felt the same way.

"Do we have a name?" I asked.

"Yes." Gently, Griff stroked the little one's cheek with one finger. "Bastian." He looked at me. "Bastian Everett."

I raised an eyebrow at him, not because I didn't like what I was hearing, but because he'd made no mention of the middle name before.

"Everett means strong," Griff explained. "I want our son to be strong and brave."

The sentiment made me smile as I leaned down to kiss Griff's forehead. "Like us?"

He grinned. "Exactly."

"I like that," I said, my heart swelling as I looked at both my omega and my son. Griff was kind and sweet, but he'd had his fair share of demons to battle to get here and I couldn't have been more proud of him. Of us. We'd put our fears aside to be with each other. It hadn't always been easy, but the result was so worth it.

I kissed him again, this time on the lips, feeling happier than I'd ever been. Griff was my love, the second half of my heart, my best friend and the father of my child.

He was my home, and I was never going to leave again

Epilogue

GRIFFIN

About six months after our son's birth, my alpha tried to surprise me again. I'd just put the baby down for a nap when he walked into the door with a heavy-looking box in his hands. An hour ago, he'd told me he needed to go out to help his cousin with some errands, but I couldn't see how the box he was holding now related to that.

And what was even weirder, he didn't put it down to give me a kiss, like he usually would. No, he just stood there and looked at me expectantly.

"What's in the box?" I asked, deciding to take the bait.

He gave me a small smile. "A present."

"For me?" One of my eyebrows went up. Not that I didn't like presents—I loved presents!—but it wasn't my birthday, or even Omega Day.

"Yes." His smile turned a bit more confident. "It's for you."

I looked at the box again. "It's not wrapped in gift paper," I chided him.

"Wouldn't want to cut off air supply," he said with a grin.

Air supply? I studied the box more closely—and noticed the small holes at the top, and that it moved.

What the hell was in there? Suddenly, I had a suspicion that I knew.

I'd told Dean once or twice that I was a pet person and wanted a pet, but... We'd never seriously discussed it. Could he have...?

Dean laughed. I glared at him. "Your eyes were so wide just now!" he pointed out.

I stuck my tongue out at him. Yes, I was a daddy now, but if you ever expected me to turn into an adult, I don't know what to tell you. That was never going to happen.

"Go on, open it," Dean said.

"If you insist," I responded, as if my curiosity wasn't killing me.

Dean only smiled, giving me no further clues as to what I should expect. The box moved again as I approached, almost jumping out of his hands. Whatever was in there, it was definitely alive. Gingerly, I took it from Dean and set it down on the table. Then I started opening the lid of the box. A yipping sound came from it as I did so.

A dog!

I opened the lid all the way and peered inside.

Awwww.

Dean had gotten me a boxer in a box! Genius! I laughed looking at the dog. He was the cutest little thing ever. He had the squishiest nose, and the biggest, most innocent eyes as he looked up at me. "I can't believe you bought a dog!"

"I adopted him." Dean was still grinning. "I went to the shelter just to have a look and he was perfect."

"He is!" I agreed, lifting the dog out of his box. He promptly proceeded to lick my hands. "Aren't you just the cutest?" I nearly cooed. He was so *warm*. "Can I really keep him?" I asked, turning to Dean with a smile, feeling like a kid again. My man had brought me a dog! "Can I call him George?"

Dean laughed. "Anything but that, please!"

"Anything?" I raised an eyebrow at him while holding the dog to my chest and petting him. Oh, how I loved that dog smell and the feel of fur beneath my fingers. I'd missed it more than I realized.

"Can I call him Captain Stinkyfeet? Officer Dogbreath?"

Dean scoffed, even though he was still smiling. "You're watching too many cartoons."

"Please, there's no such thing as too many cartoons. Besides, you knew what you were getting into."

Dean's smile softened. "Yeah, I did." He took a deep breath. "Did you even notice the jewelry box on his collar?"

Jewelry box? I scanned the dog's collar with my eyes, and, indeed, there was a small box attached to it. "More presents?" I asked. And *jewelry*? Really, what was the occasion?

"Just a small thing." Dean licked his lips. For some reason, he seemed to be getting just a little bit nervous.

Well, time to find out what this *small thing* was that he was talking about. "Hold still, doggy." I detached the black box from the collar and set my new furbaby on the floor where he sniffed my leg as if to determine whether it was edible. Oh God, we needed dog food. I looked at Dean. "Do we have anything to eat for him?"

"I bought some stuff. It's still in the car." He glanced at the front door, then back at me. "Don't you want to open the box first?"

Right, the box. I'd nearly forgotten about it. But now that I looked at it again, I noticed that it was the perfect size for a ring.

Oh!

Was this...?

My heart started pounding as I opened the box.

It was empty.

"Uh..."

My eyes darted to Dean, then back to the empty jewelry box in my hand. "There's nothing in there?" Was Dean trying to pull some really weird prank on me?

But no, he looked just as surprised as me, if not more so. "What?" He stepped up to me and took the box out of my hand. "Oh shit." His face went pale. Okay, so he wasn't trying to pull some sort of prank on me. His eyes flitted back and forth between the dog and the jewelry box.

Oh no.

Slowly it dawned on me what might have happened.

"Was there supposed to be a ring in there?" I asked, biting my bottom lip. I'd hoped Dean might propose to me someday, but... I'd never expected it to play out like this. I wasn't sure what to think. Did I want to marry Dean? Hell yes, but I also wanted a ring. More specifically, I wanted to know that my new dog hadn't eaten my ring. I was all for letting your pets participate in the ceremony—to a point! Call me old-fashioned, but I'd prefer to know that my engagement ring had not passed my pet's bowels.

Dean gulped. "There was," he admitted.

Poor Dean. I was sure this scene wasn't playing out like *he'd* imagined it either.

"Where do you think it went?" I asked. "Do you think...?" I glanced at the dog. We both did.

"I was sure I'd put it in the box," Dean said. "Oh God..."

I picked the dog up. "Maybe we need to call him the lord of the rings, huh?" I tried to make a joke. Dean's smile seemed forced. Yeah, I didn't think I was being particularly funny either. I kissed the doggy's squishy face. "Did you eat it? Did you eat my engagement ring?" The dog only licked my cheek in response.

I looked back at Dean, who was frantically searching his pockets and then the inside of the large box the dog had come in. "This is so not how I planned this to go," he muttered.

"Don't worry about that. Do you think it can hurt him? Swallowing the ring, I mean." The boxer looked healthy enough to me, but you never knew. "I'm going to call Eli," I decided, handing our puppy to Dean. "Don't let him eat anything else not dog appropriate."

"Promise." He held the dog tight as if to make extra sure.

And then, of course, the baby started to cry. "You go to him," I told Dean while I fiddled with my cell phone. My alpha looked the tiniest bit overwhelmed, but he'd brought this on himself. Honestly, he'd just given me an empty jewelry box!

But as Dean dashed off into the nursery, I had to suppress a laugh at the absurdity of my situation. Honestly, a part of me was loving this. My house certainly didn't feel empty anymore. Smiling to myself, I called my brother.

"Griff?" he answered the phone after a few rings.

"Yeah, hi. What do you think I should do if my dog swallowed my engagement ring?"

"Your what swallowed your what?"

Now I *had* to laugh. My poor brother was so confused. "Dean adopted a dog," I explained. "You have to see him! He's the cutest thing!"

"You got a dog? That's great! What kind? What are you naming him? Can I come over?"

"A boxer. He's so small and squishy and warm and..." I stopped, because Eli and I could talk about our dogs all day, but this was not what I'd called for. "You can maybe come over later but right now we're having a bit of an emergency. We think the dog might have swallowed my engagement ring."

"When did you get *engaged*?" Eli asked, instead of focusing on the problem. Not that I blamed him. I *was* giving him a lot to process.

"I didn't," I said. "Dean doesn't have a ring to propose with right now."

"Oh. Oh God." Eli burst out laughing, finally seeing the whole picture. "Sounds like you're off to a great start with this dog."

"I know, right?" I smiled because my brother's laughter was contagious, and yeah, he was right, this situation was kind of ridiculous. "What do you think we should do?"

"Dogs eat tons of shit they're not supposed to. I'm sure the ring's not going to hurt him, but take him to the vet anyway. It'll probably pass naturally, though."

Pass naturally... Yay. "Okay, thank you."

When I got off the phone with my brother, Dean sat on the couch with Bastian in his arms and the boxer on his lap. Part of me was tempted to fetch my camera and take a shot. What could be sexier than a hot alpha cuddling a dog and a baby? More specifically, my dog and my baby.

"What are you smiling at?" Dean asked.

"Nothing. Don't move." I snapped a picture with my phone. Not as good as a pro camera, but better than nothing. "This one's for the family album."

Dean grimaced. "Is this a day to remember?"

"Oh, definitely. Bastian's gonna love hearing this story when he grows up."

"And you'll tell it over and over, won't you?"

I only grinned at him in response.

He sighed. "Okay. Fair enough. What did Eli say?"

"To go to the vet." I took my furbaby from Dean. "Honestly, I can't believe you're making me rush him to the vet so soon!"

Bastian babbled something incoherent as if to agree with me, then one of his tiny hands reached out to the dog,

"You wanna pet the doggy?" I asked, holding him so

Bastian could put his fingers on the soft fur. My son studied this fascinating new creature with big eyes. He had Dean's eyes, which I was glad for. They were so gorgeous and expressive. I was sure I had the cutest baby there ever was. The dog sniffed his arm and Bastian laughed. *Aww.* Instant friendship. My heart melted a little.

"You picked well," I told Dean.

"You think so? I'm glad." He leaned over to kiss my cheek. "I'm sorry I messed up the rest. This was supposed to be special."

"Oh, it is."

"If you say so." Dean allowed himself a smile as he got up from the couch. "I'm going to get my coat and call the vet."

"Okay." I set the dog down so I could take the baby from Dean. "You like the new doggy?" I asked my son, softly rocking him in my arms. He replied in coos and gurgles and a short giggle. "I'm going to take that as a yes."

Dean came back into the living room after only a moment–without his coat or his phone. I shot him a questioning look. He didn't respond to it, instead, he simply walked up to me and went down on one knee.

What...?

"You found it?" I asked, when my brain caught on to what was happening. I was getting my proposal after all!

He only grinned and took my hand. "You're not only my best friend, but the love of my life, the father of my child, and the most beautiful, kindest omega I've ever met," he said, and he looked so sincere I nearly blushed. He truly meant every word he said, I had no doubt about that. "Every day you give me a reason to smile, to laugh, even when things go wrong," he went on. "You make my life brighter for being in it, and I don't ever want to part from you again. Griffin Stephens, would you do me the honor of marrying me?" In his free hand, he held the ring, the light of the living room reflecting off it in a way that made it shine. It was beautiful.

"Of course I will!" I exclaimed before I could tear up. Him, the dog, the baby—this was everything I'd ever wanted, and to be honest, I still couldn't believe my luck.

Dean slid the ring onto my finger, and then he stood and kissed me, making my whole body tingle with joy.

"Where did you find it?" I asked Dean when we parted, staring at the ring on my finger.

"Coat pocket," he said sheepishly.

I snorted. "Oh, you."

"Will you marry me anyway?"

"Are you kidding? I'm glad I'm not the only silly person in this relationship." I kissed him again. Between us, Bastian laughed, as if amused by his parents' antics.

I had a feeling he was going to see a lot more of those in the future, and I couldn't have been happier.

ABOUT THE AUTHOR

Ann-Katrin loves to write, read and dream. In her spare time, you can often catch her hunting wild plot bunnies in the fields of her imagination. In her other life, she's a mother and a translator, but writing about men and the men they fall in love with is so much more fun!

LIKE THIS STORY?

Want to be updated whenever a new one comes out?

Sign up for Ann-Katrin's mailing list for sneak previews, cover reveals, and bonus content!

Sign up at *http://eepurl.com/bVJCqT*

And get two free bonus shorts—A Dragon's Christmas, and a Mercy Hills Valentine's!

OTHER BOOKS BY ANN-KATRIN

Mercy Hills Pack

Mating the Omega (Book One)
Abel's Omega (Book Two)
Duke's Baby Deal (Book Three)
The Omega's Alpha (Book Four)

Still to Come:

Legally Mated (Book Five)

Fires of Fate

Under the Dragon's Spell (Book One)
The Dragon of His Dreams (Book Two)
Dragon's Love Song (Book Three)
Dragon's Miracle (Book Four)

Oceanport Omegas

The Omega's Secret Baby (Book One)
A Baby for the Firefighter (Book Two)

41866115R00169

Printed in Poland
by Amazon Fulfillmen
Poland Sp. z o.o., Wroc